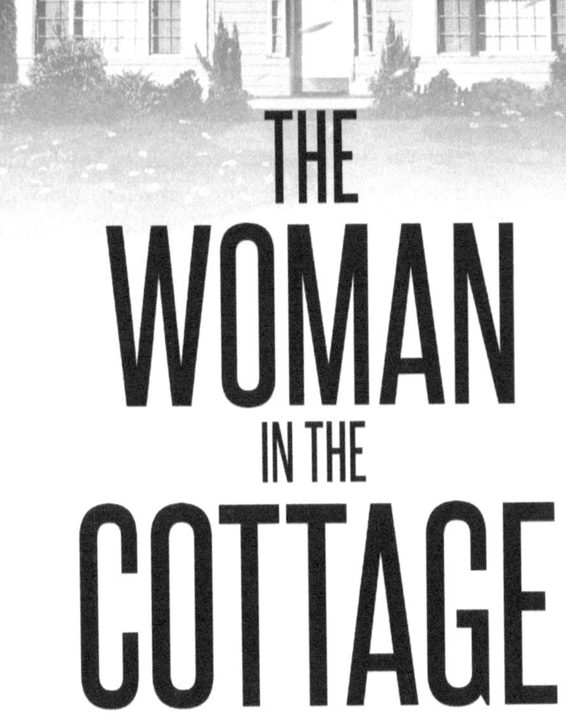

THE WOMAN IN THE COTTAGE

CARA KENT

FAIRYTALES DON'T OFTEN COME TOGETHER ON THEIR own. In the real world, they don't just fall into place naturally. They're made of hard work, sacrifice, and lots of resilience along the way. Kate learned that lesson the hard way years ago when her mental health had caused a bit of damage to her life. Nothing permanent or long-lasting, of course, but enough that it was a chapter of her life she was endlessly grateful to have moved beyond. With those demons slayed, though, she was happy with her life. Now she lived contentedly, with a good job and a wonderful husband who was working hard to build their dream home. It made life that much more fulfilling.

Of course, it did help that they added a lot of sweetness and love along the journey. She sang along to a romantic song that afternoon in her kitchen as she made herself and her husband their favorite turkey sandwiches paired with heart-shaped peanut butter cookies she had baked that morning and fresh strawberries straight from their garden.

Kate's work as a writer allowed her to be home, which gave her some freedom when she wasn't bent over her latest book. She used that time to do the things she loved, like baking and cooking. It just happened to be that her husband loved those things about her too.

It made her happy to make him happy. Especially considering all of the work he was putting in lately to make their dream home come to life. Kate packed all of her creations into a canvas bag printed with her favorite literary quotes in various fonts, then headed out to the car.

The spring day kept her company as she drove to her future home. Pink dogwood trees lightly coated the ground, bending slightly under the gentle pressure of the breeze. Tulips and daisies grew along the path that she took to get to the 10-acre lot they had bought a couple of years ago.

It was always a thrilling experience, going up the driveway to the fairytale-looking cottage in progress. It was cozy, yet decently sized at 2,000 square feet, allowing plenty of room for the family that they were trying to grow. And considering the fertility treatment they were paying for, they both hoped they'd be making use of that space soon.

In the meantime, Kate was content for things to be just the two of them. They made plenty of happiness on their own. And sometimes she had to stop and really take a deep breath, ground herself, because it felt like she was living in a dream that she feared she might wake up from at any moment.

Sometimes she thought she might go back to the days when she was much sadder for no apparent reason. When they weren't making a lot of progress because her mind was holding her back. When Tyler had to soothe her through all of it, alongside the help of her friends, getting her through those dark days to where she was now.

Yet as she stepped outside her car and smelled the refreshing scent of spring settling over their patch of heaven in Connecticut, she realized how alive and *real* everything felt. It was as if nature was trying its best to convince her of her new reality. And she believed it. She embraced it.

A harsh whirring noise cut through the peace. Kate couldn't understand how those who were working on her house could stand the noise and commotion that such projects required, so she was even more thankful that her husband was in charge of this.

She started walking toward the front door, then paused. For a moment, she had a distinct feeling that someone was watching her. It was uncomfortable and made her nervous. Their eyes tried to pry into her soul, leaving her feeling vulnerable—like maybe she was missing something important that she should be on the lookout for.

She took a deep breath and shook the feeling off. Of course, there were people all around the property right now. Contractors, electricians, drywallers, plumbers. She wasn't sure of the details of who was doing what and when—Tyler had tried to explain it seven or eight times, and it just soared over her head—but she knew she had to trust them to build her dream home. It wouldn't be strange if someone was watching her. Though at that moment it seemed that everyone was inside the house anyway.

She chalked it up to just having an overactive imagination as a writer and went into the house where the noise was nearly unbearable. Hammering, sawing, drilling, and all manner of sounds in a raucous cacophony. Though the exterior of the house was a beautiful shell by now, the interior still had some work to be done. It was coming along quickly and would be wrapped up soon, but there were paint buckets, carpet swatches, and tools to navigate around for now. She didn't mind though. Every swatch was a seed of the great future that was to come.

"Hey, love," a familiar voice cut through the racket. "It's so good to see you!"

Tyler walked over to her with a bright smile on his face that touched his blue eyes. His medium-length brown hair was a little messy, sweat and dust dotted his forehead, and his clothes were paint-stained and wrinkled. Yet he was still so handsome, taking Kate's breath away every day.

"Hey, darling," Kate drawled, wrapping her arms around his neck as he lifted her in a bear hug. "It's good to see you too.

I always love stopping in to see you and check in on how the house is coming along."

"It's coming along well so far," he assured her. As he set her down, he brushed her dark curls out of her blue eyes. "We should have a lot of the painting wrapped up in time for the new flooring to come in next week. It's really starting to look like a house in here. All the guys on the team now know our plans, so they can keep working even when I'm not around. It's all coming together perfectly. I can see our vision coming to life."

"I can see it too," Kate whispered, placing a sweet kiss on his lips. She looked her husband in his eyes as she held him. "I'm so thankful for you and all you're doing to make this dream a reality. For all you've ever done for our family."

"And I'm thankful for you," he promised her. "You're doing just as much hard work holding down the fort while I'm doing this. Keeping my spirits up is what's allowed me to work on the house and do my best. Don't ever underestimate how valuable you are. And how much I appreciate having you as my wife."

They kissed again, and Kate felt so warm and loved in that moment. Sure, she and Tyler had their rough patches as all couples do. But they had mostly worked through them by this point as they reached this calmer period in their life, and it was nice to enjoy each other and the peace that went along with that.

"Come on," Tyler said, "I'll give you the tour of the house."

Kate took his hand as he led her through the various rooms that were shaping up into something that would one day be a real place for them to live. As he described it, she could vividly imagine every detail coming to life. It was as if he were painting a picture for her to live in, and she was overjoyed to be there with him.

As she walked through, she made sure to stop and greet some of the builders to thank them for their hard work. Most of them seemed happy enough to chat with her, and they even got her involved a little, showing her the whole process so she could be part of it in some small way. A few did seem to be avoiding her, though, so she let them be. She didn't want to be in the way.

By the time they finished their walk-through, Kate's hopes were higher than ever as she pictured the life they'd be living in their new cottage. For now, she just enjoyed these moments with Tyler as they walked back outside away from the noise.

The backyard was already charming with the perfect area for a garden, patio, gazebo, and in-ground pool. Kate and Tyler walked to the white gazebo which had fairy lights and tiny, white flowers draped across it. They laid out the blanket Kate had packed with their lunches and sat on it together.

"These are adorable," Tyler said, taking a bite out of the heart-shaped cookies. "And absolutely delicious."

"And meant to be eaten after lunch," Kate teased, though she, too, ate one of the cookies.

"Yeah, yeah, yeah. You know I can never resist your baking. Tell me how your latest story is shaping up. Have you settled on a theme yet?"

Kate nodded. "I'm getting there. The research is going well into dark psychology. It's a deeply fascinating subject, and I'm grateful to have the chance to explore it more fully. It's tragic to think of the crimes that have been committed due to a troubling mental illness. Especially when such things maybe could have been prevented if they were caught earlier and treated properly.

"I think that's the purpose of my book. That's the ultimate meaning I'm striving for. I want to show people how dangerous it can be when mentally ill people aren't getting the proper treatment they need. I think I'll try to use some of the research to advocate for mentally ill people because the available resources aren't always great and they tend to be quite limited."

"I love that passion within you," Tyler replied with a smile. "I can tell how much this means to you by the way you talk about it, and I admire that. Not everyone has what it takes to follow their interests like that."

"Thank you." Kate smiled. "You also follow your passions, too, though. I guess we're matched well like that. We fit together like puzzle pieces when it comes to our ambition. I truly believe that's how we've gotten to the place where we're at. Where we're comfortable and happy."

"I couldn't agree more."

At that, they both shared more about their recent passion projects before parting so they could get back to work. Though they sometimes worked long hours in their pursuit of a better life, they always made sure to touch base like this, which made it easier to focus and take those big steps.

They didn't know it was the calm before the storm.

Kate was refreshed as she got back home and fired up her laptop to continue her research. Her most recent case study was that of a man named Daniel Jenkins who was diagnosed with borderline personality disorder and schizophrenia after he had murdered his girlfriend. The combination had resulted in disaster, and Kate was fascinated by how it played out, especially since this particular patient had undergone intensive mental health treatment since his arrest.

He had been detained in a mental institution for years, and it was said that he had made a full recovery. Doctors were even discussing if he might be able to be released. Kate thought this was perfect. He might be able to reflect on what he had done and his experience better than others could, providing a wealth of information.

But as she researched this, she found she wanted to do more than just research. Her first book had been successful, but she felt like it was missing something. This one was starting to feel the same way, and Kate hated that feeling. She wanted to be totally satisfied with everything she wrote.

After thinking about it further, she realized what she needed was hands-on experience. She wanted to hear about these stories directly from the mouths of those who had suffered from the disorders. She wanted to help them tell their stories in a more genuine way.

So, she paused her work to make a call. Her heart pounded in her chest. After a quick conversation with the receptionist, she learned she could talk to Daniel that day if she wanted to. He tended not to receive too many visitors, so the receptionist thought he might be happy to have the chance to talk to someone outside the institution.

Kate took a moment to deliberate on this. This would be huge. It would help elevate her writing and her story. It would give her firsthand information and insight that would make this story more compelling.

What would it actually be like, though, to talk to a murderer? It was certainly a heavy topic, and she had to wonder if she was really up to the task. Was she the type of person who could handle this?

"Would you like to schedule the appointment?" the receptionist asked.

Kate hesitated as she considered if she truly wanted to go through with it.

After her phone call with the institution, she made herself a cup of tea to reflect on her decision. As it was steeping, she got a call from her best friend, Allison. She answered right away, grateful that her friend tended to have the best timing.

"Hey!" Allison started. "I was just on my way home thinking about you. I'm out of work early today. I was wondering if you'd want to grab a drink or something. Maybe go for a walk. I'm antsy to shake off my workday."

"You know, I would love to," Kate told her, "but I actually have plans today. Very last minute. I'm actually on my way out the door."

"Sounds interesting," Allison replied. "What you up to?"

Kate hesitated. She wasn't sure how Allison would react to her plan, as it wasn't something she'd normally do. She rarely kept anything from her friend. They told each other everything no matter the circumstances.

"I'm going to be talking with Daniel Jenkins," Kate admitted.

"Who's that? I don't think I've heard you mention his name before."

"I haven't," Kate replied. "Because I've never talked to him before. He's going to be in my book, though, so I thought it would be helpful to interview him."

"In your book? I thought your book was about the dark side of mental illness? Isn't it about criminals or something?"

"It is. Daniel is…" she paused for a moment, trying to word it in the best way, "…suffering from a mental illness that is said to have contributed to him killing his girlfriend."

Allison was quiet for a minute, which made Kate wonder if maybe she was making a mistake.

"That sounds dangerous," Allison pointed out. "What if he gets fixated on you or something? What if he comes after you? Talking to a murderer isn't some small, simple thing."

"He's currently in a mental institution," Kate assured her. "He's not some uncontrolled mass murderer, Allison. That's part of the stigma that I'm trying to break. He's a man who suffers from a disease, but now that he's getting treatment, he's in a much better place mentally than he was. So, I think he's the perfect person to talk to when writing a book like this."

"I just worry about you. I don't want to see anything bad happen. You have to be careful, especially with something like this."

"I will be. I won't give any personal details or anything. I'll keep it all professional and remember who I'm talking to. You don't have to worry about me. I promise."

"As your best friend, I will always worry about you. But I'll try not to. Even if I think you're a little crazy for doing this."

Listening to Allison's suspicions made Kate feel a little crazy about taking the risk to talk to Daniel. But she tried to push those fears aside. She couldn't be a genuine voice for people struggling with mental illness if she feared talking to them. That wouldn't be fair to them and wouldn't make her a good ally.

She had to be willing to open herself up to their struggles. She had to be open to listening to them and getting to know them without any judgments. As much as she appreciated Allison's input, she couldn't be swayed by her. Kate knew she had to do this.

CHAPTER TWO

After getting off the phone with Allison, Kate was feeling a little less certain about her decision. But she was still determined to do this, so she finished up her tea and drove over to the mental health facility.

The building itself was a tall, imposing block of brick, tucked away in the trees just on the outskirts of town. It could have been a prison or a high school, for all she knew, and while there was a yard out front with a few trees and greenery, most of the area was a drab gray that matched the parking lot. The sight made her a little nervous. She had never had an encounter like this before, so she wasn't sure what to expect. She only knew this felt right—like she might finally do her book justice.

Walking into the facility reminded her of why her work was important. She wasn't a doctor, so she couldn't say too much about it. But the environment she stepped into didn't seem conducive to healing or preparing patients for reentering the outside world.

Rather, it felt like a sterile hospital that was meant to keep patients indefinitely with stark white walls, gray tile floors, and a general air of coldness. The place didn't seem very warm or welcoming at all. Kate imagined that a more natural setting would be more helpful for healing. But she decided that was extra research she would have to do as her book progressed. She was passionate about advocating for positive changes for patients.

She walked up to the front desk and checked in. The front desk receptionist looked at her strangely when she mentioned the name of the patient she was coming to visit.

"I'm sure he'll be happy to see you," the receptionist said hesitantly. "He doesn't get many visitors. I think his family abandoned him."

That was a trend Kate had noticed in her research. Those who struggled with such intense mental health issues were often abandoned by their friends and families even before they committed a crime. She noted that it didn't seem like there were many chances of rehabilitation.

At the very least, as she was led through the hallway that stretched past the patients' rooms, the décor in the area the patients were living in was a little warmer. It still had that sterile feel to it, but the walls were navy blue instead of white, and there were even a few plants in plastic pots to give the false appearance of life.

She was led to a visitor's room with a few black plastic tables, white chairs, and a few children's toys she imagined to be for keeping young children occupied through their visit. It wasn't as bad as she imagined visiting someone in prison would be. Yet it didn't seem like a far stretch from it either. This mental health facility felt much like a prison, and it was unsettling.

I have to be a good ally. I can't fear the realities of the situation these patients find themselves in. I can't be afraid of them.

The thoughts ran through Kate's mind on repeat as she sat down at a table by the window. Yet it was difficult to keep those fears at bay as she waited to talk with Daniel in this unsecured place where anything could happen if he just so happened to snap. What if she was his next victim? What if he wasn't as reha-bilitated as his doctors said he was?

As she looked out the window at the garden below, she took a moment to assess her own mental state. She thought about what would happen if she ever became so mentally ill that she might do something terrible without even realizing it. She wondered how much control someone would have over themselves in that state. She wondered if anyone could switch into that mental state without realizing it.

Thankfully, Daniel entered the room before Kate could ponder that too intensely. It was enough to distract her from all of her thoughts as she guiltily noted he didn't look how she assumed he would.

If she was totally honest with herself, she'd been expecting someone who was a bit disheveled. Perhaps someone with hol-low cheeks and dark circles under his eyes. He had been institu-tionalized for years. She imagined being able to see that imme-diately in the physical effects it would have on him.

That was far from the reality of the situation though. Daniel's clothes were simple, just a black shirt and grey sweat-pants. But it didn't make him look not put together. He just looked like he was relaxed, preparing for a day spent at home. He looked comfortable.

His dark hair was neatly brushed, his brown eyes were alert and awake, and his posture and stance were generally relaxed. He appeared prepared for a normal conversation with her. Kate noted that if she had seen him just walking down the street, she wouldn't think anything of it. She certainly wouldn't have guessed he was a murderer.

It was unsettling to be faced with the reality that she wouldn't be able to recognize a dangerous criminal just by looking at him. It was something she was already aware of, of course. No murderer goes around with a sign plastered to their forehead. Still, being directly confronted with it like this caught her off guard.

She stood as he approached and offered her hand. He accepted it with a firm and steady handshake.

"I'm Kate Larose. It's wonderful to meet you."

"Daniel Jenkins," he replied. "It's great to meet you too. I have to admit, though, that I don't have many visitors all that frequently. So, I was surprised when I heard that someone requested to see me. Especially when I found out that person was a stranger. I was intrigued and also confused."

They both sat down, and Kate was once again struck by his calm and steady tone and demeanor. Though she had done a lot of research into those with mental illnesses, she realized that she had still clung to some of her bias about what that should look like.

She was grateful in that moment that she had decided to do this. She needed this extra level of empathy in her work that she didn't even realize she was lacking before. She needed to see those suffering from these types of illnesses as normal people whose suffering too often remained hidden.

"I can understand why that would be confusing," she admitted as she met his curious gaze. "I probably should've written to you before I just barged in, so you'd understand why I wanted to speak with you. But I was doing research on your story, and I just felt the urge to meet you right away. I wanted to discuss your story with you."

"My… story?" he asked, crossing his arms over his chest. "My story is a particularly brutal one. I'm certainly not proud of it. What about it could possibly lead you to want to meet me?"

"I'm writing a book," Kate explained. "It's about mental illnesses and the dark effects they can have on the people suffering with them, as well as those that are in their lives. Your case caught my attention because it fits the topic perfectly. You see, I want to humanize the people who suffer from these illnesses. I want to show why we need better treatment for them, to illustrate why intervention is important. I thought that actually talking to people affected by mental illness, and centering their perspectives, would be the best way to tell this story."

"Interesting." He sat back in his chair and looked like he was analyzing her, trying to decide how much he wished to share. "That is a compelling topic. And I'm surprised that anyone is exploring it from that angle. Most people don't try to understand the humans behind the mental illness. I think it makes them uncomfortable to try to face something they don't understand.

"Though I'm not sure *we're* the ones suffering—at least those who have committed crimes aren't the true victims of mental illness. I suppose I am suffering in my own way, but not as deeply as Alyssa did. Wouldn't you rather capture her story instead?"

"I think your mental illness is part of her story. But there are so many out there who only focus on the effects of it on others. I'm interested in your experience. I think it's all connected," Kate told him.

"It was still my responsibility to treat it. I don't want to sound like a victim. Sure, I was driven by mental illness, but it doesn't excuse what I did. I've done a lot of work to take responsibility for my behavior through therapy, meds, and general treatment. I don't want that to be erased."

"I completely understand," Kate replied, impressed by his determination to take full responsibility for it. "I won't suggest that you're a victim. I simply want to understand how things led to your crime."

Daniel nodded. "I guess I don't even know where to start."

"Perhaps at the beginning," Kate suggested.

"Yes, the beginning," Daniel nodded. "I'll give you a quick rundown and then go into details after. I guess it started with a tough upbringing, as all of these types of stories do. My mother was an alcoholic. Distant. Cruel. Always fighting with my father for one reason or another. Money, usually. They'd beat each other up all the time. Sometimes me too."

"Jesus," Kate whispered. "I'm sorry."

Daniel shrugged, his face impassive as if he were recounting a story he'd read and not his own horrific childhood. "She spent more time drunk than sober. Got pretty good at hiding it. One night she got behind the wheel and wrapped the car around a telephone pole with my dad in the passenger's seat. He didn't make it. I was put into foster care when she was arrested, and that's a whole other bout of trauma."

"Was it hard for you?" It felt like such a simple, obvious question to ask, but it was worth asking, in Kate's opinion.

"Everyone knows the foster care system can be brutal. I had a bad time with the first few families. Until I finally found one that I fit in. That's when I noticed I was different. Because once

I bonded with the family, I bonded so strongly. I was terrified of them leaving, which caused a whole host of issues."

"That was later linked to borderline personality disorder, right?" Kate asked.

"Yes." He nodded. "Though at first, the doctors didn't see it that way. Later I went on to try to get treatment for it when I realized what I was doing to Alyssa. But women are more likely to have BPD than men are. So, it's often misdiagnosed as something else, especially in men. For me, I was simply thought to have anger issues. But it's so much more than that.

"Having this disorder... I still can't find the words to describe it, even though I've become more aware of it since I've been treated. It's like having all of your emotions turned up to one hundred, especially when you care about someone as much as I tend to care about people, even though I know that's difficult to believe now.

"My love for them is intense, but when they do something wrong, the hatred is just as all-consuming. I can't handle rejection in any form, and any criticism is difficult for me to face and accept. It seems like when someone criticizes me, they're ripping through who I am as a person. They're telling me I'm not good enough. Which is a deep, almost crippling blow. Sometimes I can't even fully connect to who I am. I tend to shift and change to suit whomever I'm interacting with because I don't have a fully realized sense of self. People say that I'm manipulative, and maybe I am. It's a protective thing though—to keep myself from being abandoned when I know I'm particularly difficult to be around. I don't try to hurt people, but that's what I end up doing anyway. I'm always hurting myself and the ones I love."

Kate was blown away by what Daniel was saying as he went into more detail about what his childhood was like and the intensity of terror and fear and rage he'd felt at various times in his life. His awareness was more than she ever expected. It would be a gold mine for her book.

Yet it led her to wonder how such a tragedy had happened. If he was so aware of it now, how could he be so unaware of it back then that he was deemed legally unable to control his own actions?

"This all culminated into something toxic when I met Alyssa," Daniel explained, his eyes shimmering with tears. "At first, everything was amazing. I still think she's the most incredible woman I've ever met. She was so loving, kind, smart, passionate, thoughtful, just… all the things you could want in a person. And she was so beautiful. I still couldn't believe that she chose me.

"That was the problem though. I couldn't believe that she chose me, which really got into my head. Why would she choose me? I was so damaged. I didn't understand what she saw in me, which made me feel insecure. I was certain that someday she would leave me once she realized I was unworthy of her love and attention.

"This led to emotional dysregulation. Some days I would worship her, and I would be the best boyfriend ever. Other days I would blow up over the smallest thing and tear her down with words I never meant to say. They would just come out and cut her. Destroy her. Before my own brain could even catch up, the words were already out of my mouth. I always felt bad for it after. Yet, I couldn't seem to gain control over myself. This is something that only grew worse once the voices started."

"The voices," Kate noted. "The schizophrenia."

"Yes, though at first, it was just my insecurities talking. Telling me she was going to leave me, she secretly hated me, she was conspiring against me. Then, the voices began to take a life of their own, talking to me like I had another person living in my head.

"People get the wrong idea of schizophrenia sometimes. It's not always these huge, crazy hallucinations. Sometimes it's just a whisper. A shift. I stopped sleeping. I ate far less. I became preoccupied with these conspiracy theories that turned me against Alyssa and caused a great rift between us.

"Then, that night came. When she finally decided to leave me, and for good reason. The voices in my head were acting up that day, telling me she was conspiring against me. She not only wanted to leave me, but she also wanted to harm me. And the thing was, she had bought a gun somewhere along the way. To protect herself. I wonder to this day if it was to protect herself from me. Because she knew how dangerous I was. She had it by her side as she was preparing to leave, like she was afraid I'd try to harm her."

Kate saw the true suffering in Daniel's eyes as he spoke. She believed he genuinely felt terrible about this. It genuinely hurt him that Alyssa thought she'd have to protect herself from him, even though it turned out she was right.

"The voices became so loud," Daniel whispered. "So chaotic. They said I had no choice. I had to kill her, or she'd kill me. I grabbed a knife when she wasn't looking. I hid behind our bedroom door. And the next time she walked in… well, you know what happened."

Kate had seen the crime scene photos as she was researching the story. Their bedroom had been awash in blood. Daniel had sliced through her neck and then continued stabbing her body well past when she was dead.

Then, he dismembered her. He never even tried burying her. It seemed like at some point he awoke from his shocked state and called the police, confessing to the whole thing in tears. He was arrested without a struggle, and after his trial, he came here.

"Doctors have noted that you seem to be rehabilitated," Kate said, once she found her voice again. "Do you think that's honestly the case?"

For a moment, Kate thought she saw hesitation flicker across Daniel's eyes. It was enough to make her feel unsafe. She silently hoped he wouldn't be released. At least not until more time had passed. Maybe not ever.

"I honestly do believe that I have been," he said with conviction, making Kate wonder if she had even sensed that hesitation or if she was making it up in her mind. "I don't get obsessed with people in the same way that I used to. I don't hear voices. I'm not as emotionally dysregulated. I'm properly medicated.

"I will have to live with my mental illness forever, especially the borderline personality disorder because there's no specific medication that targets that. But I've learned better coping skills through therapy. I've learned how to better manage my disorder. I'll never be cured, not entirely. But I can have as much of a life as I'm able. I have to be grateful for that. Even after what I've done."

He seemed to be truly remorseful. But some part of Kate's mind still lingered with doubt.

"Can you go over your treatment plan with me?" Kate asked, needing to gather as much information as needed for her story. But as she listened, her mind flickered back to Alyssa's brutalized body, and she couldn't help but wonder if any treatment was enough to cure someone from doing that ever again.

CHAPTER THREE

K ATE WAS IN A DAZE BY THE TIME SHE LEFT THE MENTAL institution. As Daniel was talking, she had become so completely invested in his story that it was difficult to pull herself back to reality. Her mind was buzzing with all the new information as she considered the best way to fold it into her book.

She doubted her abilities as she considered this. It was such a complicated topic that she hadn't even realized the full scope when she'd started. She thought she knew enough about the topic to write a whole book on it, but now she was wondering if she could authentically represent people struggling with these disorders without doing them a disservice.

"I'll make sure to capture their stories better," she mumbled to herself as she got into her car. "I'll do my due diligence to make sure I'm being authentic. I'll do the proper research this time to get it right."

She felt better as she assured herself of this out loud. She was setting her intentions, and she was sure to exceed them. It would be her best book yet, and in this search for empathy and understanding, she would become a better person along the way too.

Pleased with this, she turned the key in the engine, but before setting off toward home, she checked her phone, which had been on do-not-disturb mode while she was in the institution. That's when she noticed a call from an unfamiliar number she had received. She copied and pasted the number into her phone's search and discovered it was the local hospital.

Why would the hospital be calling her?

Her heart suddenly leaped into her throat. She quickly called them back and waited, her knee jiggling incessantly, as she was placed on hold and transferred to a thousand places.

Finally, someone was able to speak to her for more than two seconds.

"Hi, this is Kate Larose. I missed a call?" she started.

"Yes. We notified you because you're the emergency contact for Tyler Larose," the receptionist told her.

"He's my husband," Kate said hesitantly. Her heart pounded as she grew increasingly worried. Why would a hospital be calling her about her husband? "Has something happened to him?"

"It's best if you come here so we can talk to you in person," the receptionist answered.

"Um. Okay."

Kate wanted to demand answers right away. She didn't want to have to wait to get them. Driving there would be torturous. She needed to know if something had happened to Tyler right now. Yet she also didn't want to waste time talking to someone on the phone when she could be seeing her husband.

Seeing Tyler was what she needed most right now. She needed to hug him. She needed him to assure her he was fine. So, she hung up the phone and went straight to the hospital.

She tried to keep her cool and remain focused on the drive. Yet wave after wave of horrible possibilities flooded her mind and tears came to her eyes. Her hands began shaking in terror of what might have happened.

"Please be okay," she whispered. "Please be okay, Tyler. I need you to be okay."

She felt like a disheveled mess as she went into the hospital and frantically went up to the receptionist's desk. She quickly gave them her information.

"We'll need you to take a seat," the receptionist said. "Tyler's doctor will be out to talk to you soon."

"I don't want to talk to a doctor," Kate insisted, her voice raising in fear and anticipation. "I want to see my *husband*. Just let me be with him, and we can talk to the doctor together. I just need to know he's okay. I need to know he's okay."

"You'll just need to give us a moment," the receptionist answered. "The doctor will explain everything in a—"

"Do you not hear what I'm saying?" Kate interrupted. Usually, she was kind to workers, but this didn't seem to be a moment for politeness. She simply wanted answers. "I need to see my husband."

At that, the doors opened, and a young, female doctor stepped into the lobby. "Kate Larose?" she asked, looking at Kate.

"Yes," Kate said, nearly falling in relief.

She left the receptionist's desk and went straight to the doctor. "You must be treating Tyler. Can you please take me to him?"

The doctor looked at her with this awful look of pity that left Kate horrified. She was starting to feel like something was horribly wrong with Tyler, and her mind raced to catch up. She knew he had to be okay. Nothing that terrible could happen to him. Her love would protect him. Their life was too great to be interrupted.

"Come with me," she said. "I'm Cathleen Sullivan, and I treated your husband."

"*Treated?*"

Before Kate could get answers, she was following the doctor through the doors which calmed her. She hoped Cathleen would bring her to her husband's room. No matter how badly he was injured, she wanted to see him. She knew he'd make it through. Once she was there, she could lend him her strength, and he would heal.

Instead of going to see Tyler, though, the doctor led her into a small blue and white room with a couch, a couple of plush chairs, and plants desperately trying to make the space seem welcoming and comforting but failing to do so. It wasn't lost on her that it felt almost exactly like the visiting room at the mental facility she'd just come from.

"Please, take a seat," Cathleen said.

Taking a seat was the last thing Kate wanted to do, but she hoped it would get her answers sooner, so she complied. Once she sat on one of the chairs, Cathleen sat facing her.

"I'm sorry, Kate. But your husband has passed."

Kate froze, then began shaking. The words were foreign. They couldn't be true. Time beat in her ears, blocking out everything. Suddenly, she was trapped in a nightmare she desperately wanted out of.

"No," Kate whispered. "You're lying. You must be lying. That's impossible. I saw him earlier today. He was fine."

"I'm so sorry," Cathleen repeated. "Your husband had an accident at the job site. He fell off a ladder and hit his skull on the concrete driveway. He was brought in unresponsive and with massive internal bleeding to the brain. We couldn't revive him."

A heavy wave of guilt and terror overwhelmed Kate. "If I had been here, he would've been revived," she insisted. "If he had heard my voice, sensed my presence. He would've pulled through. This is my fault. He can't be dead. He can't be dead. No…"

Someone was breathing heavily in the room, shaking and hyperventilating loudly as if barely holding back a panic attack. It took several seconds before Kate realized that person was her.

"I assure you there's nothing you could've done," Cathleen said. "His fall killed him. There's nothing anyone could've done."

"No, let me see him. He'll come back to life if you let me see him. He'll realize I need him, and he'll fight. He will be alive."

"I'm sorry, but with the state he's in, we can't let you see him right now."

Kate shook her head. She denied it. She couldn't face it. But even as she refused to accept the truth, the tears fell. It was the most overwhelming state she had ever fallen into. Darkness engulfed her. She willed herself to wake up, but it seemed too real. It seemed like maybe this wasn't a dream. It seemed like maybe this was her new reality.

"I'll give you some privacy," Cathleen finally said.

And in this small room in the hospital, Kate broke. She sobbed like her heart was bleeding, shards of her old life digging into her skin, killing her. The truth hit her as her life changed completely for the worse; she was shattered into a million pieces. She would never be able to recover from this. The old her died as she faced the horror of this new existence.

Her husband was dead. Her dream was dead.

How could she go on living?

CHAPTER FOUR

T HERE'S SOMETHING ABOUT DEATH THAT FREEZES those who are closest to it. The amount of distance between the one left behind and the person who died determines how quickly life returns after someone has passed.

For widows, time stalls. The closeness they have with their husbands means they're completely encompassed, drowned, dragged down by an immense devastation that consumes everything so completely that there doesn't seem to be a way out of it. They're completely frozen. Or at least, that's what it meant for Kate.

For days, she didn't stop crying. The shock made her incapable of doing anything. She was shipped off to her parents' house to stay with people who loved her. She stayed on the couch and cried. She stayed in the guest room and cried. People came and went to try to comfort her, and she barely acknowledged their presence. She ignored their frantic whispers about her and just sobbed. No matter where she went, she couldn't seem to soothe the tears that she was drowning in.

Every thought she had was about him. Tyler's words, his face, his touch played in her mind in a torturous loop. All of their memories, their dreams for the future were like a sick reel of a horror movie that was now tainted and ruined. She thought of how much he loved her and how she loved him.

She knew she would never find a love quite like that again. She was separated from her soulmate, and deep down, all she wanted was to be reunited with him again. Even if that meant they'd both have to go to the next life.

Kate had long since left her suicidal days behind her, but following Tyler's death, she contemplated it. Without him, the days stretched out with no purpose; it was too much to bear. She simply couldn't handle it. So, she dreamed of any way they could be together again, even if that were under the worst circumstances. Even if she couldn't do that to her friends and family, being with him again was a comforting thought.

After a few days, though, there were a few things that broke her out of the overwhelming devastation. Every thought was still a painful reminder of Tyler. But certain things tore her out of it. Like when a group of people knocked on her parents' front door.

"You have visitors," her mother said, walking into the living room where Kate sat watching a horror movie and not really processing any of it.

"I don't want visitors," Kate mumbled.

"These ones have come a long way to see you."

Kate was curious about that. Before she could protest, Allison came in with Brad, Jasmine, Timothy, and Jade. Kate sat up in surprise, shocked to see them, and a little embarrassed about the state she was in.

"What are you guys doing here?" she asked, standing to hug each of her college friends.

"Allison called us," Brad explained. "She told us what happened, and we knew we had to be here for you, just like in the old days. We couldn't let you go through this alone."

In college, Brad, Allison, Kate, and Timothy had all formed a cozy group of friends that had stayed platonic and close over the years. When Timothy started dating Jasmine and Brad started dating Jade, they were quickly included in the group as well, and they went through everything together. A couple years after college, Tyler had come into her life, and he fit naturally into the group, even if they didn't get the chance to go out and party every single week anymore.

They shared their histories, their future dreams, and had fun making memories whenever time allowed. They were there for each other's weddings, when Jasmine and Timothy had their baby, and the untimely death of Allison's parents. And now they were here once again for Tyler's death.

"I can't tell you how good it is to see you again," Kate said. She was surprised to find that she truly meant it. Plenty of other people had stopped by to give their condolences and Kate at times found herself irritated by them. No one ever knew the right things to say, and she didn't have the energy to respond in the polite ways she knew she should.

Yet this group of friends were people she felt like she could be herself around. She knew she wouldn't have to fake being happy around them. She wouldn't need to be full of energy to join them.

"It's great to see you too," Timothy said. "You know we'd always be here for you. We're all down to go out if you want to. If leaving the house would be best for you. But since things are still new, we thought you might want to stay in."

"I don't know," Kate looked away. "I guess right now, I'm honestly kind of boring to be around. I know you guys don't live super close by, so I feel bad for you making the trip when I'm like this, but…"

"But we knew you'd say that," Jasmine said. "So, we brought some things to make all of our time more pleasant. Besides, it's always great to see you—even when you aren't your best self."

At that, they went back out to their cars and came back with chocolates, ice cream, chips, cookies, pizza, and a wide variety of drinks. The friends set up in the living room, and soon enough, an impromptu horror movie marathon was underway.

Kate really was glad to have them there. It almost felt like old times again, like everything was normal. But then she would turn to give Tyler a peck on the cheek or ask him to pass the popcorn, and he wasn't there. Then the memories would flood back in, and she got so overwhelmed by thoughts of Tyler that she just broke down in tears. When those moments happened, her friends paused the movie and surrounded her with hugs, words of encouragement, and all the love she could ask for.

They gave her space to vent when she needed, to work through those tough feelings. And when she needed to talk about something else to get her mind off it, they shared what was going on in their lives. They talked about their various hobbies and interests.

In some ways, everything had changed. But at the same time, it felt like a blast into the past, which Kate found comforting. It was familiar in this world that had become so foreign to her. It was just the comfort she needed.

Her friends stayed at a hotel in town while Kate went through the process of funeral planning, of all the last-minute details that widows need to take care of. They helped with what they could and supported her through the rest.

Then, the painful day to bury Tyler came. Kate felt like she was putting on the show of a put-together widow, a part she was reluctant to play. She orchestrated a beautiful ceremony for Tyler, complete with flowers and beautiful words, but it still didn't feel like enough. It still didn't provide her with the closure she needed. She still felt a little empty following the ceremony.

By the end, she felt completely defeated. She was no longer able to fully cope with the pain, so she sank into the arms of her friends and cried the whole night. Her parents checked in on her as well. She relied on their strength. But at the end of the night, when it was time for bed, she found herself in her room alone.

"I miss you, Tyler," she whispered into the darkness. "I love you, and I always will. I wish you were here with me."

She closed her eyes, and for a moment, it felt like he was with her. Then, it faded. And she was stuck in this nightmare without him, wondering if life was really worth living.

CHAPTER FIVE

KATE NEVER THOUGHT SHE WOULD BE A WIDOW AT THIR-ty-three years old, having been married to her husband for eight years before their bliss ended. She always thought they'd have more time together. She thought they'd raise a family together. Build a fairytale.

It was shocking how in one moment, her whole life had changed. Kate didn't want anything to do with this new life. She would give anything to go back.

Now, five months after his death, things were changing yet again. Kate couldn't truly say there was hope yet, but there was this feeling that she had to start living again. She had to get her life together somehow. She had to figure out how to move forward from this.

She was grabbing coffee with Allison when the topic of how to get back on track came up again. The low lighting in the shop mixed with the scent of coffee and the whirring of the machines created a perfect mix of calmness that allowed space for uncomfortable things to be brought up in a safe way.

The warm, sunset-orange walls brought a certain energy that made Kate feel something close to living, though she still felt dead most days. She felt distressed that she still sometimes wished she was dead with him. The depression was haunting, but at least she felt like she could breathe again.

"How's the book going?" Allison asked, sipping her latte.

"It's going... okay," Kate answered. "I guess it's been a little difficult. Since some of the people I interviewed for my book killed those they loved because they were suffering from a mental illness. It just involves a lot of death and unpleasantness. You know I've already been dealing with depression. And, you know, after Tyler... I find it more difficult to be sympathetic to that. I want to be. I know I should be. I still understand that mental illness can drive people to do awful things. But to take away someone else's loved one... I'm not sure I can look past that, now that I know how horrifying it is to lose someone."

"Yeah, I get it," Allison said with an empathetic nod. "You've been through a lot. It makes sense why you'd need to take a break from it. Does that mean you're not going to complete the book?"

For some reason, that question caught Kate off guard. She hadn't thought about it fully, but that was the only reasonable outcome. If she couldn't continue with the research, if she couldn't open her mind to it, then there was no way she could complete the book.

That meant the time she had sunk into it so far would be for nothing. Her idea would have to be scrapped. She hated the sound of that. It didn't feel right. Yet she was having difficulty writing at all. Her heart wasn't in it anymore.

"I'm not sure yet," Kate decided. "It's still something I'm considering. I don't want to scrap it all. I just don't know how I'm going to handle it yet."

"Well, you have plenty of time to consider it," Allison assured her. "No one expects you to make any major decisions right away. How about the cottage?"

That was another obstacle Kate hadn't yet come to deal with. She hated being reminded of these things, though she knew they were essential to work through.

"The cottage is just about completed," Kate replied. "We already had everything paid for upfront, so the work never stopped. I could move into it as early as next week if I wanted to."

"Do you want to?" Allison asked. "Or are you planning on selling it?"

Kate considered it. "I haven't thought too much about it," she admitted. "It was the dream I had with Tyler. We were supposed to live in it together with the family we hoped to grow. It would be strange to be there on my own. I think it would feel like something big was missing. And yet, I don't know. I think it could be a good thing maybe. Maybe I need to get out of the house we lived in together for so long. Maybe I need to get out of that town. Maybe I need to start fresh."

As Kate said it out loud, she became more confident of the idea. It was still an uncomfortable thought. She still didn't want to live there without Tyler. But she didn't want to live anywhere without Tyler. And the cottage was at least a better place than being trapped in the memories of the home they'd shared for so long. It didn't have the same past imprinted upon it.

"That sounds like a fantastic idea," Allison said. "I'll call everyone, we'll all help you get settled in. The guys will help you with the moving, you and me and Jade can sit back and supervise. We'll have a moving party. It'll be great."

Kate wanted to insist that she didn't need help, but she knew what a challenge it would be to do this on her own. So, she simply thanked Allison.

"I can't tell you how much I appreciate how supportive you've been," Kate said. "Truly. Your help has meant everything to me."

"What are friends for, right?" Allison assured her with a broad smile. "Let's focus on getting you moved in."

Despite herself, Kate chuckled. It wasn't exactly a happy chuckle, more of a nervous one, but it was the closest thing she'd had to a genuine laugh in so long.

It took a couple of weeks to finalize the plans, but finally, moving day came. Once again, Kate's friends from college came out for the weekend to help. They hired a U-Haul to move the furniture and helped her put all of the less personal things in boxes.

The pictures, memories, and special tokens were up to Kate to take care of, and that was a challenge of its own. It was one she was certain she'd never be ready for. Going through all of her and Tyler's things left her feeling drained and trapped in memories.

She was certain she would never escape the grasp of her past, and she wasn't sure she ever wanted to. She would rather just stay there with him, unable to leave. Unable to move on.

It didn't help to see the couples around her being loving. As much as she didn't want to be bitter, seeing Timothy and Jasmine all cuddly and sweet reminded her of Tyler. She wished he could be here with her. They were supposed to do this together.

As they continued moving things and packing, though, she thought she noticed some distance between Brad and Jade. It was unlike them to bicker so often. There seemed to be just a general air of tension between them and relief when they were apart.

She and Jade had never been particularly close, so she didn't feel like it was her place to ask Jade if something was going on. She was much closer to Brad, but she didn't think it was appropriate for her to be having those kinds of conversations with another woman's husband, so she decided to just let it be and not bring it up.

Still, she found herself gravitating more toward Jade and Brad than Jasmine and Timothy because they seemed less loving, and she felt guilty about that. Her life had become a whole well of clashing emotions, and some she felt guilty for, angry about, or devasted by. None of it made sense.

But she didn't want to dwell on that. She was simply happy to have them all surrounding her as they helped her transition into this new part of her life.

"I know I couldn't have done this all my own," she said, once they were back in the cottage and all of the boxes and furniture had been moved in.

"You deserve every ounce of help we've given," Brad assured her. "You were there for me through a really rough time, and I'm grateful to return the help."

Kate thought back to when Brad was struggling with depression in school and how she always made sure to listen to him and encourage him to see a doctor and a therapist. He eventually did so, improving his mental health drastically. She couldn't have been prouder of him for it.

"You've been there for me through everything," Allison agreed.

"Me too," Timothy said. "When anxiety was getting the best of me in school especially, you were there every step of the way. Remember, you helped me reorganize my whole schedule so it wasn't as overwhelming. You've done so much for everyone else. You deserve this help for yourself."

"Thank you," Kate replied, feeling warmed with love for them. "I appreciate that. I really do. You know… it still gets dark sometimes living without Tyler. It's been by far the toughest thing I've ever gone through. And I know I couldn't do it without your support."

"We're more than happy to give it," Jasmine assured her.

That night they all went out to dinner to celebrate the move. Kate spent the night at Allison's house after the friends all got a little too drunk to go home. Though Kate vowed that night that the next day she would spend the night in her cottage and fully move forward with her life.

She had to at some point, didn't she?

CHAPTER SIX

K ATE STOOD IN FRONT OF THE WALNUT DOOR THAT reminded her of the entrance to a fairy house and took a deep breath. Her friends had gone back to their lives, leaving her alone in this, and she wasn't sure how to fully face it.

She reminded herself she had to do this though. So, she took out the key, unlocked the door, and made a wish that this would be exactly what she needed. Then, she stepped inside.

The arched windows allowed a ton of light in, splashing against the cozy crème, red, and orange walls that made the house look like it was raised from the earth to provide a hobbit-style home to live in. The wood floors were covered in boxes, but the cheerful demeanor of the home persisted. The assortment of furniture they had collected over the years made the space feel like home.

Kate walked inside and did a quick walk-through of the house as it slowly settled in that this was her home now. She was both delighted and intimidated by it, an odd mix of emotions she wasn't quite able to process.

She stopped at her bedroom door then stepped inside. The canopy bed with its bedframe shaped to look like tree branches sat in the middle of the room dressed in gold and red coverings that went nicely with the crème-colored walls. Her matching vanity, dresser, love seat, small bookshelf, and bedside tables sat bare, waiting for her to cover them, while her walk-in closet seemed full of possibilities to be filled with.

There was so much unpacking to be done that Kate didn't know where to start. So, she decided to just dig into the first box she found in this room. She opened it and found it was a box of clothes, so she set to work hanging them all up in her closet.

Her mind wandered to what her future might look like as she hung the clothes—until she got to the bottom of the box and grasped something that made her stop. She pulled out a button-down navy-blue shirt and held it close to her.

"Do you remember this, Tyler?" she whispered as she closed her eyes. "I got it for you to wear to that fancy dinner on Valentine's Day, and you kept it ever since. You said it was your lucky shirt. You said you loved it so much just because I bought it for you. You always loved every little thing I did for you."

At that, the tears started to fall again. She brought the shirt to her face and breathed the smell in. It still smelled of his cologne with that mixture of sandalwood with a hint of nutmeg intertwined in it.

Hugging it was like hugging a phantom of him. He had always been warm and comforting, the place she called home. And now she was devasted knowing that the most she could cling to was the ghost of him.

Still, the ghost of him was worth the world to her. So, she clung to him for a moment longer before putting the shirt on the hanger. She hoped that it would always smell of him, but she decided to do a little digging just in case the smell wore off.

After going through the boxes a little more thoroughly, she found his bottle of cologne packed next to his watch. She took them both out and set them on the vanity. She dreamily gazed at them there, as if they were waiting for him to come by and put them on at any time, idly wondering if this was a healthy thing to do.

She had kept all the photos in their frames hung on her walls, most of his things, and all the little tokens of him. It was almost like her home was a shrine to their marriage, and she wasn't sure if that was conducive to moving on. She wasn't sure if she was ready to change that yet though.

At the very least, unpacking soothed her soul a little bit. She had worried that it would unleash the memories, and it did. But it unlocked them in a healthy way that allowed her to process them.

She worked throughout much of the day until she realized it was time for dinner. Then she ordered takeout and made her nightly tea. As she ate, a strange feeling overcame her. Her mind raced with possibility. She paused midway through her meal and grabbed her laptop, propping it up in front of her.

It was as if a door that was slammed in her face was now unlocked. She opened up the document she had been working on, and without even a moment's hesitation, began writing. Her fingers ran over the keyboard like they were meant to do this sacred dance. The words tumbled out of her like they had been waiting for this all along, anxious to pour out of her and into the document.

The moment didn't last long. After about twenty minutes, the well of inspiration dried up again, and she didn't have the heart to continue as thoughts of Tyler broke the trance she had been in. But it was still more progress than she had made since he died. It encouraged her, making her feel like maybe she could live again.

After finishing her tea, she felt sleepier than normal, which came as a surprise to her. Since Tyler died, she'd had trouble sleeping for more than a few hours. She was chronically exhausted, yet somehow never sleepy—or at least not sleepy enough to allow herself to rest.

That night felt different though. She felt calm in a way that she hadn't since he died. She felt at peace.

Though it was before her bedtime, she decided she would try to get some sleep. She went into the master bathroom with its stone walls, chrome fixtures, and soothing colors, and reached for her sleeping pills before deciding that maybe she wouldn't need them that night. Maybe she was sleepy enough already.

She still took the antidepressants that she had been prescribed following his death. Then, she turned off the lights and slipped into her bed, exhausted in a good way with the hope that she might sleep at least a little better than she had been. Just as she was dozing off, though, she got a distinct feeling that someone was watching her.

The curtains rustled just a little, which gave her pause. It wasn't like the windows were open, and the house wasn't designed to be drafty.

She turned the lights back on. She was alone.

As she turned the lights off again, she thought of the things people had said to comfort her after Tyler had passed. They assured her that he'd be watching over her, that their love wouldn't die. He wouldn't fully leave her.

Kate had trouble believing in all of that and even became frustrated at them for saying it even though she knew they meant well by it. Her husband was gone. Couldn't they see that? It was the end of her world. She didn't have him there to soothe her anymore. He was dead.

Now, she felt a bit of comfort from their words. She let herself dare to dream for a moment that maybe he was still lingering near her as a ghost. Maybe he hadn't fully left her. If his spirit could be there with her, she knew he'd find a way to make it happen.

"I love you, Tyler," Kate whispered, feeling silly even as she said it. "If you're here with me right now, I want you to know I love you. I always have. I always will. I miss you with my whole heart, and I'll try every day to make you proud. Until we meet again, darling."

She snuggled into her bed feeling like once again someone was watching her. Someone was there with her; she was sure of it. But she welcomed the presence. And the thought of it was comforting enough to make her fall asleep quickly and peacefully, almost as if he were there with her again.

CHAPTER SEVEN

KATE WAS SHOCKED WHEN SHE WOKE UP THE NEXT morning feeling energetic and well-rested. She'd woken up feeling so good it caught her completely off guard. She lay there for a moment, unable to quite believe it.

She had slept through the whole night. It was the first time since Tyler died that she had slept through the whole night. And when she woke up, she felt refreshed, energized, and ready to get on with her day in a way that she hadn't since he left her.

Part of her felt alive again. She was still grieving him, but she didn't feel as stuck in an all-consuming, black hole. She didn't feel as weighed down with sadness. She felt like she could breathe again. Like maybe she could somehow live again. Like maybe there was a purpose to living.

"Maybe I don't want to die," she whispered.

The thought helped her get out of bed, though the guilt that followed her into the shower was brutal. She questioned herself as the hot water ran over her.

How can I begin to feel happy when he's gone? Does this mean that I'm moving on too fast? How can I want to live when he's not alive? Does that mean I want to be without him? Am I a bad widow? Was I a bad wife?

She tried to work through those thoughts as she exited the shower and got dressed for the day. While she was getting ready, she noticed that Tyler's cologne bottle had been knocked over, so she righted it.

"Just the fact that I kept this shows I'm not fully moving on," she assured herself. "So that means I'm still okay. I still love him. I'm not being a bad widow. I'm just trying to live again. That's what he would want me to do."

That knowledge soothed her for the moment, though guilt still nagged at the back of her mind. She worried that wanting to live again was some sort of betrayal. Yet she couldn't fully face that. So, she tucked it in the back of her mind to wrestle with later.

It helped when she got downstairs to stand in front of the upgraded built-in coffee machine Tyler had ordered for her before he died. Allison had already stocked her pantry with high-end gourmet coffee grounds, so Kate was all set for success.

She made her cup of coffee, then brought it upstairs to the office that was meant just for her. There were still boxes to unpack in here as well, but the sunset orange walls, ornate wood furniture, and walls with built-in bookshelves made the space feel professional. Tyler had built her the perfect work environment.

A skylight allowed fresh sunlight to wash over her mahogany desk that looked out of the bay window overlooking the garden. Writing was important to Kate, which in turn made it important to Tyler. He had ensured that her workspace was set up so she would not only enjoy it but would also be successful while working within it.

Hoping to rekindle some of the magic she'd felt the night before, she opened up her laptop and started her research. She started investigating more cases of people whose mental illnesses had contributed to their doing terrible things.

She started off with a story of a woman who was suffering from schizophrenia and bipolar disorder. She had three children and had only been diagnosed with bipolar disorder after their births. Schizophrenic traits hadn't shown yet, and they wouldn't appear until much later.

However, with each child, the woman had been stricken with postpartum depression that affected her severely and got in the way of her functioning in her day-to-day life. She continually noted that something was wrong. She went to a doctor and a therapist, trying to fix the disorganization scrambling her thoughts and making her life more complicated.

As things got worse, though, the woman completely stopped attending appointments. She became a recluse, and the next time anyone heard from her was when she was investigated for murdering her children.

More cases like this followed. There was another man who was abused by his mother throughout his life. He was constantly berated for his behavior and made to feel so much guilt until one day his mind snapped when he and his girlfriend got into an argument. Her head was found in the basement. Her body had yet to be recovered.

Kate paused after this story to grab breakfast, needing a break from the disturbing content. She found that being able to work again revitalized her, even if it was on something that wasn't exactly pleasant. It reminded her of her passions. It reminded her that she was still living. Still feeling.

So, despite eating the bare minimum since Tyler died, that morning she made herself a full breakfast. She cooked up some eggs with spinach, made some whole-grain toast, and chopped up some fresh fruit to go along with it.

Having a full, healthy breakfast left her with more energy than she'd had in a long time, so she sat there for a few minutes, considering what she would do with it. She thought about her old self and tried to figure out how she might be that person again. She found that she missed that person. Even though she knew she'd never be quite the same again, she wanted to at least try to get back to some sort of normal.

These thoughts brought her back to the research she had been doing right before Tyler died. She thought back to the interview with Daniel Jenkins and how helpful that had been. She began to ponder the possibility that maybe she'd want to do something like that again.

Allison's warning came back into her mind that talking to criminals might be dangerous. But Kate cared even less about that now than she did before. She still wasn't fully committed to the idea that she wanted to live after her husband's death, so dangerous things felt far less threatening to her now.

After a bit of thought, she looked a little further into the patients she had been learning about. She made a few calls, and at first, she was denied the right to visit any of them. But she was persistent, and eventually she was able to make an appointment to visit an inmate the very next day.

Feeling pleased with her success, she sat back in her chair and looked out the window. With these new plans in mind, she was starting to feel more alive again. She wasn't sure how to process that. But all of a sudden, this warm and cozy house felt a little too small to contain all of the strange things she was feeling.

For a moment, it felt like someone was watching her again. But this time it felt like they were judging her. They were silently shaking their head at how she was moving on, telling her it was too soon for that. She had no right to be happy when he was gone.

Kate thought back to the cologne bottle that had been knocked over. Was it a sign that she was doing something wrong? Should she be holding back?

To avoid these thoughts that she worried might derail her, she forced herself out of the house, deciding that she needed to get out and see the town. She was going to have a semigood day, at the very least. She was determined to rinse herself of the dark waters of the past and somehow emerge again out of the ocean of sorrow she found herself drowning in.

CHAPTER EIGHT

T HOUGH KATE HAD VISITED TYLER WHILE HE WAS working on the house plenty of times before, she had never explored the surrounding town much before she moved into the cottage, so she knew little about what it had to offer. It was a sleepy, little, coastal town steeped in history, or so she'd heard. Driven by that need to get out of her house and escape the sorrow and memories that trapped her there, she decided to go on a little adventure. She hoped it might clear her mind of the guilt and confusing feelings as well as provide some inspiration. She always found that she did her best writing when she remembered to go see what life was like outside the page.

She felt more at ease as the ocean came into view, slowly reaching out across the sand to convince her that someday, things would be okay again. She was getting to that place where maybe she could find happiness.

In the spirit of this quest for happiness, she drove farther into the town and found a place to park her car along the street. She got out and marveled at the cute little shops, the cobblestone sidewalks, and the general cheerful demeanor that surrounded the area.

Willow trees with long fingers and blue and white flowers broke up the stones as she walked, providing that extra pop of color to the charming scene. Though the colorful shops seemed to be doing fine on their own in that regard. Kate popped into a few of them, marveling at the paintings from local artists, the hand-knitted scarves and socks, and the unique finds she couldn't have purchased where she used to live.

She picked up a few handmade candles, a cute little succulent with yellow flowers, and some natural soap for a bubble bath before coming to a stop in front of a bundle of sage. She debated getting it in the spirit of cleansing her home, even though she didn't exactly believe in that sort of thing. She thought it might be good symbolically to get her mind in a better place. Part of her was still slightly convinced that Tyler's ghost was joining her, though, and she certainly didn't want to banish him just in case. So, she let it be and went to check out with the young woman wearing a wide-brimmed hat and seashell jewelry who was standing behind the counter.

Kate's stomach unexpectedly rumbled as she stepped out of the all-natural shop, so she slipped into the first café she found and immediately decided upon entering that she made the right decision. The bright, cheerful, yellow walls mixed with the white tables and daisies decorating the space helped lighten her mood a bit. There were enough patrons to fill the room with lively chatter, but not so much that it was noisy and overcrowded. It was simply pleasant in the way that Kate was longing for.

Since she was able to seat herself, she chose a seat by the window where she could look out at the bright blue day and try to chase some of the depression away. She looked over the homemade choices on the menu and was immediately charmed by the fun, whimsical names they had.

Soon after, she was greeted by a waitress. The young woman looked to be in her late twenties with a strong smile, a dark ponytail that moved in time with her enthusiastic steps, and blue eyes that were bright with energy.

"Morning!" she chirped with a bright and cheerful voice. "I'm Amanda, and I'll be your server today. You know, I don't know if I've seen you yet. Have you ever been in to join us at Barb's Café before?"

"No, I haven't," Kate admitted. "I'm actually new to the area. So, I'm still trying to explore and get a feel for what's around."

"Well, you've started at the perfect place," Amanda assured her. "Our coffee is all roasted in-house, and our food is made fresh with local ingredients from farmers in the area. We try our best to get to know everyone who sticks around—to make it a community."

As if to prove her point, the chime above the door tingled, and Amanda's eyes flitted up; she offered a finger wave to the newcomer before returning her attention to Kate.

"Seems like you have a lot of regulars," Kate observed.

"We always welcome new faces though. And if you ever need anything, you can ask me for recommendations, help with any questions, anything at all. Even if you just need a friend. I'm always eager to spread the love of Juniper Bay to new faces. I came out here to pursue a career as an artist, and I fell in love. This place really just bursts with inspiration."

"I sure hope so. I'm a writer, so I'd love to be inspired as well."

Kate and Amanda talked for a moment more before Kate placed her order. Then she was alone. She dropped into a sadness she was familiar with. She was used to having meals with her husband. So, being without him now reminded her of all the things they were missing out on doing together. She knew he would love this place.

Before she could sink too deeply into that sad space, though, an older woman with grey hair and brown eyes who was sitting at the table next to hers turned to her. She gave her a warm smile that immediately put Kate at ease.

"Hi there," the woman started. "I hope I'm not intruding, but I overheard you saying you're new to Juniper Bay?"

"I am," Kate nodded.

"I suspected as much," the woman noted. She pointed to herself and a man about her age sitting at the table. "We're the owners of this café, so we've seen about every person who has walked in. I'm Barbara, and this is my husband, Frank. It's a pleasure to meet you."

"It's a pleasure to meet you too," Kate replied. "I'm trying to connect to other people in town, so it's always nice to come across a friendly stranger."

"Hopefully we won't be strangers for long," Barbara smiled. "I hope you enjoy it here. We may not have all the things a big city has, but we look out for one another here. We don't want anyone feeling lonely when we have such a great community. And we're always open to conversation."

"Absolutely," Frank agreed. "We've run this place for thirty years and always try our best to make sure everyone is welcome here. People bring their kids, those kids grow up, and then they bring their own. We host events and community spaces here. So, if you ever need anything, please, feel free to stop by anytime. We can put you in touch with just about anyone in town, whether you need a dentist, a handyman, or a good ole fashioned apple pie."

Kate laughed, feeling strangely assured by this. She still didn't know these people well, but it made her feel less alone to have some sort of connection with the people in town. Ever since Tyler died, there were plenty of times when she felt like she had to face the world on her own, despite the incredible support she'd received from friends and family. There were simply things that fell squarely on her now—burdens that she used to share with him. She assumed navigating Juniper Bay would be one of those things since she didn't know anyone here. So, having this resource was a relief.

They spent a little while getting to know each other and discussing the various spots around town and the best people to talk to about certain services. Then Amanda came back carrying Kate's lunch: a roast beef sandwich with a side of Caesar salad and a blue, twisty drink. Kate was released back to her own thoughts as the couple turned back to their meal.

She was feeling better after having socialized a little. She felt empowered. Like maybe she could build a life for herself in this town. Maybe she could find her place.

As she began to eat, though, her thoughts dipped again. She thought about what Tyler might say if he were eating with her. She thought of the jokes they might tell, the loving remarks they'd make, and the way everything would be so much better if he were there.

It made her heart ache for him, and she realized that though she could handle having lunch on her own, she'd much rather be having lunch with him. She would rather explore Juniper Bay with her love by her side. There was still that feeling of emptiness, that feeling that she was merely going through the motions of life instead of actually living.

But instead of dwelling on those thoughts like she normally did, Kate found that she wanted to do something about them. She wanted to make progress in her life. She didn't want to sit in sadness. She desperately wanted to leave it, to transform into something better.

So, after some thought, she came up with an idea to get her body moving. She waited until the waitress came back to give her the check.

"You know, I think I could use some exercise," Kate admitted to Amanda. She hadn't gotten any real exercise in weeks, aside from the effort of lifting boxes and pushing furniture around. She missed the way her body felt when it was moving in a direct, active way. "Do you happen to know of any good running trails nearby?"

As she said it, it felt right. Kate loved running. It helped her come up with new ideas, run away from the stress, and escape into the safe bubble in her mind. She'd found moving her body to be a great way of fighting depression in the past. She suspected it would help at least a little bit now.

"I do!" Amanda said. "Usually I run along the beach, but sometimes it hurts my feet after a while. So, when I'm not running along the coast, there's this park I love to go to. There's a great trail there. I'll give you the address and my number in case you ever want someone to go running with."

Amanda provided her the information, and Kate thanked her with a big tip and a promise to reach out. As she left the café, she decided that she wasn't ready to go running quite yet, so she found herself down by the water instead, walking barefoot on the beach.

She thought it might be refreshing to be by the ocean, and it was to some extent. The footprints she made on the fine, white sand reminded her that she was alive. She still left an imprint on the world. She still existed even if she existed in a different form than she was used to.

The waves colliding into each other gave her something else to focus on as she thought about what might be hidden in the deep, blue water. She allowed her imagination to explore until she reached a patch of sea grass and stood among it.

The water trapped her in a trance, calling out to her. It reminded her of Tyler. Everything reminded her of Tyler. And she thought for a moment of what it might be like to go swimming. If she swam deep enough, would she find him again? Would they somehow be reunited?

She brushed the delusional thought away as soon as it entered her mind, but it still caught her off guard. She was surprised to find her mind still going to that dark place sometimes. Even with things getting better, she still wasn't nearly over what had happened.

To escape any further disturbing thoughts, she continued about her day. She went grocery shopping, explored a few more shops, then headed home and got some writing done. Despite the frightening thoughts that had flashed through her mind while she was at the beach, it seemed to inspire her. Or at least getting out of the house had shifted something within her.

She could focus again like she hadn't been able to before. For a brief moment of bliss, nothing else mattered aside from the words she was writing. It allowed her to block the rest of the world out completely as she focused on the important issues she was trying to tackle through her work.

Eventually, she found her eyes getting tired, and her brain was suddenly exhausted and foggy. She leaned back in her chair and looked over at the clock to realize she had been working nonstop for four hours. She needed a break.

Kate thought back on the conversation at the café. She had asked for that running trail recommendation for a reason, yet now she found herself reluctant to force herself outside and get her body moving.

It was difficult to leave the house again when she was so used to staying home. Plus, the thought of exercise was exhausting. She wasn't sure why she had come up with that idea in the first place. She reasoned that she could just wait until a day when Amanda could go with her. She didn't have to make use of the trail right now.

Yet even as she sat there internally complaining about the idea of going on a run, she knew it would be good for her. She wanted to start taking more steps toward a life that would be good for her. So, after a long internal struggle, Kate got ready to go for a run to see if she could escape some of her problems.

CHAPTER NINE

T HE SUN HAD NOT QUITE SET WHEN KATE EMERGED from her front door. Everything within her warned her not to go for a run. She was too tired. She was still too sad. She couldn't do it. She would go tomorrow or wait for Amanda.

She fought hard against that thought by repeating over and over in her mind that this would be good for her. She reminded herself she had to take these steps that would be good for her, and eventually, she believed she would feel better. Eventually, the grief wouldn't weigh her down as much as it did now… even if it would hold her hand forever.

Strangely enough, though, as she pulled up the location of the trail on her GPS, she realized some of the trails through the park linked up to her house. There was a trail that ran next to her property line. So, she wouldn't even have to drive if she didn't want to. She could just start running and find the place on her own.

Something within her told her she couldn't do it. She wasn't healed enough to run. Exercise would only drain her. But she mustered up the courage anyway, and she started walking to where it said the trail should be.

The colors of the fading summer joined her as she walked under the thick canopy of leaves. It wasn't quite autumn yet, but there were traces of gold among the leaves, so she got the sense of a new season coming. On the horizon waited a colder season full of color, transformation, and spooky Halloween stuff.

"Am I ready for a change?" she asked herself. She shook her head. "I'm not sure, but a change is coming regardless."

As she walked, she listened to the sounds of little critters moving through the forest, feeling the last of the sun's rays touching her skin as the day slowly started to crawl away from her. The scent of summer clung to her, reluctant to let go.

Finally, a dirt path came into view just where her internet search said it would be. It was a hidden gem, tucked away among pine and maple trees with blueberry and raspberry bushes growing alongside it.

Kate decided to just try walking for a bit. She picked the berries and ate them, enjoying the warm juices on her tongue as she walked casually. She enjoyed the feeling of even this simple movement and the refreshing shift that just being in nature awakened within her.

Then, a rustling noise in the woods distracted her. It sounded like something larger than a squirrel was in the woods, and she again got the distinct sense that someone was watching her. It felt like their eyes were following her every move. Despite the trail appearing to be desolate, she felt like she wasn't alone.

"Tyler?" she whispered. "If this is your ghost, it's starting to get a little creepy. I know you're not meaning to scare me, but..."

She glanced around but couldn't see anything. The noise had stopped anyway, but it was enough to almost convince her to turn back around. It was her sign that she shouldn't be out here. She should be home being sad, not trying to combat it by running.

Running. As her mind stumbled over the word, she realized that was what she should be doing. If she ran, she could get away from that strange noise. She could escape the feeling that someone was watching her. She could run away from all the monsters.

The urge was suddenly so great that even though it was the last thing she'd wanted to do before, Kate started running.

She regretted it pretty soon after she started. She was quite out of shape, and she quickly got winded. Her lungs worked overtime, but it still felt like she wasn't getting enough air into them. Her legs complained that they weren't strong enough for this after having neglected them for far too long.

It was almost enough to stop her. Almost. Yet something within her was stronger than the old voice saying she couldn't do it. So, she persisted. She pushed through the things trying to hold her back, and eventually, her body adjusted.

Given a bit of time, it felt good to run again. It felt good to push herself like this. It felt like she could escape some of the stress in some small way. The tiniest spark of pride filled her as she continued and proved to herself that she wasn't giving up no matter how tough it was.

As she ran, she found a creek that followed the trail, so she focused on that as she continued running until she reached a little clearing with a tiny park. An old wooden playground sat abandoned with peeling picnic benches around it, a sandbox, and a small pond with willows draped over it like they were gently caressing the water.

Kate decided to stop for a break and strolled through the park a little. As she reached the lilies floating along the pond and heard the frogs croaking, she noticed a doll with a red dress sitting on the side of the pond in the grass, clearly forgotten.

She picked up the doll and played with its blond hair, smiling at its blue eyes. She thought of the little girl who was probably sad now missing her friend, which made her sad as well. It reminded her of all of the times she and Tyler had tried to get pregnant. All the hope that had come and gone throughout the process.

To some extent, she was thankful now that they didn't have children. At least now she wouldn't have to deal with the stress of being a single mother on top of everything else. Yet it also made her sad.

If they'd had children, at least she would have a piece of him still with her. Since they didn't, it felt like he hadn't really left much behind at all. It felt like every bit of him was gone. No matter what material things she clung to, she could never quite grasp him ever again.

Kate wiped away a few stray tears. She didn't often have the same all-consuming sobbing fits that she'd had in the first few weeks, but she still found herself crying from time to time when the feelings became too much to bear. It was still no easy feat to get used to. The horror of her life still remained too big to comprehend.

One tiny silver lining she'd learned was that if she allowed herself to experience the emotions, they passed by a little quicker than if she tried to bury them. They were easier to manage that way. They didn't become quite as unreasonable and overwhelming.

So, she allowed herself to be sad. She allowed herself to dwell on what could've been. She imagined what their children would be like, what having a fully formed family would be like. She allowed herself to grieve.

Then, she brought the doll over to the swing set and set her gently on the swing so she'd be easily visible in case the little girl came back for her. She walked around a little longer and explored the tiny park until the sun dipped lower into the sky.

Lovely traces of pink, orange, purple, and gold began to stretch across the dimming light, warning her that night would soon be falling. She admired the colors as she started running back through the trees again, following the creek back home.

She no longer had the sense that someone was watching her, which was a nice feeling. There was freedom in that. Instead of running away from something, she was just enjoying moving her body. She was running toward a new life. She was going in the direction of pursuing things she would enjoy.

As the cottage came into view, she realized she needed to do this more frequently. She needed to allow herself these pockets of time to heal. She needed to start focusing on truly getting better in whatever way she could.

She reached inside her pocket to find her keys as she approached the house and froze. Her fingers poked into her pocket, but it was empty. She continued walking toward the house, but panic started to set in. Had she dropped the keys on the trail while she was running?

Kate assumed she must have, which would be a problem considering she hadn't made sure to hide any spare keys yet. She glanced back at the trail. By then, the sunlight had dripped off of the sky, making room for a growing darkness. Out of the cover of the leaves, the world was grey. But on the trail, it would all be black.

How would she ever see her keys? Even more importantly, was it safe to be on the trail this late? Kate thought about the wild animals that might come out at night. She was alone with no way to protect herself. She didn't want to be in the middle of the woods in the dark.

She considered calling a friend to spend the night with, but she felt bad about that. She was no longer living close to any of her friends, and they would have to come all the way here to pick her up. It just wasn't practical. She supposed she could call Amanda, but that would be quite an imposition on someone she'd just met that morning.

As her mind went into overdrive in panic, something else caught her attention. She walked closer to the steps and saw a hint of glimmering light reflecting off her back porch. Kate bent down to grab it, sure things couldn't have worked out so perfectly.

Yet there they were. Her keys were right on her steps. It was as if someone had been watching her, saw that the keys had fallen out of her pocket, and brought them back for her. Kate thought back to when she felt like someone was watching her.

Was she truly imagining it all along? Or was there some validity in that feeling? Maybe she wasn't being suspicious. Maybe someone *was* following her.

She shook her head to clear the paranoia. The more reasonable explanation was simply that her keys had fallen out when she was still standing on the steps. She must have put them into her pocket too hastily, leaving them to slip out without her even noticing it.

It was difficult to convince herself this was the case. Still, it made more sense than the worry that someone had been following her and had brought her keys back to her. Surely if someone were following her, they'd mean her harm. They wouldn't make her life easier like this.

"Who would want to follow me anyway?" she wondered aloud. The sound of words to break up the silence made her feel a little better. "I'm really not that interesting. It's not like I do much with my days. If someone were following me, they would get bored very quickly and learn to stay away."

With that assurance, Kate unlocked the door and stepped inside her home, making sure to lock the door hastily behind her. Regardless of how her key had found its way to her doorstep, she was lucky it had. It saved her from having to make a very unfortunate phone call to have someone come save her.

Still, something about it lingered in Kate's mind. To calm her nerves, she walked over to her stainless steel, electric kettle and turned it on to make herself a cup of tea. It had a safety feature that meant she didn't have to be near it the whole time while it was heating, so she decided a shower was in order. It would be just what she needed to calm her overactive imagination.

The hot water running over her sweaty skin proved to be the perfect distraction; it was perfectly soothing and refreshing. There was nothing quite like the feeling of washing off a run, knowing she had pushed herself, knowing she was doing everything she could to get better. It made her feel stronger and more in control of a life that she felt like she was losing control over lately.

As she fell into a smooth state of happy serotonin absorption and bliss, the sound of something crashing knocked her right out of it. She panicked. Was someone in her house? Could that be why she had been feeling like she was being watched?

Maybe someone had been watching her this whole time. And now the person had followed her into her house. Her mind raced with terror and ran through countless visions of what could happen to her. She worried they'd broken in and were stealing her things. She worried they'd come to vandalize her new home. She worried they'd attack her and she had nothing to defend herself with. She realized in that moment how vulnerable she truly was.

Kate grabbed a towel and wrapped it around herself. She wanted to get dressed just in case someone was in her house. But if someone were in there, she reasoned she'd be wasting valuable time, so she walked out of the bathroom with just a towel on.

As she left the bathroom, she reminded herself that her door was locked. Her windows were always locked. There was no reasonable way for someone to get into her house. She tried to convince herself that something had just fallen. There was a safe explanation for this.

Still, her senses remained heightened as she walked downstairs to where the sound had come from. She glanced around to see if there were any signs that someone was there. One by one, she went into each room, trying to figure out where the sound had come from, but she didn't find anything. Nothing in the bedroom, or the spare room, or the office, or the living room.

Then she spotted it. Her kettle had fallen to the floor in the kitchen, knocking over her tea supplies in the process. Kate scanned the kitchen for any signs of an intruder that might've knocked over the kettle but didn't see anything.

"I guess I must've just put it closer to the edge than I thought," she mumbled to herself as she walked to the kettle and righted it. "I am tired. Maybe I put it so close to the edge that the movement of the water knocked it forward. That's the only explanation that makes sense."

Still, Kate was on edge as she cleaned up the mess and started the kettle again. Feeling like someone was watching her, finding her keys on her doorstep, and now the kettle falling all combined into one eerie feeling that was difficult to shake.

She was aware that she was probably being paranoid. There truly wasn't anything to worry about. And yet it was difficult to convince herself of that. Especially when she felt as exhausted as she did because of the long day she'd had.

She was curious and nervous as she went back upstairs to finish her shower after putting the kettle well away from the edge of the countertop. She decided that if it fell again, she was going to call the police. Then there would be proof enough that someone was in her home and she would do whatever she could to protect herself.

Thankfully, her shower concluded in an uneventful manner. She got dressed and went back downstairs to heated water. She finished up her cup of tea and relaxed a bit before heading to bed, already drowsy and hazy even without her sleeping pills' help.

Once again, as she drifted off, she got the sense that someone was watching her. She convinced herself it was simply Tyler's ghost and said goodnight to him before turning out the light.

In a sleepy, dreamy state, Kate shifted in her bed. Something had disturbed her. But as she moved, a soft touch comforted her as the world blurred around her.

A muscular man held her body close to his as he traced his fingers down her back in a soothing motion. She snuggled against his chest.

"I love you, Tyler," she whispered.

For some reason she couldn't understand, she felt desperate for him to know that. It felt like she might lose him at any moment. It felt like it had been so long since they had seen each other last, and she was ecstatic that they would be reunited.

Tyler didn't say anything, but his presence assured her enough to make her sleepy again. He was here. He was safe. She could faintly recall a nightmare she had been trapped in where she lost him. But it was just a nightmare. He had found her and gathered her in his arms. Their love story could never end.

He kissed the top of her head, and she felt more content than she had in a long time. Perfectly at peace, she fell asleep in his arms. So grateful to be with him. Everything felt okay again.

CHAPTER TEN

AMANDA WAS MORE THAN HAPPY TO BE REUNITED with her boyfriend after a long shift at work. There was nothing quite like a hug from him; it always made her day a bit better. She needed the distraction. She needed to be rejuvenated after the exhaustion.

She was happy to see that he was already at her apartment building when she pulled into the parking lot. They had discussed the convenience of moving in together recently, and though she had been a little reluctant about it before, now she was starting to think it'd be a good idea.

What she loved more than anything was art. She saw all the beauty in the world and wanted to capture it. That was her passion. Moving in together would allow her to save more money, affording her more time to work on her art. It would be exactly what she needed.

Tonight's the night. I'm going to agree to moving in together. It's time. I'm comfortable. I trust him. I'm ready to take the next big step.

Those pleasant thoughts kept Amanda company as she walked to her front door. She was surprised to find it unlocked but assumed David had simply let himself in using the spare key she had given him; he probably just forgot to lock the door behind him.

It was one of those things that irritated her about him. That carelessness had made her reluctant to want to move in with him.

She decided not to nag him about it that night though. That night was going to be when the talks of their future began. She didn't want anything to ruin it, even if internally she worried about moving in with him when he couldn't even manage to lock the door behind him.

The unlocked door was just the start of the strange evening though. It was almost like he was trying to creep her out with the low lighting and the fact that he didn't even greet her when she first walked in.

"David?" she called. "You are here, aren't you?"

For a moment, she considered the possibility that maybe she shouldn't have walked into her apartment when the door was unlocked. What if David wasn't here? What if a stranger had broken in and she was walking straight into his trap?

"I'm here," he called out.

Amanda followed his voice into the living room, turning on the lights for comfort along the way. She was automatically concerned with the way his head was in his hands, his face completely covered by his brown hair as he sat on the couch. When he looked up at her, his brown eyes expressed thoughts she didn't want to hear.

"We need to talk," David said in a somber voice.

Amanda wasn't ready for the kind of talk it seemed like he wanted to have, so she tried to keep things lighthearted as she set her purse down.

"I was thinking the same thing," she replied. "I had such a long day at work today. Crazy busy. And it got me thinking about how we spend so much money living in separate apartments. It seems like a waste. I think I'm finally coming around to your line of thinking. I'm finally seeing why it might be useful for us to move in together. I really want to start moving forward in a future with you."

But the look of pain on his face told her everything. He didn't want to talk about them moving in together, and from the moment she'd walked in, she'd known that deep down. But she hoped that in some way, she might be able to avoid hearing things she didn't want to hear by directing the conversation like this.

Things didn't have to go like this. She was desperate to stop it. She started babbling about the benefits of moving in together, but it felt like she was running out of time.

"I just think it would be really great, you know, we could find a more central place—"

"Amanda, that's not what we need to talk about," David finally interrupted her by saying those words she was fearing all along. "I'm sorry, but I don't foresee that in our future. I guess I just… I don't foresee a future with you at all anymore."

"What do you mean?" she asked, blinking back tears.

"I mean, this isn't working for me. It's not working for you either—I can see it. You just don't want to admit it. We're not right for each other. We fight way too much, and it's draining. Our goals don't line up. We deserve more than this. We deserve to be with someone who makes us happy, who we're on the same page with. That's just not us. It's not right. I wish it was, but it's not. We're not right for each other."

Amanda started taking quicker, more shallow breaths. After the long day she'd had, this was the last thing she wanted to come home to. They had been together for nearly two years now, so it was serious. She was attached. The thought of breaking up ripped her heart apart.

"Please, don't do this," she whispered. "We can fix things; I know we can fix things. We've been through rough patches before. We've always fixed it."

"That's the problem, though; don't you see it? There have been too many rough patches. Too many fights, too much drama. Love shouldn't be this difficult. We shouldn't have to force it."

She couldn't believe the words he was saying as her heart was breaking. Sure, things hadn't always been easy for them. But she'd really thought he was her forever. She never imagined it would come to an end.

Despite her pleading, though, nothing she said could change his mind. He was done with the relationship. He had given up. There was nothing left for her to do but give up on them as well. But it wasn't so easy for her. She wanted to cling to it.

As he left her apartment, it felt like her world was crashing down. The pain in her chest was unbearable. She couldn't just sit with it. She had to do something. She couldn't handle this.

Tears began to fall, and Amanda knew if she didn't do something about them, she would drown in the sadness, finding it difficult to resurface. She tended to struggle with letting people go.

But before she could fall down that dark hole, a conversation from earlier that day came to mind. She remembered talking to Kate and suggesting the running trail to her.

At that moment, the running trail seemed alluring. She thought maybe if she could just run fast enough, she could escape the pain. She could feel better. She needed to feel better.

Amanda quickly got changed and pulled her running shoes on. As she left her apartment building, she noticed the colors falling from the sky like teardrops from the heavens. The sun was setting, and it would be dark soon. Usually, that would be enough to deter her.

That night, though, she was too desperate to let the darkness hold her back. She needed that escape, no matter what time of day it was. She needed to be free of this.

Part of her was so sad she didn't even care what happened to her. She could barely think of it. Her thoughts were too distracted by the sadness over the breakup. She reasoned with herself, making excuses to do what she was always going to do regardless.

It's not a crowded trail anyway. It's safe. We're in a safe town. Nothing ever happens here.

Soothed with that knowledge, she started making her way to the trail. About halfway there, she thought about the possibility of getting attacked by a wild animal while on the trail. Then, she assured herself that wild animals are usually more afraid of humans than humans are of them. They wouldn't come after her.

Besides, she was going to be back at a reasonable time anyway. The sun was setting, but it wasn't pitch black yet. Night hadn't fully fallen. She didn't need to be gone for that long, she just needed some time to run. Some time to get away from all of this.

She kept running until she reached the part of the trail that was barely visible next to the road. She turned onto it and found herself on the main trail, covered in leaves and random bits of nature and decorated with the sound of the creek bubbling alongside her.

That sound calmed her racing heart a little. It was grounding when her mind was threatening to fly away from her unwanted situation. She was overwhelmed with heartbreak she didn't want to settle into. So, she ran. She connected to her breath, the feel of her body pushing and moving, the cool, night air around her, and the sound of crickets in the forest.

As her breathing grew quicker, her heart grew calmer. She realized that as much as this hurt, she could get through this. She was strong. She was independent. She would pour her heartbreak into her art and allow it to inspire her. She'd make sure something good came of it.

As she neared the tiny park tucked away in the middle of nowhere, she started to slow some. Her thoughts had won their race and were now able to rest. She was felt a little less on edge.

The growing darkness helped. Though she had feared it before, the blackened surroundings made her feel more at peace. It made her feel alone, which was exactly what she wanted right now.

Fireflies flickered among the leaves, chanting a soothing, silent song that it would be okay. She watched their glowing lights as she slowed to a stop. She felt in tune with her surroundings.

That's when she noticed it. It felt like someone was watching her. She could feel their eyes traveling over her body, assessing her. But for what?

She tried to convince herself she was just being skittish because of the darkness. There was no true reason to believe someone was watching her. She hadn't come across anyone on the trail at all.

Then, she heard the distinct snap of a branch. She turned to face the noise, but before she could see what was behind her, there was a loud thud as something crashed against her head, causing the most horrible pain to erupt in her skull.

She let out a scream, but the sound was distant, as if it came from far away. She collapsed on the ground, and the whole world went black.

—

When Amanda came to, the world was blurry and hazy. It was mostly dark around her, aside from a glowing light that created shadows that looked like they were leaning in to harm her. She was confused and disoriented.

Where am I? What happened?

As she took in her surroundings, an eerie picture formed. She saw a swing set moving in time with the wind and a strange doll with a red dress sitting on it, looking like one of those haunted toys from a horror movie. Frogs croaked in the distance while she felt grass against her back.

"Good morning, sweetheart," a deep voice whispered.

Amanda looked up in horror at a tall, dark figure staring down at her, mostly obscured by the shadows. All she could really in the darkness was the glimmer of the knife in his hand and the sickest smile she had ever seen.

"I was wondering when you'd come to," he continued. "I wanted to see you, see her. You look just like her, you know. So, why is it that I want to kill *you?*"

"W—what? What are you talking about?" she stammered. "Who are you?"

He tsked at her. "Ah-ah-ah. Do you really think I would make it so easy?"

She took in a deep, shuddering breath and realized the coldness she felt on her face was blood from her head wound. She tried to stand up but couldn't get her legs under her. "Please, don't kill me," she begged. "I've got so much life ahead of me. I—I'm too young to die. I don't deserve this."

The man glowered at her and bent closer, holding the knife just inches from her face. "I wouldn't be too sure about that," he sneered in a voice that sent snakes wriggling down her spine. "Everyone has a dark side. Perhaps everyone deserves to die. It just happens to be your time."

"Please, please, please," she whimpered.

The man continued as if she hadn't said anything. "You see, I would never do this to *her*. I love her. I'd cherish her if she were mine. But she can't be mine, at least not yet. These things take time. That brings me a certain … frustration. And I have to take that out on someone, you know. But I don't want to accidentally harm her. You're honestly saving her life. You're a hero. You should be proud of that."

"I don't want to be a hero," Amanda sobbed. "I just want to go home. I've never done anything to you. Please, don't do this."

"Your pleading is sweet," he admitted. "I do feel bad about it. I do wish I wasn't like this, you know? I wish I didn't have this sick drive. It would make me more worthy of her. I know she'd run and scream if she knew the real me. But this brings me closer to her. Until it's time to be with her. I'd like to think she'd understand."

"She wouldn't," Amanda insisted through the mixture of tears and blood dripping down her face and head. "She wouldn't approve. B-b-b-be worthy of her and let me go. I promise I won't tell anyone what happened."

"Sure, you won't." He rolled his eyes. "You're a liar. I can tell that. I can sense liars easily, having been lied to so many times before. I hate liars more than anything. You'll go to the police. I'll be arrested. I'll be locked away from her. Sorry, darling. It has to be this way. I can't fathom a world with her so far away."

In an act of desperation, Amanda remembered the pepper spray she kept on her keys for emergencies. She wasn't sure she'd have time to reach it before he could attack her. But he was going to kill her regardless. She had nothing to lose in trying anything to get out of this deadly situation.

So, she rolled to her side, her fingers clawing at the dirt, as she reached for the pepper spray. She moved faster than she ever had before, trying to find some way—any way—to escape.

But he was quicker.

CHAPTER ELEVEN

K ATE HAD BEEN WORRIED THAT THE ONE NIGHT OF great sleep was a fluke. She was certain that she'd go back to sleeping horribly again. That for one night the exhaustion had caught up with her enough to make her sleep so deeply, but there was no way that could last.

To her pleasant surprise, she woke up feeling refreshed again. She took a deep breath as she thought about how great it was to not be exhausted upon first waking up. The day didn't seem as daunting that way. She felt like she could actually face it without so much trouble.

Then she remembered her dream. She remembered feeling Tyler cuddling her and closed her eyes as fresh waves of pain crashed around her. Her heart ached to hold him again. She longed for their cuddling session to be far more than a dream.

"It felt so real," she whispered. "Tyler, it felt like you were right there beside me. Is visiting me in my dreams your way of showing me you're still here with me?"

She didn't get an answer, of course, but she held that belief close to her. She clung to the hope that maybe Tyler was still with her. Maybe he was trying to reassure her that she wasn't alone.

It was a sweet thought, regardless, which made her feel warm and supported. She held the memory of him close like a comfort blanket as she got ready for the day, which would be a special one—the day she'd be interviewing her latest patient of interest.

Once she was freshly showered and dressed, she sat down with her coffee to write down some questions she had for the woman she would be interviewing. It was a bit overwhelming as she tried to think of the proper way to broach such a topic and prepare herself for what was to come.

It was even more intimidating, considering the person she would be interviewing this time was in a prison cell rather than a mental institution. She had pleaded not guilty to murder due to legal insanity, but she was found guilty anyway. Not everyone believed the mental illness had contributed to her children's death. Kate was determined to find out for herself.

Despite her determination, Kate found herself wanting to turn back around once she finally reached the prison. The tall, intimidating brick walls seemed to glare down at her, judging her for visiting an inmate. The barbed wire-topped fences reminded her of cattle being trapped before the slaughter. Everything about the building made her want to run away.

"I've got to tell their story," Kate reminded herself. "I can't run away from this. They can't run away from this. I can't run away from them."

Having hyped herself up a bit, she finally stepped into the prison and went through the standard visiting protocol procedure. She hated every minute of it. The way the prison staff looked at her and analyzed her with casual cruelty. They knew she wasn't a worried relative of an inmate trying to hold together a broken family. They knew she wasn't a harried attorney trying to negotiate with a client. They looked at her with a level of disdain reserved for "murder junkies"—for thrill-seekers trying to get a fix by placing themselves in these situations. It almost made her feel like she was a criminal too. Like there was something wrong with her for wanting to visit a prisoner.

Is there something wrong with me? Is there something wrong with wanting to tell these people's stories? Why am I so fascinated by this? Is this a sign of inner darkness?

The doubts crowded Kate's mind, getting louder as she went into the small room where the visitation would take place. She was expecting more people to be there to visit their loved ones, but there were only a couple of other people: a young woman with tears in her eyes, a middle-aged woman with two children at her side, and an elderly couple who huddled together for strength.

The room itself was pretty barren, with white walls, a white floor, and flimsy white tables and chairs. It could almost be taken as a sign of purity, but instead, it reminded Kate of a level of coldness. It was like whoever was running this operation didn't want the prisoners or their families to feel too comfortable throughout their visit.

Not like that would happen. They were in prison. There were reminders of that everywhere. It made Kate squirm in her seat as she tried to talk herself down from her anxiety. She wanted to appear cool and calm in front of Isabella Langdon. She wanted to come across as someone easy to talk to.

Her anxiety spiked, though, as the inmates were finally let out. After her encounter with Daniel Jenkins, she wasn't sure what to expect. But Isabella certainly looked worse than Daniel had.

Her long, blonde hair was a bit knotted and looked like it had lost its shine. Her green eyes were red and sunk deep into her face in the telltale sign of exhaustion. She was much thinner now than she had been in the pictures Kate had seen of her online.

She still moved gracefully, but in a worried sort of way. Like each step she took might be misinterpreted. She didn't meet anyone's gaze until she sat in front of Kate and finally looked up at her.

"Who are you, and what are you doing here?" Isabella started, skipping right over any false pretenses.

"I'm Kate Larose," she started. "I came so I could… hear your story."

Isabella scowled. "And why do you care so much?"

Kate gave a tight, nervous smile. "I'm writing a book—"

"A *book?*" The heat in Isabella's glare seared into Kate, but she pressed on.

"It's—yes—it's about the dark side of mental illness, about how it can lead to harm."

Isabella rolled her eyes and grunted. "Great. Another true crime junkie…"

"No," Kate shook her head. "It's not like that at all. I'm trying to center the stories of mentally ill people to better advocate for compassion and treatment. I want to understand how your mental illness impacted you. I want to understand what happened the night you killed your children."

Isabella winced at the words, and Kate wondered if she had pushed too far. Maybe she shouldn't have mentioned the killing part. But she needed clear answers, and she worried that to get those, she would have to be super direct. But something in Isabella's face changed.

"There's a lot to understand," Isabella admitted. "And it goes far beyond that night. There's more to it, if you really want to understand the role mental illness played in their deaths. It's not like it started that night."

"I understand that," Kate said. "At least as much as I possibly can. I'm willing to take the time to listen to your full story. For whatever length of time we have, anyway. I'll even come back for another visit if needed. I want to get this right. I want to be able to move away from the sensationalistic stories and tell the truth."

Isabella held Kate's gaze for a moment as if she were trying to peer into her soul and figure out her true intentions. Kate wanted to look away. She wasn't used to being looked at so intensely, and it was uncomfortable.

She refused to look away though. She suspected this was the only way she'd gain Isabella's trust, so she allowed the scrutiny.

Then, Isabella leaned back in her chair. She nodded as some of the intenseness finally faded. "Okay," she relented with a heavy sigh. "I'll talk to you."

"Thank you," Kate said. "Since we do only have a certain amount of time, I'm going to suggest we get right into how and when your issues with your mental health began."

"Jumping right into things," Isabella grunted. "Maybe with the time constraints, that's for the best. I struggled with depression on and off throughout my life. Nothing too intense. It was always pretty manageable. I got on a low dose of medication starting when I was fourteen. It helped some, I guess. I never really paid too close attention to it."

Kate looked down at her notes. "I understand you had to go off the medication during your first pregnancy?"

Isabella nodded. "That led to me struggling with my emotions throughout my pregnancy, which then turned into postpartum depression once my first child was born. I even did all the right things. I sought out help. I went to therapy. I couldn't be on medication at first because I was breastfeeding. But as soon as I could get back on, I did. It all took a toll on me, but I made it out okay. A couple of years after our first was born, I was feeling much better. And Cody and I always wanted to have multiple children. He had grown up an only child. He didn't want that for our kids. So, we got pregnant with another child almost three years after my first was born, thinking it was safe by then."

"How was that?" Kate asked.

"This pregnancy was a lot more difficult. I didn't realize how much my medication had helped me with my stability until I went off them again for the pregnancy. I got so dark and down that my doctor wanted to put me back on the medication even while I was still pregnant, thinking the benefits would outweigh the risks.

"My husband was adamantly against that though. He would've been furious if I would've gone on that medication while I was pregnant. He worried it would interfere with us having a healthy baby, so I didn't go back on it, and the depression worsened. So, when postpartum hit…"

Isabella closed her eyes, but Kate caught the pain within them before she could hide it. This was torturing Isabella, recalling all of this again. But Kate hoped it would also be cathartic in a way. At the very least, she suspected her story would help other people who might be going through the same things. So, she hoped it would be worth it.

"If you've never dealt with depression, it's a difficult thing to explain," Isabella stated. "You'll never fully understand it, no matter how many people you talk to about it. It's nearly impossible to fully express the extent of suffering that comes along with it."

She held Kate's gaze for a long moment, but it was like she was looking straight through her. "It's like this darkness that just engulfs you. Everything becomes difficult as the world collapses in around you. It's hard to eat, sleep, do anything, because it doesn't seem worth it. I wasn't even actively suicidal, but I did often question the point of living. I often wondered if there was any point at all. Or if things would be better if I was dead."

That chilled Kate more than anything else Isabella had said so far. Because she could relate to it. She thought back to the dark days of depression following Tyler's death. To the thoughts she still struggled with about what was the use of living since he was dead.

She started to question herself. Sure, she had sought help, but was it enough? It wasn't like she was seeing a therapist or anything. But certainly, things couldn't get as bad as they had with Isabella. She would know to stop it before that happened.

"Cody was supportive for a while," Isabella continued. "He helped take care of the children. He helped take care of me. But I think there's only so long someone can do that without building resentment. I don't think that makes him a bad person. He was just experiencing compassion fatigue. So, after a while, he grew a bit distant from me. I couldn't quite place a solid finger on what changed, but something changed. I could sense it. I *felt* it. Yet every time I brought it up to him, he assured me that nothing was wrong. It was all in my head.

"I don't remember how long I dealt with it. Every day kind of just blended into the next. I was forgetting to take my meds. The depression put me in a fog that made me forgetful, including forgetting my birth control pills. Thanks to my carelessness, we got pregnant with our third child."

"My husband was furious at me for it. Yet he still supported me through the pregnancy. He tried to keep his true feelings under control. But I could feel his resentment, and I knew it wasn't just in my head. Our family was being destroyed. His love for me was dwindling. And after little Daisy was born, I began hearing the voices."

Kate grabbed onto that. Her own mental health wasn't so bad. It wasn't like she was hearing voices or anything.

Then, she thought of the dream that didn't feel like a dream. She thought about how often she felt Tyler's presence. She thought about how often she talked to him—which seemed normal enough. But sometimes it felt like he was truly there. She was starting to believe it.

So, where was that line between sanity and something darker and different? How would she know the difference? Was she missing something vital she would later regret?

"The voices said awful things about my husband and children," Isabella said. "They tried to convince me that my husband didn't love me and was going to leave me. And the children were monsters in human form. They were the devil reborn. That's why things got worse with their births. Because they were sent to torment me.

"I fought against these thoughts. I told myself I was delusional. I reminded myself it was just the depression. But one day I found out they were right about something—because two weeks before the incident, my husband left me."

"I'm so sorry," Kate whispered.

Isabella paused and took a shaky breath. Her body started trembling, and Kate worried she wouldn't be able to continue. Yet, she closed her eyes, and when she opened them, she revealed a sort of new determination.

"He sat me down and told me he was leaving," Isabella said. "It was a sudden thing too. All out of the blue. He admitted that while I'd been deep in my depression, he had fallen in love with someone else.

"And honestly, that was just too much to bear for me. I couldn't stand the thought of him being gone. I couldn't handle the thought of him being with someone else. So, my mind twisted it into something that made more sense than the fact that he just didn't love me anymore.

"The voices conspired against my family. They said this was proof that the children were monsters. My husband saw how monstrous they were. That was the real reason he was leaving. Because he couldn't be around them anymore—it had nothing to do with me. And if they stayed, those devils would drive everyone away.

"So, one day, the voices got so loud I couldn't ignore them anymore. These monsters were ruining my life. They were the reason everything was going terribly wrong. The only way I could fix things was to get rid of them. And then… well, you know what happened next."

Kate nodded. She didn't want to make Isabella talk about it. She didn't want to hear a firsthand account of the murder herself. Because that fateful day, Isabella had suffocated her children. She tried to burn their bodies in the backyard as a way to purge them of their demons and allow them to go to heaven in the wake of their deaths.

Afterward Isabella took a bunch of sleeping pills and anti-depressants. She was found unresponsive when the children's father came to pick up the children. Paramedics were called to attend to her. While they were assisting her, the children's father went looking for the children. That's when he saw their burned bodies in the backyard.

It was difficult to reconcile the fact that the distraught woman in front of her had murdered her children. Kate couldn't quite connect the two together. Isabella didn't seem like someone who could do something so horrific. But the illness she suffered from had eaten her from within and destroyed everything she loved.

For a moment, Kate thought of the danger her own mental illness might pose. Would there ever be consequences for the way she was suffering? Would it ever cause her to do something she'd regret? Would it lead her to do something she felt like she wasn't in control of?

"Thank you for sharing your story with me," Kate said. "I know that must have been difficult, but I appreciate you being so open and honest."

Isabella's eyes shimmered with emotion and resolve, but she kept her face steady. "I want you to know that I'm not a monster. I was just ill. I was acting on the nightmare the voices made in my head. My normal self would never want to harm my children. I still love and miss them so much. My well self would never do something like that."

"I know. That's why I'm writing this book," Kate promised. "I want people to know how harmful the stigma can be. How people affected by these things are human too."

"I hope you do," Isabella replied. "Because this can happen to anyone, even though you might not believe it. When your mind turns against you, there's limited options for what you can do. Maybe someday it might even happen to you."

CHAPTER TWELVE

SABELLA'S FINAL, HAUNTING WORDS STUCK IN KATE'S MIND as she drove away from the prison. She couldn't help but worry that she was right. Kate was vulnerable, especially after her husband's death. She didn't have the best state of mind. Would it ever get to the point that she would lose control of her actions?

She liked to think she was stronger than that, but considering some of the more recent happenings, Kate decided it might be time to take a second look at her medication. She thought it might even be time to see a therapist. She had to do whatever was needed to ensure that her mental health improved. She was determined to never end up like the subjects of her book. She'd never let things get that far.

If she had control of that kind of thing, of course.

With that worry in mind, Kate was grateful when she got back home and saw that while she was at the prison, she had missed a call from Allison. She made herself a cup of coffee, took it outside to the patio, settled herself onto a chair, then called her friend back.

It was so nice to hear a familiar voice that grounded her in reality rather than the darkness talking to these patients had put her in. Allison had always been her lifeline, and even in this mess, she continued to be. Talking to her always made Kate feel better.

"How are you doing?" Allison asked after they exchanged the usual greetings. "Enjoying your new home?"

"I love the town so far," Kate enthused. "Being here has been extremely good for my mental health as well."

"That's really great, Kate. I'm glad."

"I find myself being more productive, sleeping better, and just in general being more alert and happier. It's like I'm stepping out of a fog I had been trapped in. I mean, it's still a struggle. I still miss Tyler. But it's getting easier."

"You don't know how happy I am to hear that," Allison told her. "I know it will take time. But it really sounds like you're making progress, and I'm so glad for you."

They chatted for a little while about inconsequential things. It was nice, even briefly, to feel somewhat normal again.

"I even went back to interviewing convicted criminals for my book again."

That gave Allison pause. When she finally responded, her voice sounded like she was being careful and hesitant. "I'm glad you're getting back to work, but … don't you worry about interviewing these people? They could be dangerous."

"They're *ill*, Allison. Not just dangerous. Mentally ill people are far more likely to be the victims of violence than the perpetrators of it. Yes, part of it is that they could be capable of horrible things, but if we're going to break the stigma, we have to understand that these things aren't so black and white."

Allison huffed. "I just worry about you. I know there's a lot of nuance to it, but at the end of the day, these people are still murderers. Right? I mean, please tell me the person you talked to wasn't accused of anything too serious."

Kate bit her lip as she stared out at the garden. She thought about how she needed to plant more flowers and should do that next. She thought about ways she could bring more color into her life. Then, her mind came slamming back into this unpleasant conversation.

"I can't tell you that," Kate admitted. "She was accused of murdering her children."

"Her *children*, Kate! How could you ever want to talk to someone accused of murdering her own children? That's vile. There's no excuse for that."

"I'm not saying there is an excuse," Kate insisted. "I know there isn't. I would never even try to justify her behavior. I'm just saying that mental illness contributed to it. So, I'm curious to see what part it may have played in this tragedy. Because if mental illness is a contributing factor, it can be treated. It needs to be understood, and their stories need to be told."

Allison was silent on the other end for a moment. Kate worried she had hung up because she offended her friend so badly. She felt awful for it, yet she always knew that not everyone would respond to her work in the best way. She simply wished Allison was a little more understanding of it.

"I'm sorry," Allison finally said. "I didn't mean to jump down your throat about it or anything. I understand that you're trying to make a difference, and there is value to the work you're doing. I just want you to be careful when you're talking with killers. Mental illness or not, I don't care about the reasoning. I don't want to lose you."

"You won't lose me," Kate assured her. "The people I've been talking to are locked up in prison or mental institutions. There's no way for them to get to me, even if they wanted to. Which, I can't understand why they would want to. I'm just helping them tell their stories."

"Sure, but maybe they'll become attached to you somehow. Maybe they'll become obsessed or something, thinking you understand them, so they become fixated on you. Which is actually a reason I called. The guy you talked to, Daniel Jenkins? He was released last week. I saw the news online."

That gave Kate pause. She had known before she'd talked to Daniel that his being released in the future was a possibility. She just didn't think he actually would be released, especially not so soon after she talked to him.

"I hadn't heard," Kate admitted.

"I was worried about that—" Allison answered, "—that you wouldn't know. Though you really should've kept on top of something like this. If you were going to talk to someone like him, you should've been following when he was going to be released—*if* he was going to be released. That's my whole problem with this. You're not taking the proper precautions. You're not being careful."

Kate considered this for a moment. Was Allison right? She had to admit that perhaps she wasn't being as vigilant as she should, but it was difficult to care so much about her safety when she didn't care as much about living after Tyler's death. She just didn't have the same attachment to her life anymore that she used to. She wasn't actively suicidal, but she wasn't thrilled at the thought of living without him either. Not that she'd admit that out loud to Allison, of course.

"I'm sorry," she said, knowing Allison was just scared and not trying to be offensive. "I should be more careful, and I will be in the future. I'm just really invested in telling these people's stories. I think the best way I can do that is by talking to them. I've got to hear about their struggles through them directly if I want to convey them correctly. It's part of writing the perfect book. That's really all I'm trying to do. I'm trying to write the perfect, all-encompassing book."

"I understand that. You just have to take care of yourself in the process. No book is worth risking your life for." Allison paused. "Now, be honest with me. Do you think Daniel Jenkins is a threat now that he's been released? Do you think you're safe from him?"

Kate gave that some thought because she knew it was important, and as much as she didn't want Allison to worry, she also refused to lie to her.

"I think I'm safe from him," Kate decided. "He was cleared by his doctors. He didn't show any signs of attaching to me or anything in a positive or negative way. We had a simple conversation that wasn't emotionally charged or anything. He'd have no reason to come after me. I feel safe even knowing he's been released."

"Okay," Allison replied, sounding relieved. "I'll trust you on this, but I still want you to be careful—with him and with anyone else you talk to. You're living alone, which is kind of dangerous. You need to be vigilant. Do you have any weapons to protect yourself?"

"Weapons?" Kate laughed. "What do you mean? I don't I'll need a weapon."

"You never know. You are a young woman living on her own. Haven't you watched any crime shows? You're about as vulnerable as you can be. At least tell me you have pepper spray or something."

"Not exactly. I never thought I'd need anything like that."

"Well, at least get pepper spray," Allison insisted. "Just to make me feel better. It'd be even better if you took shooting lessons and got a gun but—"

"No," Kate insisted. She thought about her suspect mental health lately and was convinced that having a gun in the house was the last thing she'd need right now. "I'm not getting a gun. That's nonnegotiable."

"Fine, I'm just saying you should consider it. Consider getting a gun just for protection. Consider learning how to use it. And at the very least, go get pepper spray today."

"I will." Kate sighed, knowing that if she didn't agree Allison would keep pushing until she did.

"Promise?"

"I promise."

"You better send me a picture of it when you buy it. I don't trust you, but I want to. I want to know you'll be careful. I want to know you'll take care of yourself. Please, Kate. For me."

"I will," Kate promised. "I know I haven't been great at that in the past, but I will be more careful. I will take better care of myself. I won't let anything bad happen to me if I can help it. I promise."

Kate stayed on the phone call a little longer, catching up on Allison's life as well. But eventually, Allison insisted Kate go buy pepper spray. So, after hanging up the phone, Kate headed down to the local store to pick up the self-defense tool she never thought she'd need.

She decided to stop at the local outdoors shop as she assumed they would have it. She felt silly walking inside to get pepper spray when she saw the guns, camping equipment, tools for archery, and other things she would never buy.

A burly man dressed in camo eyed her suspiciously as she walked inside, like he couldn't quite figure out what she was doing there, which made her wonder if she should be there in the first place. She thought about turning right back around and leaving. It wasn't like she'd really ever need pepper spray.

Then, she thought about how worried Allison was. She knew she'd be upset if she didn't do this. And she didn't want to worry her friend… nor did she want to hear her nagging.

"Good afternoon," the man said in a cheery voice that seemed at odds with his demeanor. His red hair and freckles clashed against the camo, making for a strange assortment. His brown eyes looked kind but curious. Kate got a glimpse of his name tag. His name was Henry. "New in town?"

It seemed everyone was asking that question lately.

"Yes," Kate admitted. "I just moved in a few weeks ago."

"I thought so. You didn't look familiar. We don't see a ton of new faces around here."

"Well, you got me pegged," she replied with a nervous chuckle. She blushed as she thought about how out of place she was. "Um, I know it might sound silly, but my friend is insisting I buy it, so… do you happen to sell pepper spray?"

"Pepper spray?" he asked, his eyebrows arching. Kate nodded. "Ain't silly at all. Every woman should at the very least carry pepper spray with her. I'm always sayin' they need even more heavy-duty weapons for protection, but pepper spray is a start. Come on back. I'll show you what we have."

As Kate followed the man toward the middle aisle of the store, she felt a little more assured that maybe this was the right decision. Maybe Allison's worry was for good reason. Maybe she really did need protection.

"I don't blame you, given what all happened," Henry said as he pointed out the selection in the aisle. "Damn shame."

Something about the way he said that set a rumble of worry into Kate's stomach. "What do you mean?"

"Didn't you hear? There was that woman stabbed to death last night."

"What?" Kate gasped, freezing right to the spot. That was something she never expected in Juniper Bay. It was too small. It was too pleasant and held a certain charm to it. "That can't be."

"Sorry to say it's true," Henry said. "Someone worked her over somethin' fierce. I didn't see what happened, but I heard it's pretty horrible. That kind of stuff just doesn't happen here. It's really rocked the community."

"Oh," Kate attempted, not really sure how to respond. What could one even say in a situation like this?

"There's a vigil down at the café tonight where she worked. She was really a bright light, always so friendly and willing to talk to anyone. I think that loss will stay with us for a long time."

Kate's mind went back to Amanda. It was too horrible to think about, so she didn't want to ask. Yet a darker part of her needed to know.

"What was the woman's name?" she asked.

"Amanda Flynn," he answered.

Kate closed her eyes for a moment as she thought about the young woman who had told her about the running path. She was so bubbly and full of life when she'd met her. It was a shock to think that in such a short time, she was now gone.

"Did you know her?" Henry asked.

"Not really," Kate shook her head. Though she still felt connected to her somehow. She couldn't explain it, so she wouldn't admit to it out loud. "Not well, anyway. It does make me grateful I'm getting this pepper spray though. It will at least give me some sort of protection."

Henry nodded. "We also have small handguns for sale if you'd be interested in that. Or if that's too intense for you, we have tasers as well, which could be more useful than the pepper spray."

The thought of anything more powerful than pepper spray was too extreme for Kate to even fathom, so she declined his offer and just stuck with the pepper spray instead. The thought of Amanda's murder was chilling. It followed her out of the store and all the way home.

She still felt like someone was watching her sometimes. Yet a darker voice was starting to whisper that maybe it wasn't Tyler's ghost that was making her feel that way. Maybe the feeling was the result of something far more sinister.

CHAPTER THIRTEEN

THAT EERIE FEELING THAT SOMEONE DANGEROUS might be watching her stayed with Kate throughout the day. When she got back home, she tried to shake it off. But she looked at living alone a little differently now.

"Are you there, Tyler?" she asked that night before bed. "Or am I just imagining it? Or is there something more?"

Kate couldn't finish saying what she was thinking out loud. There couldn't be anything more to it. She wouldn't allow herself to believe that.

It probably was all in her mind. She imagined her grief was creating this elaborate fairytale in her head that she and Tyler were soulmates, so of course, he lingered after death. Of course, he wouldn't leave her forever. She knew it probably wasn't true. She knew it was probably the result of some sort of delusion. And yet it was comforting to her to imagine he was there with her. So, if it was comforting, she couldn't think of a good reason why she shouldn't indulge in it a little. What could be the harm?

The night came, and with it came another evening of bittersweet pain. Another evening of imagining Tyler's arms around her, him holding her close, such vivid and tactile detail that she could swear it was real. He smelled just like the cologne he always used to wear, which made him even more endearing.

"Please," she whispered to him. "Please, don't go. Please don't leave me here on my own."

Yet when she woke up the next morning, he was gone. She was forced to face a world in which Tyler was dead and never coming back. The truth of it tortured her, sending her into a stormy ocean of tears she couldn't calm. It ripped through her body and tore at her soul.

It was as if someone had told her he was dead all over again. She clutched her pillow in desperation, hoping that one day this pain would end.

Over the next week, her days got better. She was able to be productive again. She finished unpacking the boxes. She made progress on her book. She got some work done in the garden.

Yet each night came the same dream and same nightmare ending. Though she cherished those moments when she felt his presence, she loathed waking up and knowing he was gone. It was like breaking the same bone over and over again and then having to walk on it the next day.

She was actually happy when the day came that she had to force herself out of the house to do some grocery shopping. It was usually not her favorite chore, but she decided to make a whole trip of it: going grocery shopping, checking out the shops, eating at Barb's, and taking a stroll on the beach. Some fresh air would be good for her.

She had a whole day planned for herself. And though it was going to be difficult to visit Barb's Café again, she was determined to get through it so she could offer her condolences to the couple who had been so nice to her before. She hoped that getting out and talking to people could break her from the painful cycle she was in.

"Don't you think so, Tyler?" she mused aloud as she drove into Juniper Bay. "I probably could use more scintillating conversation."

Even as she said it, though, she started to worry about herself a little more. She imagined talking to her dead husband all the time wasn't healthy, and it probably wasn't healthy for her to constantly think he was there with her.

She wondered, yet again, what the line was between sanity and a real mental health crisis. She couldn't help but worry if she had already crossed it. Was she playing a dangerous game? Was it time to reach out for extra help?

Kate still didn't have an answer as she parked her car and started walking to the familiar town square. But being able to leave her home and see familiar sights was reassuring to her. It helped her to get out of the house, away from the ghosts, and admire the unique atmosphere Juniper Bay had to offer.

After a bit of window shopping, she headed to the local whole food grocer for groceries. She decided she would try to get all of her groceries from local sources instead of a big-box store. She wanted the real, authentic experience of living in a small town, and she loved the vibes of this particular shop.

It was refreshing to her to go through the fresh produce section and pick healthy choices she knew would nourish her body. She grabbed fresh hearts of romaine, cabbage, some carrots, and even some fruits, but soon enough, she found herself in the candy aisle, looking for her new favorite chocolate bar. The emotional side of her had decided it needed something too.

She squinted, looking for a specific one she had tried last week with white chocolate, toffee bits, and almonds in it. It was an uncommon combination that perfectly suited her. She hadn't found another like it anywhere else. She was practically salivating as she reached for the chocolate bar and paused as she brushed hands with someone.

"Oh!" she gasped. Kate stepped back in shock to see a tall, handsome man with dark hair, dark eyes, and tan skin staring back at her. He was fit, looking like he spent a lot of time working out or being active outside, yet he was dressed nicely in a casual button-down shirt and well-fitted jeans.

Something about him reminded her of Tyler. It was something about the way he stood, the way he looked at her. That confident, yet kind swagger.

She looked away. She knew she was just imagining things because she missed Tyler. He wasn't looking at her in any specific way. He was probably just irritated that she got in the way of him grabbing his chocolate bar.

But he laughed gently, and she laughed along with him. It was uneasy at first, but somehow, the man's kind smile set her at ease.

"I'm sorry," he said. "I got so distracted reaching for the chocolate bar, I wasn't paying enough attention to my surroundings. It's my favorite."

"No need to be sorry," she assured him as her cheeks heated. "Mine too. Honestly, I wasn't paying attention either. It's just the best chocolate I've ever had. It's super… distracting."

Kate was super distracted by this stranger, which was unsettling. It wasn't like her. But there was something about him that drew her in. It was like he was familiar in a strange way. It seemed like she had met him before, though she couldn't recall anything clear enough to know for sure. She wracked her brain to think of where she could have seen him and came up blank. He didn't seem like he recognized her either.

You're letting your imagination get the best of you again. Maybe it's time to get that checked out. This is getting concerning.

Her inner critic was so loud she could hardly focus on the conversation in front of her. Then, he smiled, and she had to smile back. She was back in the present moment.

"It is distracting," he agreed. "Though a bit uncommon. You know, I've never met anyone else who likes it. Everyone always says it's weird, but I love 'em. You have good taste."

"So do you," she agreed.

She hated how awkward she was being. It was like it had been so long since she had conversed with a man like this that she had completely forgotten how to do it. Yet she wanted to talk to him longer. He just looked so much like Tyler that she longed to be around him.

"I suppose I should formally introduce myself, since we have the most important thing in common," he said, reaching his hand out to shake. "I'm Victor."

"I'm Kate," she replied, trying desperately to think of something interesting to say following that. She shook his hand somewhat limply, still kind of dazed by his presence.

"Are you new to the area?" he asked. "Or a tourist? I haven't seen you around is all I mean, and I tend to know a lot of the locals."

"I am new," she admitted. "I moved into my cottage a little over a week ago, so I'm still getting adjusted to everything. It's beautiful though. Juniper Bay is lovely. I love it so far."

"That's fantastic!" he enthused. "If you ever need someone to show you around or anything, let me know. I know all the best spots. And..." He reached up and grabbed one of the chocolate bars and handed it to her. "I know the best places to get chocolate too. Which is probably the most useful skill of all."

At that, he winked at her, which sent a strange feeling that was rather foreign to her flowing through her veins. She wasn't sure exactly how to explain it, but it was pleasant. He hesitated, almost as if he was going to give her his number so she could contact him if she needed someone to show her around.

"It was charming to meet you," he said instead. "See you around."

Then, he walked away, leaving Kate feeling a little off-centered about the whole thing. She stood there for a moment so it wouldn't seem like she was following him. Then, she casually walked in the same direction, secretly hoping to "accidentally" bump into him again.

As she walked, she wondered at the fact that he said he would show her around if she wanted but didn't give her his number. Was it an empty offering? Or had he been waiting for her to ask for it instead?

If he had been waiting, then Kate appreciated that. It showed a sort of thoughtfulness that he was going to let her take the lead. Though it also made her question herself. Should she have asked for his number?

The thought was enough to shock her into horror. She quickly grabbed the rest of her things without looking around to see if he was there. She didn't want to accidentally bump into him again. She didn't want to face whatever strange things he was making her think and feel.

Kate was so distressed by it that she put her groceries into the cooler in her car, then went straight to the beach. She was hungry and had intended to go to the café next, but she needed some time to walk. She needed time to process this.

As she walked along the sand, the salty mist in the air helped her feel calm enough to work through some of her thoughts. She glanced down at the smooth sand, free of footprints, having been washed anew by the tide, and she thought about her life.

It was like each day was a tiny bit of the tide washing her old life away, and she desperately wanted to cling to it. That encounter with Victor had unexpectedly shaken things up. It almost seemed like...

Kate blushed at the thought of him. It was confusing because he reminded her of Tyler, and Tyler was the person she truly missed. He was the person she wanted to be with. But she wondered if maybe she was projecting that onto him.

Had it been flirting, what they did? She wasn't too sure. There did seem to be some sort of connection though. She questioned herself further. Was it all in her head?

She was starting to get to the point where she wasn't sure what was real and what she was making up anymore, which worried her.

"It's time," she promised herself as she walked along the beach. "It's time to get real, professional help. I can't keep living like this. We need to figure this out."

She turned around to head to Barb's and paused. Trailing her footprints were a second set of footprints, following slightly behind her. It was almost as if someone had followed directly behind her, keeping as close to her footfalls as possible, but their larger size was a dead giveaway. She was sure they hadn't been there before, but she couldn't recall hearing or seeing anyone else there.

Something about it dug into her skin. It mingled with the fear that someone was watching her. She glanced around the beach but found no one nearby. She looked at the trees on the coastline and wondered if maybe someone had been following her, then had hidden in the trees when she turned around and was now watching her from afar.

Am I losing my mind? Or is someone following me?

Not knowing the answer was enough to make Kate leave the beach in a hurry, constantly looking over her shoulder so she could be aware. She didn't want to be terrified of what she'd find there, but she couldn't help herself.

As she sat in her usual table at the café, Kate felt safer and grounded. Her stroll had helped her work through some thoughts, but seeing those footprints was eerie. Now that she was safe within the walls of Barb's, she started to feel silly about her reaction.

The beach was for the public. It was a great spot to take a walk and enjoy the ocean. Of course, it wouldn't be a surprise if someone else had joined her and then left before she did. There wasn't anything wrong with that. It was just another normal day.

I'm safe here. The worst thing that could happen has already happened. I'm safe, and nothing like that will touch me again.

Kate played those thoughts like a loop in her mind, clinging to them as assurance that she would be fine.

Then, she ran into Barbara and Frank, and all her other thoughts vanished. They looked like their world had been rocked as they came out into the dining room to sit at a table by the window. Kate worried about disturbing them but decided that talking to them was the right thing to do. She stood and slowly approached them.

"Hi," she said. "I just wanted to give my condolences. I heard about what happened to Amanda, and I'm sure it's been difficult for everyone who knew her."

"It has been," Barbara admitted, taking Frank's hand from across the table. "She was like a daughter to us, but I feel worse for her family. We're taking this week's proceeds and donating them to her family to help them pay for the burial and anything else they need. I wish we could do more."

"I'm sure it means so much to them," Kate said. "Could I add to the money you're giving them? I'd love to be able to help in some way."

"I'm sure they would appreciate that," Barbara said. "You can add it to your bill. Now, do tell me you're being careful as you're getting adjusted to life around here. I never thought Juniper Bay could be a dangerous place, but apparently, it is. We don't want anything like this to happen to anyone else."

"I just got pepper spray to protect myself," Kate told her.

"That might not be enough," Frank replied. "I don't mean to be pushy, but our daughter is offering a self-defense class at the local gym. Maybe you might want to join her? We're recommending it to all the women we meet. You can't be too safe."

"I'll look into it," Kate nodded. She took down their daughter's name and number.

For a moment, Victor popped into her head. She thought about asking if they knew him. Just because she was curious about him, and he did say he knew a lot of people in town. Perhaps he had run into Barbara and Frank before.

Then, she realized the timing wasn't great. She didn't want to ask about some guy when they were still grieving. It wouldn't be the best time or place to bring something like that up. So, she decided to keep those particular questions to herself.

Her food had just been delivered to her table anyway. She went back to her seat to eat. As she ate, she thought about Amanda, and she texted Barb and Frank's daughter Lisa to sign up for self-defense classes, a move she never thought she'd make.

CHAPTER FOURTEEN

T HAT NIGHT, KATE HAD ANOTHER ONE OF HER DREAMS of a man holding her close. He smelled just like Tyler, and his arms felt similar. So, she assumed it was him, just as she had ever since she started having these dreams.

Yet that night, she turned in her dreamy haze and saw a strange face obscured by the shadows. His features were different from Tyler's, and at first, she was scared. Then, she recognized him, and a fog faded over her. She was calmed by the feeling that things would be okay.

"Victor," she whispered.

He smiled, and she was immediately confused enough to slightly pierce through the fog. How could he have gotten into her bed? Why was he in her house? Why was he cuddling with her?

Then, she noticed how the world kept fading in and out. Everything was a little blurry and disorienting. It was okay. It was only a dream. She reached out to him to see if he was real, but before she could touch him, she fell into darkness.

Kate woke up to the sunshine drenching her with guilt that slid over her body and cemented her to her bed. She remembered her dream of Victor holding her, and she was horrified by it. It felt like she was betraying Tyler by even thinking of another man. Especially because she knew deep down that she was attracted to Victor. She was drawn in by him.

The dream was further proof of what she had been trying to deny. He reminded her of Tyler, so it felt like less of a betrayal. But he was still another man. She was attracted to another man.

Did that make her a bad widow? She was certain that was the case. She was a bad widow thinking of someone other than her husband. She felt horrible about it.

That feeling was only made worse when she went to her dresser and noticed her husband's bottle of cologne had been knocked over again. She couldn't imagine what could've bumped into it while she was sleeping, so she was certain it was a sign from him. It proved that he had probably seen the dream or picked up on her attraction to Victor.

"I'm sorry," she said. "Tyler, you have to know that I don't mean it. I couldn't actually love anyone but you. I'll be faithful to you even after death."

She righted the bottle of cologne and got ready for her day, hoping to wash some of the guilt away in the shower. Being a widow was a strange thing. It seemed to give birth to a distinct amount of guilt every day, no matter what she did.

Guilt descended upon her in abundance. Happiness was something she had to work for. This was part of her journey, and she hoped someday she would find happiness again, but she wasn't sure how to yet.

To help her shake the dream, she decided to go for another run. She had gone running only once after her initial run, even though it made her feel good. It was difficult to always do things that made her feel good, so she wanted to commit to doing that more in her life.

She made sure her keys were secured to her this time as she took off down the trail. This time, she didn't get the sense that someone was watching her, so she was able to enjoy her run more than before. She didn't feel like she was running for her life. She felt like she was simply running because it felt good to do so.

She focused on the movement of her body, on nature surrounding and grounding her. She focused on the air as it went in and out of her lungs. She noticed the way that her run was a little easier this time. She wasn't having to strain as much. She felt stronger, yet somehow lighter.

She enjoyed the feeling as the small park came into view. But she paused just before reaching it and slowed. Last time, she didn't go near the park. It seemed too haunted by a ghost.

Her conversation with Henry at the store replayed in her head. This was where Amanda's body had been found. She wondered if it was disrespectful to visit a park where someone had died. Then she thought maybe it was wrong to avoid it just because Amanda had died there.

It was a frustrating thing that happened all too often for Kate now. She found it more difficult to make decisions since Tyler's death, as she often felt out of touch with life. It was like she was hovering outside of her body and trying to control a robot that didn't want to listen to her all the time.

No matter what decision she made, she often second-guessed herself. But this time she decided to just do it. She continued running to the park. It felt like she needed to be there after everything that had happened. It just seemed right.

As the park and pond came into view, she stopped again. She recognized a man standing by the water, looking thoughtfully out into the distance.

It was Victor; Kate was sure of it. He was still far away from her, far enough that he wouldn't notice her. But she recognized his dark hair, his coat, and his particular way of standing that reminded her so much of her husband that she wanted to cry.

She debated going up to him just to say hi. It would be the polite thing to do, and then she could gauge if he wanted to talk to her again—if his offer to show her around was genuine. She reasoned that maybe she could make a new friend, and she could use more friends in Juniper Bay.

Then, she thought of the dream she'd had. She thought of the strange ways he made her feel. The guilt crept back in. She shouldn't be interested in any man besides her husband.

So instead of approaching him, she turned back around and started running.

—

"The dissociation started off in small ways at first," Mark Donaldson told her. "I'd forget things like what I wanted to say, where I placed something, if I left something on the stove… little things like that. Then, I started feeling out of touch with myself. Like I was an outsider looking in. Sometimes I felt completely out of control, like I was simply watching a movie and wondering what would happen next."

Kate had to take a deep breath. She grounded herself while sitting in the mental hospital. The white walls, blue tile, and uncomfortable seating brought her back to the present. She had to remind herself that this conversation wasn't about her. It was about learning more about Mark, trying to understand the mental illness that had landed him in this hospital.

"Life felt a bit surreal," Mark continued. "That feeling got worse. That night was the most intense moment of things feeling surrealistic. The real me would never take an axe to my parents' heads. I love them. I honestly can't relate at all to the person who did that. I don't remember doing it. I simply know I did it because they told me I did. And it makes sense, considering everything I was going through before it happened."

"What were you going through?" Kate asked.

"I wasn't sleeping. Barely eating. I was losing chunks of memory. Small ones at first, but they got bigger and bigger. I lost days. Weeks. Sometimes my memories came back, but sometimes they didn't. I lost my job because I just stopped showing up. I had people reaching out to me, and somehow, without my own knowledge, I kept telling them I was okay. But I wasn't."

"Did you know you were lying to them?"

"It's hard to say. Maybe I thought I was okay. Looking back now, I can see that it was my responsibility to get help even though I didn't. But it's so difficult to be honest with yourself like that. It's difficult to accept the signs and acknowledge you're unwell—especially since it is technically all in your mind. The symptoms aren't physical, and therefore, aren't taken as seriously.

"I really applaud those who can see those signs before it gets to the point where it did for me. I admire people who get help beforehand. I suggest everyone do that. If there's anything anyone can learn from my story it's to get help when you need it—before you think you need it. Because if you wait, it might end up being too late."

To Kate, this conversation confirmed she was doing the right thing: she was seeing a therapist directly after her interview with Mark, and she saw her psychiatrist the day before.

It had been a week since she'd seen Victor at the park, and things had only gotten worse from there. She still dreamed about him at night and woke feeling increasingly out of touch with herself and the world, as if a deeper part of her was punishing her for thinking of any man but Tyler.

The paranoia hadn't stopped. Every once in a while, she would still get the sense that someone was watching her, though she never caught sight of anyone or anything out of the ordinary. She was starting to be more forgetful. She lost things more. It felt like part of her brain was in a fog.

It was strange that she was still able to write through all of this. She was able to do better research than ever, writing with more conviction and passion. It seemed part of her was very affected by these strange occurrences while another part of her was unfazed. She wasn't exactly sure what to think about it all.

All she did know was she needed help. So, after the interview, she went to her therapist and discussed all of her symptoms and the way she had been feeling since Tyler's death.

"I can see where that's all distressing," Doctor Talley said as Kate finished venting about all her feelings and thoughts. "However, that doesn't mean there's something wrong with you. It's simply the result of being a widow and the trauma associated with that. I assure you that what you're going through is very normal, even if it seems abnormal and overwhelming to you. Many widows are forgetful, disconnected, afraid, and guilt-ridden. There are so many emotions that can come up when we lose someone we love, especially someone so close to us."

She looked at Kate with kindness in her eyes.

"I want you to try to have more compassion for yourself. Stop being so hard on yourself and expecting so much. You went through something life-changing and traumatic. Your reaction makes perfect sense. The sooner you accept that and accept these changes, the quicker you can learn to cope with these things and manage them."

"I'm not sure I can accept it," Kate admitted. It was easy to admit to her weaknesses in this office with its soothing green walls, earth-colored furniture, and an assortment of art coloring the space in a creative way. It felt like a safe space, somewhere she could tell her secrets without fear of judgment. "I want to be my old self again. I worry this mental illness might make me do something I'll regret."

"What do you mean by that?" Doctor Talley asked.

Kate thought back to the people she had been interviewing. "I don't know. That's the problem. I don't know. I don't want to be one of those people who gets so delusional that I don't realize it until it's too late. I don't want to keep making these mistakes."

"The fact that you're aware of this is a great first step," her therapist assured her. "And you're getting help, which should prevent things from spiraling out of your control without you realizing it. I'll support you each step of the way, but you need to let go a little. You're doing great, so focus on that. We'll work on helping you feel even better and get more in control of your life again. For now, you should be proud of yourself and how strong you're being. Know that this will pass as you work through the grief and begin to rebuild your life."

The therapist's words did help soothe Kate's worries, and she left the office feeling less distressed than she felt when she first arrived. Knowing what she was going through was normal for widows made her feel less worried about possibly losing control and becoming so out of touch with herself that she would end up like one of the people she'd been interviewing.

She certainly never wanted to hurt anyone. As much as her life was tough, she didn't want to be a danger to herself either. She just wanted to find peace somehow. She wanted to come to terms with Tyler's death without betraying him in the process.

These hopes and worries collided in Kate's head as she went home that afternoon. She was so thoughtful, in fact, that she barely noticed that her door was unlocked. It took a few seconds before the realization came over her, and that realization sent panic through her.

There was no way she had forgotten to lock her door. She never did that. She was always very careful to lock her door before leaving the house.

She considered calling the police. That would be safer than investigating this herself. But her state of mind lately stopped her from doing so. It was dangerous to walk right in, but being proven that she was wrong was more than her pride could bear.

Kate got out her pepper spray before stepping into her house. She slowly closed the door behind her and peered around the entryway. Since her things were unpacked, all of her familiar decorations greeted her. Nothing seemed disturbed.

Still, she wasn't about to let her guard down yet. She kept the pepper spray out as she went from room to room, trying to figure out where the intruder was hiding. Because there *had* to be an intruder. There was *no way* she left the door unlocked. What had they stolen?

The fear that welled up inside her as she worried for her life and well-being subsided after she had searched the whole house twice and didn't find a single thing out of place or any signs that anyone had been in her house. Nothing was touched. Nothing was altered. Everything was fine.

"I really left the door unlocked," she said out loud as she made herself a cup of tea to calm down. "I really did that. With a murderer in town. I left my door unlocked for any stranger to come through and do whatever strangers do. I can't believe I left my door unlocked."

Hearing herself admit to this out loud was extra chilling as she thought about the various things that could've gone wrong. Anyone could've come inside her house to harm her. Things could've been stolen. It was simply dangerous to leave her house unlocked like that. She still couldn't believe she had done it.

She thought about what her therapist said about how this was normal. Widows usually act like this. She had nothing to worry about.

Still, she couldn't help but chide herself for this dangerous mistake. Sure, widows might normally act like this, but she wanted to get her life together. She wanted to stop acting like this.

Despite all her therapist had said, Kate worried and wondered about her mental health as she settled down for the night, still feeling like there were prying eyes settling over her.

CHAPTER FIFTEEN

ESPITE THE CHAOS GOING ON IN HER MIND, KATE tried to live a normal, fulfilling life as she tried to find her new routine and peace in the aftermath of her devastation. Work was going a bit slower, but that was okay because she wanted to focus on balancing it with living her life as much as possible. She started attending the self-defense classes, hoping they would make her feel more secure and less paranoid. She ran regularly. She cooked healthy meals and started doing yoga, meditating, and journaling. She did all of the things people are supposed to do to heal. Slowly, she started to get a little better, but she still didn't feel healed.

So, a couple weeks after she forgot to lock her front door, she decided to take a detour to the library to get out of her house for a while. She hoped that it might help her make connections in the community, or at least have a safe space to go to work and explore her literary side. She hoped that getting out more might make her less paranoid.

She automatically felt soothed as she stepped into the modest, red brick building and was surrounded by rows and rows of books stacked all the way to the ceiling. Stories seemed to leap out of the pages toward her, reminding her of how much she loved reading. She hadn't gotten to do much of it lately, being so consumed by work and dealing with everything in her life. She realized she needed to dive into a new book to help distract her from the sad feelings when they came. It would be like a bandage over a bullet wound, but it was a start.

The warm red walls against the light, hardwood floors reminded her of home, while the posters of literary quotes by some of the greats inspired her as always. There was a handful of people perusing the library and working on their own thing, which motivated her to do the same.

Kate went toward one of the old-fashioned-looking wooden desks with a stained-glass lamp on it and got out her laptop. She found that she worked far more efficiently in this space, focused as she drenched herself in her work. The words came much more easily here as the sadness faded away to give her room to breathe and think.

After a couple of hours, she needed a break, so she decided to find a new book to read. She started in the fiction section, finding some silly fantasy story that she hoped would carry her away to a far-off land. Then she moved over to the non-fiction section to look through some crime books for inspiration.

As she browsed through the shelves, she noticed him again. Victor. He was standing right in front of the section she was going to be looking at. She hesitated, wondering if she should approach him. But at that moment before she could decide, he looked up and smiled at her like he was expecting her to come talk to him.

"Hey," he said.

Kate took a deep breath. She couldn't ignore him now. Still, she reminded herself to keep her head straight while she talked to him. She didn't want to have any more crazy dreams about him. She didn't want to have that same attraction. She reminded herself of Tyler as she approached him. She couldn't betray her husband. So, she just smiled.

"It's funny to catch you here," Victor said. "I realized after I ran into you at the store that you're the author of the last novel my wife and I ever read. We used to read out loud together. I wanted to commend you on your excellent writing. It's so exciting to meet the author of a book she cherished."

Kate picked up on that tone, that way of phrasing it. She had used it herself many times since Tyler's death. But it couldn't mean what it sounded like. There was no way he had lost a spouse like she had. That would be too strange of a coincidence.

"She especially loved the section about how your main case study's desire started off pure, but his greed was his downfall in the end. His unquenchable thirst and desire for happiness was insatiable, eventually ruining him until he became a shell of his former self. That transformation." Victor shook his head. "It's powerful stuff. You chose a good topic. It really resonated with me and my wife before she passed."

Kate got a lump in her throat that was difficult to swallow. He was a widower. Strangely enough, even though she was a widow herself, she didn't know exactly what to say to him. She knew there wasn't anything she could say to make it better. So, she stuck to the basics.

"I'm sorry to hear about her passing," Kate offered lamely. She wondered if she should tell him about Tyler but hesitated. It felt too personal to share with him yet. She always hated the pity and awkwardness that followed whenever she told someone of Tyler's death. It wasn't something she wanted to deal with if it could be avoided. "That must be incredibly tough."

"It is," Victor admitted. Then he smiled. "You'll have to sign a copy of the book for me. I think she would love that. I'll head over to the bookstore right after this conversation to get a copy, and next time I see you, could I get your autograph?"

Kate blushed at that. She had signed a few books before, but it was still a strange experience. She couldn't quite fathom anyone wanting her autograph.

"How about I go to the bookstore with you?" she offered, surprising herself by it. "I could sign a copy of the book while we're there."

It was a lame excuse when deep down she knew she just wanted to spend more time with him. She had this strange desire to get to know this man better. He still reminded her of Tyler. Being near him reminded her of being with her husband, even when she felt the sting of the betrayal because of it.

"That would be fantastic." He smiled a huge smile at her that made the offer worth it. Despite her hesitation, she thought she had made the right decision. She knew how tough it was to lose a spouse, and if she could help ease the pain in any way whatsoever, she wanted to do that. Maybe it would help ease her own pain too.

They chatted idly as they checked out their books together, then headed out to the sidewalk to walk to the bookstore. Being with him was an oddly familiar feeling that Kate tried not to read too much into.

"I should share that we did once have a copy of your book," Victor said, thankfully filling the silence that had fallen between them. "But after my wife passed, I left all of her things with her sister. The reminder of it was too painful."

"I can imagine," Kate said. But she didn't have to imagine, she knew it all too well.

"After she died, I left everything behind. I came back here to my hometown to be with my family again. I needed them after everything that had happened, and I especially adore my little niece. She's five years old, and I love taking her to the park, the beach, out for ice cream. Anywhere, really. Evelyn and I never had children, but we wanted them. So, it's nice to be her favorite uncle. Even if I'm her only uncle."

Kate forced a laugh at that, though internally she was thinking of her own struggles to conceive. It was incredible how this stranger's life so perfectly mirrored her own. She suspected he would understand her on a level that others couldn't. If she could only find the strength to be as open with him as he was with her.

"I admire your honesty," Kate told him. "Your pure openness. It's incredible, though,… you seem so carefree and easygoing after experiencing such a horrible tragedy. I hope that one day I'll get to that place myself again."

Kate's demeanor dropped at that as she thought about Tyler. Was it right for her to keep living while he was dead? She still wasn't sure about that.

"Again?" Victor repeated curiously. "If you don't mind me asking, what has gotten in the way of that for you? What changed your happier self?"

Kate hesitated, her cheeks flaring at the slipup. She wasn't one for sharing so much of herself with a stranger. It felt odd to open up to him about her deep struggles. What if he found it too much to handle?

Then, she thought of how open he had been with her. She reasoned that he could probably relate to her more than anyone else could. And his openness made her feel safe enough to share her thoughts and heart with him.

"I… I understand what you went through with your wife. Because my husband also passed away."

"Oh. I'm so sorry for your loss," he said, his happy demeanor noticeably turning to a softer tone. "It's one of the worst things anyone can go through."

She chuckled silently through the tears slowly dropping. "Yeah."

He didn't prod, didn't ask questions, and didn't make her uncomfortable. He merely reached a hand to her shoulder for support, and she accepted it. She sniffled and brushed it away, giving him a wan smile. "Sorry," she offered.

"There's nothing to be sorry about," he told her. "I know exactly how brutal it can be. And though it's nice to know I'm not alone, you never want anyone else to experience the same pain as you."

"It is challenging," she admitted. "Horrific. It's something I've wondered if I could live through. That's why I admire you so much. You're so strong, keeping an upbeat attitude. One day I hope I can smile and laugh as easily as you do."

Now it was his turn to smile wanly. "Don't be fooled by my easygoing demeanor," he warned her. "It took me a while to get to the place I'm at now, and I still struggle with her death. There are still nights that seem endless and days where I miss her deeply."

"Been there," she admitted.

He nodded. "I've just put a lot of effort into healing. I know she would want me to be happy and move forward in my life, so as I do that, I know I'd be making her proud. Deep down, even though I couldn't always admit it to myself, I have always wanted to be happy and move forward in my life despite how much my heart broke by not having her in it. So, I listened to that little voice until it grew stronger, and I reached this state of mostly happiness. Mostly."

Kate admired him more than ever as he spoke his truth. She wondered if maybe she was like that too. Maybe there was a part of her that had always been there that wanted her to be happy and move forward. Maybe she could use that to get to the place he was at now.

As they approached the bookstore, Victor paused and took out a pen and a slip of paper. Kate looked at him with curiosity. "Are you a writer too?" she asked.

That made him bark out a laugh—a genuine one. "Oh, no. I'm a carpenter," he explained. "I always keep a notepad on me in case I have to make note of something. It's just helpful to have around."

He wrote his name and number on the paper and handed it to her. "You don't have to reach out," he said. "But you can if you'd like to. There are only so many people in this little town to talk to. And I've found that most people our age can't relate to losing a spouse. I know it's a difficult thing to process. So, if you ever need someone to talk to, please feel free to call me anytime. It would be good for me, too, to make that connection. It could be the start of a helpful friendship."

"I appreciate that," she said, accepting the note and tucking it away in her purse. "I definitely will reach out. It's so refreshing to talk to someone who understands what I'm going through."

At that, they stepped into the bookstore and found her book. Seeing her own book on shelves still shocked Kate. She still couldn't quite fathom that she had reached that level of success. It reminded to her to be proud of all of her hard work.

Victor bought the book, and she signed it with a note thanking him for being a friendly ear and wishing him the best, hoping for a good friendship with him.

"I really should be going," she said, not wanting to get too close as she remembered the dream she'd had of him before. She didn't want to risk that happening again. She didn't want to have to suffer through that feeling of betraying her husband. "But it was wonderful seeing you again, and I definitely will reach out."

"I hope you do." He smiled. "It was wonderful to talk to you too."

At that, they gave each other a friendly hug. Kate paused as she was in his arms. She breathed in a scent that was achingly familiar. He was wearing the same cologne that Tyler used to wear. It only attributed to that feeling of familiarity that he served as a greater reminder of Tyler.

For a moment, it felt like Tyler was right there with her. She wanted to cling to him tighter. She wanted to close her eyes and pretend it was her husband instead. But that would be taking things too far. She forced herself to let go so it wouldn't be weird.

With that, they went their separate ways, but Victor stayed on her mind more than she wanted to admit.

CHAPTER SIXTEEN

KATE WAS DISTURBED AS SHE RETURNED HOME AND realized she was still thinking of Victor. She convinced herself it was just because he reminded her of Tyler. Yet if she were honest, there was more to it.

He genuinely seemed like an interesting guy. He was kind, funny, and compelling. Plus, the fact that they had gone through a lot of the same things added to this attraction. She felt connected to him, like he was the only person she knew who could really understand what she was going through.

As she settled down that night with her usual cup of tea, she found herself itching to text him. She needed to check in. There were so many things she wanted to say to him.

She longed to connect with someone who had lost a spouse like she had. She wanted answers about how he had become as happy as he was, how he'd learned to cope with the pain. She wanted to learn from him. She desperately wanted to reach the mental and emotional state he was in.

Instead, she decided to wait an appropriate amount of time before reaching out to him. She didn't want to seem desperate by texting him so quickly. She also didn't want to make it seem like she wanted anything other than friendship.

Sure, he was handsome, charming, and compelling. But she was married to Tyler, and she still felt a strong connection to her husband. It would still feel like a betrayal to be with another man. She simply couldn't stand the pain of that.

That night she had a dream of Victor again, and though it was still foggy and hazy, it seemed more vivid than before. She could make out his facial features a little better, she breathed in that familiar scent, and she soaked in his warmth. In the dream, it felt like this was normal—like she was meant to sleep next to him every night.

And when she woke, the guilt returned as it always did. She still couldn't quite come to terms that she dreamt of another man. She wasn't sure why her mind was betraying her heart like this. Her brain knew the torment she was going through. Why wouldn't it simply stop the nonsense?

As Kate ate breakfast that morning, she decided that Victor was fulfilling some sort of need within her that wasn't being met in other ways. That's why he was so compelling. He was offering something to her that she had been longing for.

So, she got down to journaling to try to find the source of what drew her to him. The initial thing was the fact that he did remind her of Tyler. She realized she was projecting onto him a bit, which was unhealthy and a bad coping mechanism that she wanted to break.

After having talked to him further, though, she realized she also really enjoyed connecting with another person who had lost their spouse. As sad as it was that he had gone through the same pain, and she would never wish that on anyone, she was glad to not feel alone anymore in it. He knew that pain intimately, and he modeled the type of person she eventually wanted to be.

Keeping that in mind, Kate decided to search for a group for widows and widowers. After a little bit of digging online, she was pleasantly surprised to find that there was going to be a meeting that night in Juniper Bay. She decided to at least give it a shot.

She pulled out her phone, thinking that it had been long enough that it wouldn't be weird to text Victor. Then she stopped herself. She couldn't talk to him when she was already growing so attached. She would try to form other connections instead right now. Then she would reach out to him later if it still felt right.

Instead, she tried to distract herself from thoughts of him by writing, taking her self-defense class, working in her garden, and baking some homemade cookies. It was still strange cooking and baking for one person. She still always made too much. So she went for a run, allotting herself permission to eat more cookies and stress-eat away her feelings.

As evening approached, she started to question herself. She was feeling better that day with fewer thoughts of Victor to interrupt her. Maybe she wouldn't go to the group tonight. Maybe another time. She didn't want to leave her house.

Besides, she worried that it might be painful to talk about her husband to strangers. She couldn't imagine that she'd actually feel support from them. She figured she'd just be an outcast, which would make her feel even worse.

Yet again, she tried to force herself through. But it was no use having these constant self-doubts. The anxious part of her was surprised and panicked as she got into her car, but her determination to get better drove her forward. She was going to take the steps to be like Victor. It was time. She needed to do this for her own growth and healing.

Still, Kate second-guessed her decision the whole way to the library where the meeting would be taking place. She even hesitated when she parked her car, still wondering if it was too late to change her mind. But she forced herself inside and found the small room they had reserved for the meeting.

She took a deep breath with her hand on the doorknob. Negative thoughts flooded her mind, rendering her powerless for a moment.

I can't do this. I can't do this. I can't do this.

With one burst of strength, though, Kate pushed through these thoughts and opened the door. She stepped inside and immediately felt awkward as all eyes turned to her. She was surprised by the wide range of people who were there. Most of the attendees were older than she, but there was another woman who looked a couple of years younger than she was and a man who appeared to be around her age.

The younger woman was by a table set up with cookies and drinks. Kate walked over to her, drawn by how scared and shy she looked. Her face mirrored the mix of turbulent emotions Kate was feeling. She seemed to be hiding behind the dark hair that fell over her blue eyes.

Kate took one of the cookies and debated if she should introduce herself. She suspected the woman wasn't about to greet her. She didn't seem like the most outgoing person.

"Hi," Kate started, deciding to take the first step. Someone had to. "I'm Kate. I'm new here, so I thought it might be good to get to know a couple of people before the meeting begins."

"Hi, Kate," she replied meekly. "I'm Vanessa. This is only my second meeting, so I'm getting to know people too. It's a little intimidating."

"It really is," Kate agreed, grateful she wasn't alone in this feeling. "How has it been for you so far? Was your first meeting helpful?"

"It was. I didn't speak too much; I just listened. But I think tonight I'm going to tell my story. I think I'll benefit more from it. I am committed to getting better, so I want to do everything I can to get there. I just… I feel so lost and alone without him."

"I know that feeling. I don't know your specific situation, and no one can one hundred percent relate to everything you're going through, but on some level, I get it. We'll all get through this together. And hopefully, there will be happiness in the end. I believe there is. I have to hold onto that."

Kate wasn't sure where the sudden wellspring of strength had come from, but she welcomed it. She felt surer of herself as she talked to Vanessa and got to know her. Being there for someone else made her feel stronger than when she was just trying to support herself. It made her better able to be positive and think of the ways she could someday emerge from the dark tunnel she'd been trapped in for so long.

Soon after, they all sat down in a circle with Kate sitting in between Vanessa and the young man who was around their age. She turned and introduced herself to him.

"I'm Liam," he started, trying to smile despite the sadness in his brown eyes. Physically, he looked so strong with blond hair and features that could belong to a model. But his soul was clearly tortured. It was apparent in the circles under his eyes, his slumped posture, and his look of defeat.

"I've been attending these meetings for a few months now, and it's sad to see another new face. But I also welcome you to our safe space. I hope you'll get some benefit from it."

"I'm Kate. I'm sorry as well to see so many people here, but there is something already comforting in knowing I'm not alone."

"Absolutely," Liam agreed. "Losing a spouse can be a very isolating experience. But you've found a place where you never have to be alone. The people here are so supportive. It helps immensely."

As Kate talked with Liam and Vanessa for a few minutes longer, she couldn't help but wonder how they lost their spouses at this age. The three of them were the youngest people in the group, and when someone young dies, it's always a curious thing to know why. But she didn't dare ask.

It turned out she didn't need to, as when introductions were made, and people told snippets of their stories, she learned the reasons for their deaths. Liam's wife had died in a car accident, leaving him alone with his son who was a toddler. Now a single father, he tried his best to take on the role of both parents. But sometimes he still struggled.

Vanessa's story was tragic too. She could barely face anyone's glances as she spoke. Yet she seemed determined to tell her story.

"My husband Peter was depressed before his death," she told them. "It was a struggle he suffered with for a long time. We tried to get him help. He saw multiple therapists and psychiatrists. I researched how I could best support him. I did everything a wife was supposed to do. Or at least, I thought I did.

"I made mistakes along the way—I know it. We were so young when we got married, right out of high school. We'd been together for years. I thought we'd always be together. But there was something in him that I never knew how to help. I didn't know how to cope with something of that magnitude, and..." Vanessa paused as she wiped tears from her eyes, "three months ago, Peter committed suicide."

Kate's heart reached out to Vanessa as she took a moment to touch her hand briefly in a show of support. She thought back to her darkest days, the days she'd been contemplating it herself. She knew how painful suicide was for everyone around the person who takes their life. It made her even more determined to get better so those dark thoughts wouldn't return.

"I'll admit, I was overwhelmed with guilt after his death," Vanessa continued. "I felt like I should've done more to stop him—to help him. I felt like it was my duty as his wife to prevent it. I know that's not rational, that there's nothing I could have done. But I didn't know how to handle it. I even considered taking my own life to follow him just so I could be with him again. I didn't know how to live without him."

Whispers of support and sympathy echoed through the room. Kate knew that practically every single one of them had thought the same thoughts and felt the same feelings.

"Recently, though, I've started to feel a little more like myself again. I realized I do want to live, despite how painful living can be sometimes. I want to make the most of my life. I want to heal. And that's why I'm here. It's my first step in doing that."

Vanessa was surrounded by validation, empathy, and praise for being brave enough to continue on with her life after such a tough time. It inspired Kate to be open with her own story as she shared what had happened and admitted to the difficult feelings that had swamped her following Tyler's death.

After she finished speaking, she felt horribly vulnerable and prepared herself for rejection, even though she knew rationally it wouldn't come. All she received was an outpouring of support that made her feel a little bit better. It made her feel less alone. She smiled through the tears as they offered her warmth, and for the first time in a long time, she felt welcomed by the community.

It turned out that the support group was the missing piece she needed in her healing journey. Or at the very least, it felt like a step closer to where she eventually wanted to be. She felt refreshed after leaving, even though she had cried while she was there. The tears felt healing instead of isolating.

She realized once she got back home that it provided a similar connection to the one she had experienced with Victor, but it didn't get her mind totally off him. She thought about how he might feel alone as he still struggled with his wife's death. No one should have to feel that way. She knew all too well how painful it was, so she decided to reach out.

After way too much thought, she sent Victor a text telling him about the support group and inviting him to the next meeting. Then she went about her night trying not to worry too much about his response. She got the ping right before bed.

Thanks so much for reaching out! I'm glad to hear from you again. Thank you for sharing the information on the group as well. I'll definitely check it out! Hope everything is going well for you. Remember, I'm here if you ever need someone outside the group to talk to.

Kate re-read the text and debated how she should respond to it. She knew she was putting entirely too much thought into this, but there was just something about him that worked its way into her mind, making her think about him more than she wanted to.

Thank you for the support! Hope to see you at the next meeting.

With that, Kate went to bed, hoping she wouldn't dream of Victor again.

CHAPTER SEVENTEEN

K ATE WAS PLEASANTLY SURPRISED THAT SHE DIDN'T dream of Victor that night. She didn't dream of any man joining her in her bed, not even Tyler. It was nice not to wake up with the guilt, but it also made her feel a bit alone and empty.

The conflicting feelings were a mystery to her, so she tried to push them aside as she went about her day. Not dreaming about Victor made her feel more secure in their friendship, so she allowed herself to text him casually throughout the day, and he responded. They didn't send a lot of texts to each other, but just a few to kind of test the waters of friendship. So far, she found she enjoyed talking to him, but she tried not to get too personal. She didn't want those dreams to start up again.

For the next few days, the dreams actually stopped completely. She started feeling less on edge, and the thoughts that someone was watching her faded too. She suspected the change in medications and therapy appointments were to thank for the shift. She assumed all the work she was doing was helping her mental illness, and she couldn't be more grateful for it.

Feeling more confident again, she decided to continue the interviews for her book, but this time she had a different subject in mind. Instead of talking to yet another murderer, she wanted to explore how mental illness could hurt the people suffering from it, from self-harm to suicide. It was important to explore the less sensationalistic elements to truly capture the full scope of her subject and stop it from being yet another true crime rag.

Of course, she couldn't talk to anyone who had successfully committed suicide. But she could talk to someone who had been suicidal before and someone who was affected by the suicide of another person. Lucky for her, she knew the perfect person to talk to about this.

She was still a little surprised that Vanessa had suggested meeting at Casey's Ice Cream Shoppe; Kate wasn't sure it would be a good place to talk about such a dark topic. She wasn't complaining though. The pastel-colored shop was inviting with its pink walls, purple tile flooring, and blue tables and chairs. The employees were dressed just as brightly, and all the patrons seemed overjoyed to be there.

Vanessa was already sitting at a table in the corner; she rose to greet Kate as she approached. The two hugged for an extra moment before parting.

"Thank you for agreeing to meet with me," Kate said.

"Thank you for agreeing to come here," Vanessa replied. "I know it's a strange choice, but I figured that having ice cream while we talk might make the sadness a little easier to manage."

"I couldn't agree more."

Before getting down to their dark conversation, the two women ordered sundaes with birthday cake ice cream, marshmallow and caramel topping, white chocolate chips, and rainbow sprinkles. It was as if they were forcing a bit of happiness to help them get through the sadness that had edged its way into their lives.

It was a delicious distraction as they sat in the back corner of the shop and dug right in. They allowed themselves a few bites of ice cream before beginning the conversation.

"I'm sure this is a tough topic for you," Kate started. "So, I'm grateful you're taking the time to talk to me. You can share as little or as much as you feel comfortable with. I just ideally would want to know everything from your husband's mental health journey, the impact of his death, and how you've coped with your own mental illness following the trauma of his death."

Vanessa nodded and dove right into her story. She detailed how her husband's mental health had declined over the years and all the things they did to try to prevent things from escalating. She pointed out flaws in the healthcare system that kept him from always getting the support he needed. She admitted to how a lack of knowledge sometimes hurt them in the quest for answers.

Then she got vulnerable in sharing her own mental health struggles, her suicidal ideation, her fear of getting help, and how she had begun to pull herself out of the darkness. Kate found the whole story inspiring—and much more relatable than she'd like to admit.

"It's been an adjustment being on my own and trying to heal," Vanessa said. "I think it's made me a little paranoid, honestly."

"What do you mean?" Kate asked.

"Well, lately I've gotten the sense that someone's following me," Vanessa admitted. "Sometimes I see strange shadows out of the corner of my eyes. I just get the feeling that someone's… watching me. And sometimes things aren't always where I left them, random things go missing, items fall without reason, I hear strange noises."

Kate suddenly grew more on edge. What if Vanessa having the same experience meant that someone in town was stalking both of them? Kate hadn't had any of those strange things happen lately, but she was no less cautious about it. Maybe that meant her stalker was turning his attention to Vanessa now.

Then she reminded herself of what her therapist said. These sorts of things were typical of widows. It didn't mean necessarily that anything bad was happening. It simply meant that she and Vanessa were struggling in similar ways. It made perfect sense.

"It's a difficult thing," Vanessa said. "Sometimes I wonder if it's all in my head. While other times I'm convinced someone is stalking me. Whatever the reason, I feel unsafe. I hate living by myself. I hate having to do all of this alone. It's terrifying because I'm used to having a partner to help me through it."

"I know," Kate replied sympathetically. But she refrained from telling Vanessa her own experiences with unexplained feelings of paranoia, afraid that sharing her own experience might make the girl even more afraid. "Though I know you feel totally alone sometimes, you do have support. I'm here for you. If you ever feel scared, you can text or call me. I'll even come to your house if you need me to. I know that losing a husband is one of the worst feelings. So, I want to be there for you. We can be there for each other. We can get through this together."

"I really appreciate that," Vanessa smiled sadly. "It does make me feel less alone and more empowered. Like I can build a life without him. Like maybe I can do this."

"I know you can."

As Kate assured her, she felt more comforted herself. She was moving forward, away from the scary shadows and ghosts. And she was starting to believe that someday she would truly be happy.

As they talked throughout the week, Kate and Vanessa grew closer; Kate was also talking to Victor more as well. She was thankful for the connections she was forming with the people in Juniper Bay. She was grateful for all the progress she was making, even though she missed Tyler terribly.

Every day fell into a routine: wake up, check on the garden, spend a couple hours writing, attend the self-defense class, and then wind down after dinner with a cup of tea before bed. Occasionally she went to Barb's Café or to the shops in town, or she'd make a point to catch up with Vanessa; but mostly, she just kept to her strict schedule, hoping that eventually it would stop being an active effort and just become a regular life.

She still had the sense that someone was watching her sometimes, but the thought was still comforting rather than scary, and it occurred less often than it did before. She still talked to Tyler out loud, hoping his ghost could hear her and that's why she felt like she was being watched. He was watching over her. She wasn't ready to get rid of that yet. But now she talked to her living friends more, making her feel more grounded. Barbara and Frank seemed to make a habit of "accidentally" baking too many pastries and offering her the extras for free. Kate appreciated it more than she could say.

When the day came for the group widows and widowers meeting, she found herself looking forward to it. Though it was challenging to bring up old wounds from Tyler's death, she also found it comforting to be around other people who could relate rather than being surrounded by those who simply couldn't understand all she was going through.

Deep down, even though it was difficult to admit, she was also really looking forward to seeing Victor again. The short conversations they'd had were engaging and interesting. He still reminded her of Tyler sometimes, but he was also different from Tyler, which intrigued her to want to learn more about him.

Any possibility of romance was off the table for her. Despite her attraction to him, she just wasn't ready for that. She still needed to process Tyler's death. She wasn't ready to move on in that way yet.

She really enjoyed his friendship though. She thought they had a special connection, and she was looking forward to building upon it.

To her surprise and disappointment, Victor didn't show up to the meeting. Maybe something had come up, she reasoned. She tried not to dwell on it too much, and she felt supported and accepted in this group of people she was growing to care about rather quickly.

Unfortunately, that night she slipped into Victor's arms again. She snuggled against him, thinking he was Tyler at first. Then, she resurfaced long enough to recognize who was in her bed.

"It's been a while," she said bitterly before she could slip out of the dream.

"I know," he replied. "I'm sorry for that. But I'm here now, and I won't leave you again."

At that, Kate blacked out again. The next morning, she saw that a framed photo of her and Tyler on the wall had fallen, its glass shattered, and she sobbed, falling right back into the endless pit of darkness as she worried about Tyler's spirit being brokenhearted.

CHAPTER EIGHTEEN

ONCE AGAIN, KATE STARTED FEELING PARANOID. SHE loathed this descent back into her mental illness. She knew that healing would come with its ebbs and flows, but she just wanted to get better. She was desperate to feel okay again.

But this haunting feeling cloaked her. She couldn't seem to shake it. To her surprise, that morning she woke up to a text from Brad.

Hey, Kate. Just wanted to check in to see if you're doing okay. We've all been thinking about you and hoping for the best. Feel free to call me when you get a chance.

Kate's heart lightened a bit as she thought of her college friends. She reminded herself she had support. She would get through this. Before replying, though, she decided to go for a run to clear her head.

As she ran, she thought about her life with Tyler. The memories were still so fresh, the pain still so real. She would never see him again. That was too much to fathom.

She couldn't just dwell on the same well-worn path over and over, so she decided to take a little detour. Instead of following the path, she stepped into the woods, her curiosity piqued and a spirit of courage flowing in her veins. Was she really about to explore further? What if she got lost? What if it was dangerous to be in the woods alone?

She found that she cared more about her safety than before. The thought of dying now seemed kind of scary. She wasn't quite ready to go yet.

Still, a bit of the fearlessness remained, so she stepped into the forest and soon found herself engulfed in a whole new world. The lush green plant life around her reminded her of the life she had forsaken. The sound of little animals chattering was more inviting than any music. The peace that was found under the canopy of trees felt like walking through a safe space that was more alive and somehow easier to manage than the rest of the world. Here, Kate felt completely at peace with herself.

As she walked, she started to breathe deeper. With each inhale she imagined soaking in the comfort mother nature was gently offering her. With each exhale, she was letting go of a little of the stress that bound her so tightly that she often found it difficult to breathe.

After a bit of wandering, the trees opened a little and revealed a field with daisies dotting it. The green grass had been left to grow freely, tangled around the perfectly white petals. Kate stepped into heavenlike scene and held a flower softly in her hands. She admired how delicate, fragile, and beautiful it was.

Then, she picked it. It reminded her of the flowers Tyler used to bring her. She missed those sweet notes of affection most of all. They had done plenty of fancy, elaborate, and romantic things while they were together, but there was something about the simpler, day-to-day things that resonated with her. Those were what she missed most of all.

She continued to pick flowers and thought about how ironic it was that humans so often kill the things they're fond of, trap them, have to possess them, and keep them to themselves. Wasn't it enough to just let them live?

At that thought, she stopped adding to her modest bouquet. She sat down on the grass and looked up at the puffy clouds floating across the sky with ease.

"Someday, that will be me," she whispered. "I'll move through the world just like a cloud, making Tyler proud. I'll share the wonderful lessons he had to offer. I'll grow through the pain. I'll be stronger."

"That's a beautiful thing," a voice answered, sounding like it was far away.

Kate froze. She wondered for a moment if she was hearing things. She looked around her. She couldn't see anyone. The voice sounded so clear though. It sounded so real.

She thought of the people she had interviewed and how convinced they were that the voices they'd heard were real before they convinced them to do terrible things. They'd fallen into a whole other world of delusion. She didn't want to believe that was happening to her. But the alternative was nearly as scary.

"Is someone out there?" she asked, a little louder. She felt a little silly for saying it, but she had to know. It was driving her crazy.

At that, she heard a rustling in the trees. It sounded louder than a simple chipmunk or bird. She took a moment to consider maybe it was a wild animal. Maybe it was someone dangerous.

Something deeper was desperate to know if she was in danger or if she was losing her mind. So, without another thought, Kate dropped her flowers and started running.

She realized what she was doing was crazy as she dashed towards the sound. It was dangerous. She was taking a huge risk. Yet she still felt like it was worth it.

Adrenaline made her faster than ever. The trees spun around her. Her whole world narrowed down to that one need. She was determined to figure out if she was crazy.

Kate kept running, not spotting anything until finally, her foot caught a tree branch that sent her sprawling to the ground. Her knees cried out in pain as the dirt greeted them harshly. Her first instinct was to get up and resume her chase.

But something deeper inside her stopped her. She realized what she was doing was crazy on its own. She hadn't seen or heard anything unusual since she'd started running. It was a wild goose chase. It was more confirmation that something bad was going on with her mental health, and if she kept indulging these feelings, it was bound to get worse.

Kate got to her feet. She dusted off her knees. She started walking, but this time, it was back toward the trail. That haunting feeling followed her as she started to wonder how long it would take before this mental state really began to ruin things for her. How far would things decline? What would happen if she lost control? Would she be able to stop it before she did something horrible?

Kate was exhausted mentally and physically by the time she got back home. It was still early in the day, so she took a shower and started to get ready like she normally would even though she felt far from normal.

Still, she wasn't giving up. She decided she needed to leave her house, hoping that might help her mental health. She stepped outside and froze.

On her front step was the bouquet of flowers she had picked in the field. She stared down at them, unsure of how to react.

This was proof that she wasn't going crazy, wasn't it? Someone had been out there with her. Someone had then gathered the flowers after she dropped them and brought them here. She distinctly remembered dropping them.

Didn't she? She thought back and wondered if she had picked them back up. If she had, though, why would she have left them on the steps?

A chill ran through her. Why would a stalker bring her flowers? Was he admiring her from afar? Who would stalk her anyway?

Kate thought about calling the police. She needed to feel safer. But what would she tell them? That she had a feeling someone was following her? That flowers were at her doorstep? She doubted they would take that seriously.

So instead, she stepped right over the flowers, deciding she would deal with them when she got back. Then, she called Brad on her Bluetooth speaker as she drove into town.

"Hey!" he said, picking up the phone on the first ring. He sounded rather out of breath. "I'm so glad you called. I've been thinking of you. I know things were tough for a while, and I was wondering how you were coping now that you're all settled in."

"It goes back and forth," Kate replied. "A little better on some days, and then it feels like I've slipped back on others. Or at least, I might be regressing. Or there might be something else going on. Do you… do you mind if I vent a little, and you can tell me if I'm crazy?"

"Not at all. Vent away."

At that, Kate admitted to the strange feelings she had of someone watching her, the weird things that had occurred in her home, and the entire story leading up to the flowers on her doorstep.

"Well, I don't think you're going crazy," Brad noted. "That is concerning. Do you have any weapons to protect yourself?"

"I have pepper spray."

"That's not enough," Brad insisted. "You should get a handgun, even if it's just a small one."

"I wouldn't even know what to do with one," Kate pointed out. "I've never shot a gun before. It would be dangerous for me to have one, not knowing what I'm doing."

"How about I come out to see you soon?" he offered. "I could teach you how to use a gun, and I can check out things for you. Maybe we could check out your new town or something. It might make you feel better. I'll have to give my job notice, but I could be out in a couple of weeks."

Kate felt bad for admitting how beneficial that would be. But she also didn't want to make him feel unwelcome. She felt kind of stuck.

"What about Jade? Would she be coming too?"

"Ah, well… things with Jade and me aren't going great," Brad admitted. "I could honestly use a break from her, if that's okay."

"I don't want to step on any toes…"

"I promise that she won't mind."

Kate wasn't exactly surprised to hear this after seeing their interactions when they helped her move in. They hadn't hidden it well at all. "Well, you're always welcome to stay with me for a bit. I'd love to see you. If it's not too much of a drive."

"Oh, not at all. I've actually been staying in the area a few times before this," Brad admitted. "When I've needed to get away for a bit. I would've seen you then, but when I came I needed space and time to think. I needed time to be alone, but I'm ready to reconnect with friends. I hope you're not offended."

"Of course not," she assured him. "I totally understand how that feels. I'm glad you're getting back into life again. I'll be more than happy to have you here."

At that, the two made plans to get together in a couple of weeks. Then, they had to stop talking because Kate had arrived at Barb's and Brad had to get to work. Still, it made Kate feel so much better—like she wasn't so alone. Yet nothing could totally ease her at the moment, knowing someone was stalking her. There was no way of even trying to convince herself now that she was safe.

⟶

As she sat in the café, she made conversation with Barbara and Frank as usual. Just as they were finishing up their conversation, though, someone else caught her attention. He smiled as he walked over. Kate found herself as drawn to him as ever.

"Hey, Kate," Victor said. "It's so nice to see you again. Would you mind if I join you? It's always more fun eating with company than alone."

"Of course, that's no problem," Kate replied, a little too eager to talk to him again. "I could always use the company."

Victor sat across from her just as the waitress came over to take his order. Once he was finished, Kate and Victor shared a look that felt too familiar. It was somewhere between friends and more, even though Kate was one hundred percent sure she wasn't ready for something like that yet.

"Sorry I haven't been around much," Victor said. "I've been busy on a project up in Maine, which has kept me occupied. But now that I'm back, I'm hoping to have more time for other important things."

"Like what?" Kate asked.

"Well, I'd love to get back to work on my own house. I've had a few renovations in mind for a while now. I have a great space for a garden, so I want to work on that. Get back into running on the beach again. Spending time with my family. My niece is growing up so fast. Maybe even cultivate some new friendships."

He gave her a hopeful smile at that last comment. She couldn't help but smile back. She reassured herself that at least he had said friendships. It seemed like they were on the same page on that at least. Neither of them expected anything more.

"I'd like to cultivate more friendships too," Kate said. "I find that's so important. I've been delighted to make some new friends in town. I'm making some great connections—especially through the support group. You really should come."

"I'll go to the next meeting," he promised. "I've just been busy. And honestly, it's a little tough to face Evelyn's death in that way. I know it would be beneficial, but it's just one of those things I've been putting off, you know?"

Kate smiled. "I think it would be good for you. As a friend."

He laughed. "Oh, well, as a friend, sure. No, I'll check it out. I'm sure the support would help."

"It's like you said," Kate told him. "It's really helped me feel like I'm not alone. Like there's maybe a light at the end of the tunnel after all. It's not perfect. I'm still struggling. But I think I am getting happier. Slowly."

He smiled. "That's really great, Kate."

At that, Kate shared the progress she was making. Then Victor shared his triumphs and struggles as well. It felt so nice to relate to someone, which made Kate feel much better than she had in a while. It felt nice to have that space to vent.

Then, they moved on to other topics, which was helpful in its own way as well. She was grateful to have that distraction, and time moved on so quickly that she couldn't believe what time it was when they finished their breakfasts.

"I'd love to continue our conversation," Victor said. "Would you like to join me for dinner sometime? Maybe Friday night?"

Kate hesitated. She did enjoy her conversations with Victor, and she wanted to talk to him more. But dinner sounded a bit too much like a date. She was still uncomfortable with even the thought of that.

She had gotten dinner with Vanessa recently though. She certainly had grabbed dinner with Allison plenty of times, along with her other friends. So, she reasoned it didn't have to be a date as long as they didn't make it that way.

"I'd like that," she said, though the words still felt a little wrong as they came out. She wanted to build that connection.

"Wonderful!" Victor replied. "I know the perfect place. It's called *Lavish Lounge,* which I know is super cliché. But I promise it's not as lame as it sounds."

"After learning what your favorite chocolate is, I trust your taste and judgment." Kate laughed, surprising herself with the sound. Sure, she had laughed since Tyler died, but it was mostly forced and faked. This laugh was real and genuine.

"Fantastic," Victor said. "See you at eight?"

"I'll be there."

Having made that arrangement, Kate left Barb's Café with an unexpected spring in her step. But her mood dropped once again when she returned home and saw the daisies again. She didn't want to anger or offend whomever might be watching her in case he was dangerous, so she brought them into her house and put them into a vase, just in case.

After that, Kate sat down and pondered this. She thought about who might have reason to stalk her. Then, she came upon a chilling thought as she remembered Allison's warnings about talking to criminals.

Could someone she interviewed have anything to do with this? Kate thought she was being cautious. But she realized she really hadn't done much to protect herself, so she wasn't sure she was safe. But she couldn't be sure her mental health wasn't to blame either. So, she started writing again to escape the fear, at a loss of what she could truly do to fix anything.

CHAPTER NINETEEN

K ATE WAS SURPRISED TO FIND THAT SHE DIDN'T DREAM of Victor that night, even though he was on her mind because she was a bit worried about having dinner with him. It was as if having him closer in her life soothed some sort of subconscious longing, which was a relief. It helped her to not have to deal with the guilt.

"What do you think about me going out to dinner with Victor?" Kate asked Tyler on Thursday night as she sat drinking her tea by her stone fireplace. The flames warmed the room chilled by the fall of autumn as the tea made her feel drowsy and cozy.

"If you can hear me, Tyler, I want you to know it's not a date. We're just friends hanging out with each other. But I don't want to do anything to upset you. So, if it will bother you, just give me a dream of you tonight. I promise if you do, I won't go."

It gave Kate an out in a way. She was already hesitant about going, so if she had a reason not to go, she was going to grab ahold of that. It meant she wouldn't have to reach outside her comfort zone. She wouldn't have to face the guilt she felt about doing so.

Tyler didn't visit her dreams that night though. It both relieved and saddened her. She liked the thought that he was still there with her, but she also was grateful for the belief that if he was, he wasn't upset about Victor.

There was that lingering possibility that she had made it all up in her head. She entertained the thought that maybe Tyler hadn't been with her all along. Maybe she was truly alone in this world without him. Maybe he was gone for good.

"What do you think?" she asked the next morning over breakfast. "Before, you were leaving me signs all the time. You don't do that as much anymore. I want your opinion on things. I don't want to feel so alone."

Again, nothing happened. She was left feeling cold and abandoned. She knew he wouldn't fully leave her, not if he had a choice. So, why had he stopped sending her signs?

She tried not to think about it too much as she went about her day. She tried not to think about the dinner either because it was distracting. Regardless, she found it difficult to get work done because the thoughts were relentless and the guilt was just as demanding.

Kate almost canceled multiple times. Unsure of what to do, she decided to call Allison. She worried that her best friend might judge her for even thinking of going out to dinner with another guy. She reasoned if Allison did judge her, though, that would be another sign not to go.

"Oh, that's great!" Allison said after Kate told her about her dilemma. "I mean, it's obviously not great that you're struggling with that decision. But I think it's a good sign you're even considering going out with him."

"It's not like it's a date," Kate rushed to explain. "It's not like I'm forgetting about Tyler or anything."

"Of course not," Allison agreed. "Even if it were a date, which I believe you when you say it's not, that wouldn't mean you were forgetting about Tyler. And you can't betray someone who's dead. You're simply moving forward. He would want that for you. I know he would."

"You don't know that," Kate protested.

"Well, he loved you, didn't he?"

"Yes. We loved each other with our whole hearts."

"Exactly. And what would you want for someone you love? Would you want them to stop their lives completely and live in misery forever? Or would you want them to find happiness somehow? If you had died instead of him, would you want him to stay single, isolated, and unhappy forever?"

Kate considered her words deeply. Part of her reeled at the thought of Tyler being with another woman, even if it happened after her death. Yet a bigger part knew she'd want him to move on. She wouldn't want him to be alone forever. She wouldn't expect that of him. She'd want him to be happy.

"Of course not," Kate answered. "I'd want him to live his life and find happiness."

"Well, you said Tyler loved you as much as you loved him. So, what makes you think he wouldn't want that for you?"

Kate didn't have a response to that, so they sat in silence for a moment. She hadn't thought about things like that before, so it challenged her beliefs in an uncomfortable way. She wasn't sure how to process it.

"I hope you know you need to go tonight," Allison finally broke the silence. "I know it's difficult to move forward. I know it comes along with a lot of conflicting emotions for you. I feel for you—I really do. I wouldn't want to be in your position. It's something I'll never fully understand. But I know you. I've seen how you've dealt with this so far. I can tell that you need this. You need to get out. You need to try to move forward. That doesn't mean you're forgetting him. It simply means you're living, which is exactly what he'd want you to do."

"It just feels weird," Kate said lamely.

"I mean, it *is* weird. But it's a weirdness you can work through," Allison pointed out. "Tell you what. Why don't you go out with him, even if it's just as friends? I can come up next weekend to visit, and you can tell me all about it."

Kate couldn't protest any longer, so she agreed with Allison. She promised she would at least go out for dinner with Victor, no matter how difficult it was. She needed to do this. She was strong enough to do this. She knew she needed to move forward.

But as she was leaving to go meet Victor, that conviction wavered a little. She wasn't so sure she was ready for this. She was no longer convinced she could do it.

"I'm not ready," she said in her car as she drove to the restaurant. "I need more time. His death is still so fresh in my mind. What if Victor thinks this is a date?"

She thought back to any indication that Victor might have given that he thought it was a date. He'd never explicitly said it. He'd always acted in a friendly and respectful way. She was sure if she laid down her expectations of what the night would and would not entail, he would respect that. He wouldn't try to push any boundaries.

Assured of the knowledge that she wouldn't have to do anything she didn't want to do, Kate forced herself out of her car. She walked to the front door of Lavish Lounge where Victor was already waiting, looking handsome in a blue button-down shirt that matched her eyes, black slacks, and a general put-together demeanor.

As Kate looked down at her black dress, she realized that to anyone coming across them, they would probably look like they were on a date. She reminded herself that other people's thoughts didn't matter… as long as she and Victor knew where they stood, that was all that was important.

She and Victor hugged before he opened the door for her and they walked inside the fancy restaurant together. The low lighting made the blue walls and black furnishings look soothing and classy. Everyone was dressed nicely, their shadows being twisted by the candlelit tables into something beautiful and magical.

"Good choice," Kate said, admiring the ambiance as soft music calmed her anxious nerves. "Hopefully the food is as good as the décor."

"It's even better," Victor assured her.

They were quickly seated by a window seat that looked out at the ocean. It was just dark enough outside to make the water look gray but light enough to see the waves yawning as they stretched against the shore.

Kate caught a glimpse of herself and Victor in the reflection of the window and noted how they did in fact look very much like they were on a date. It was something that made her incredibly uncomfortable.

"So, how has your week been?" Victor asked.

They soon slipped into simple conversation that made Kate forget about her worries. They ordered food that sounded delicious and had a couple of amazing cocktails. With the alcohol helping bring her guard down, she started to get honest.

"It's so tough sometimes," Kate admitted. "Sometimes I feel like I'm making progress. Then, I slide back again. I just don't get it."

"It's not easy getting over trauma like that," Victor said. "I know I seem happy and carefree, but it weighs on me too sometimes. The pain is just carved in so deep that it becomes part of your everyday life. Part of me feels alone in this world without my wife. When I was with her, I felt like I was part of a team. My life felt more fulfilled and happier. Now, I'm getting to a place of happiness. But I still feel the guilt and sadness sometimes. I still miss her deeply."

"I totally understand," Kate replied. "I feel the same way. It's almost like living becomes a betrayal—where sometimes it's a struggle to make it through each day. You're not alone though. Not anymore. I'm here. So are the people in the support group. I know it's not the same, but hopefully, that helps ease some of the pain."

"Hopefully," he replied with a smile. "But honestly, talking to you has helped ease some of that lingering pain tremendously," Victor assured her. "You quickly became a close friend to me. I truly appreciate that. I can't express how much I value having you in my life. How much you already mean to me."

Kate thought back to her dreams of him holding her tight, embracing her, keeping her safe in his arms. He had already cemented himself in her mind more than she dared confess to him. It made her uncomfortable, and she wanted to draw away from him.

Yet he had also helped her tremendously as well. He was the first person she had to talk to who could relate to everything she was going through. She leaned on him heavily during this time, and he helped keep her afloat. His experience with widowerhood gifted her something that the other people who were close to her just couldn't offer.

"You mean a lot to me too," she whispered. "This has all been so healing for me. I've appreciated meeting you and welcoming you into my life."

She worried that would be too revealing. What if he thought that they were more than friends? She certainly wasn't ready for anything romantic yet. She wasn't sure when she would be ready, but the thought of being with someone else right now still stung too much for her to face or even consider.

"To friendship," Victor said, calming her worries as he lifted his glass of wine.

"To friendship," she said, lifting hers in return.

The glasses clinked, and the sound seemed to signal a new beginning for them. It was an assurance that things were going to be okay. She could explore this safe place that was special and important to her without having to worry about anything ruining it.

At that, their conversation shifted. To distract them from some of the pain, they talked about their lives before their spouses. Kate shared more about her childhood while Victor told her about his.

"I love my parents," he said, as the night wore on and they'd had a little too much to drink. "But the pressure from them was always ceaseless. I feel like they always demanded perfection without giving me the validation I needed. Everything had to be perfect. Everything had to be clean. Everything had to meet their expectations. It was just so toxic. That harmed me immensely until I met Evelyn. She welcomed me into her life gently. She provided the love, acceptance, and validation I had been looking for. I'll admit… I was very clingy to her for a while. I didn't know how to feel confident, and she helped me.

But now, I'm looking to find that in myself. I have to develop that confidence without leaning on someone else."

Kate's heart melted a bit. "It's funny… I know exactly what you mean," she started. Her words slurred a little bit as she found herself in awe of the enlightened things Victor was saying. "I think in some ways, sometimes I leaned too much on Tyler for the things I needed in life. Our relationship was great, but I realize now that I was so dependent on him that I almost lost my own sense of identity. Now I'm having to find strength within myself in his absence. I'm having to be stronger without him. Being on my own now, I'm having to learn how to be stronger without the other people I had in my life. I still wish he were here, of course, but I think there is something strong in letting go a little—even of people who are still alive. There's something different and empowering about standing on my own, even when I hate it sometimes."

"I totally agree." Victor nodded. "Though I hope you know you're not on your own out here either. Not completely. You have me. We can cling together a little."

She smiled at him, assured by this. Then she noticed the time as the tables around them were being cleared. She realized she had drunk far too much alcohol as her mind felt a little foggy and disoriented.

"It's getting late," Victor said, noticing her checking her phone. "But I'm not sure I'm good to drive right now. How about you?"

Kate wanted to insist that she was fine, but she blinked and suddenly found it very hard to open her eyelids all the way back up again. "I don't think I'm alright to drive either," she admitted. "I'll have to call an Uber and get my car tomorrow."

Kate winced at the price she would have to pay for this evening. She lived quite a ways from Juniper Bay, and a ride back would be costly… not to mention the price she'd have to pay to pick up her car in the morning.

"We could always go to my place," Victor suggested. "It's about a fifteen-minute walk from here. I could make you some coffee, we could relax, give you time to sober up before heading home."

Kate hesitated. She'd been afraid of this. The night had been so lovely, but now it was charged with a new potential meaning—one she didn't necessarily welcome. She worried that Victor might think this was the time for a hookup or something.

"No funny business," he assured her, raising his palms innocently. "I promise. Just time to chat a little more as friends—if you feel comfortable with it."

Kate looked into his eyes and saw a genuineness within them. She felt safe with him.

"Okay," she agreed. "Let's go to your house."

He smiled.

CHAPTER TWENTY

WALKING THROUGH THE NIGHT WITH VICTOR WAS oddly soothing. The cool air against her flushed skin brought clarity to Kate's mind. As she stood next to him, she thought about how much she missed holding someone's hand. Though she wasn't about to take that step with him.

As they walked, Victor pointed out various shops and gave her some insider knowledge about them. She liked viewing Juniper Bay through his eyes and fell even more in love with it as he explained all it had to offer.

Finally, they wrapped around to the coast. Even from the sidewalk, Kate could see the dark ocean watching them. She wondered what the waves were thinking. She wondered what Tyler would be thinking if he saw her with Victor. She wished she could just focus on her own thoughts so she could somehow make sense of them.

"This is me," Victor said, pulling her away from her thoughts.

"You can't be serious," Kate whispered in awe of the house in front of them.

It was a gorgeous modern house built of white and silver stone that caught the falling rays of moonlight and turned them into glitter splashing against the driveway. Several large bay windows faced the ocean, promising spectacular views, and the columns of the home spoke to an earlier era while the general shape of the house looked like it might belong in a museum of contemporary art with its soft curves paired with sharp edges.

"What?" Victor laughed. "Do you not like it?"

"Of course, I like it. I love it. It's one of the most impressive houses I've ever seen. It just caught me off guard is all."

"Well, I am a carpenter," he reminded her. "This is what I do for a living. It'd speak poorly of my work if my own home didn't reflect that."

"That's what my husband thought of when he was designing our cottage," Kate replied. "He was more of an architect, but he really wanted to go hands-on with building our home. My home is much more modest than yours but…"

"I'm sure it's still beautiful," Victor replied. "We've already established you have amazing taste in things. I'm sure your home is no different."

"I'm certainly happy with it," she agreed. "I love it especially because it's so intrinsically tied to him."

"That's what's most important," Victor reminded her.

At that, he led her into his home, and she was even more impressed by his work. Despite the classical elements to it, the home was still very modern with pops of color against black and white walls with light flooring. Art decorated the house but in a toned-down way that didn't distract from the expert architecture.

"This home was my passion project after my wife died," Victor explained. "It got me through the turbulent times that followed. It embarrasses me to admit we both had life insurance policies out on each other. Plus, I got money from selling the old house, so this is what I dumped that money into."

"You shouldn't be embarrassed about having life insurance on each other," Kate assured him. "Though I understand why you'd feel that way. Tyler and I had life insurance policies out on each other too. So, after he died, I got a chunk of money that I've used to help support myself until I can get back to writing again."

"I imagine it's tough," he said. He always knew just what to say.

Kate nodded. "It makes me feel like I profited off of his death, which is something I never wanted to do. But we have those things in place for a reason. They're meant to help us when emergencies happen. I'm sure you had to spend a good chunk of it on her funeral as well, and I'm sure this is what she'd want for you."

"Thank you for that," Victor said, looking grateful for her words. "I did have to spend a lot of the money on the funeral and burial services. And I do like to think it's what she'd want for me. If it was switched, I'd want her to be able to move forward. It's just…"

"It's weird to think about," Kate finished for him. They shared a soft chuckle.

At that, Victor gave her a tour of the home which Kate admired. He had clearly put a lot of time and energy into the house, resulting in a stunning home that was welcoming and artistic. The tour concluded in a bright, open-concept kitchen with updated, modern stainless-steel appliances that paired well with the marble countertops and black furnishings.

"Would you like a martini or some coffee?" Victor asked. "I have a fantastic espresso maker and an even better bar."

Kate was tempted to accept the martini. She knew what she should choose and what she wanted to choose, but both of those options were on polar opposite ends of the spectrum.

"I should probably have a coffee," she decided. "That way hopefully I can sober up enough to go home at a reasonable time. Though I must admit that I've thoroughly enjoyed our evening together. This has been the most fun I've had in a while. I appreciate it."

"Me too," Victor replied. "It's been a fantastic time. And you know, if you don't want the night to end, I do have a guest room. We could have another drink, watch a movie, and you could spend the night here."

She raised an eyebrow. "So much for no funny business," she pressed him.

He chortled. "And none here, I promise. Only a platonic friendship. Just wanna be a good host."

Kate thought back to the guest room he had shown her. It did look comfortable. It wouldn't be the worst place she could stay by far. It was welcoming, and Victor made her feel safe. He hadn't tried anything she felt uncomfortable with at all. He seemed to understand where she was at in her healing journey, and he respected that.

"I'll have a strong martini then," Kate finally relented.

"Two strong martinis coming right up," Victor said.

As he poured their drinks, he told her about his bartending skills, and they swapped drink recipes. Then, they walked into the living room together.

It was a gorgeous, open room with windows that stretched from the floor to the ceiling that looked out at the ocean, black waves tumbling below them, playing in the night. Kate settled on the white leather couch in front of the big screen TV and thought about how comfortable and safe she felt with Victor.

"You know, I never thought I'd have this feeling again after Tyler passed," Kate found herself saying as she held Victor's gaze. "This pure sense of friendship and connection with another man. It's really nice, and I appreciate it. I appreciate you."

"I never thought I'd have this with another woman either," Victor admitted. "I haven't felt so on the same page with someone since Evelyn died. It really is refreshing. I appreciate you as well. I'm grateful that you're in my life."

At that, they got even closer as the conversation continued. They followed this up with a movie, and not even half an hour into it, Kate found herself drifting off.

It could have been only a few minutes—it could have been an hour—she had no idea. But Kate's eyes fluttered halfway open to see the vague outline of Victor smiling down at her. She was curled up with her head on his shoulder. She should have minded, but she didn't.

"Hey," he whispered gently. "Why don't we get you to bed?"

"That would be nice," Kate replied, still not sure if she was even awake as she said it.

He helped Kate to her feet, and the two walked gingerly to the guest room. Throughout it all, he behaved like a perfect gentleman, helping support her but never touching her in any inappropriate way. She slipped out of her shoes and right under the covers in an instant.

"Goodnight, Kate," he whispered, watching her for a moment longer. Then he left the room to let her sleep in peace.

When Kate stirred to life again, she was in Victor's bed. His arms were around her in the same way they always were in her dreams, yet as she turned, his touches grew more daring. His fingertips explored her skin in a new, intoxicating way.

At first, she froze. She panicked at the thought of betraying Tyler by being with another man. Then, she realized how fuzzy and surreal everything seemed. It wasn't drunkenness either. This was different.

Somewhat strangely, Kate had enough cognitive ability to recognize she was dreaming. She suspected that once she realized that, she would wake up, but she didn't. Instead, she stayed in this dream and maintained the capacity to make decisions. And that was just fine with her.

As Victor touched her, she realized being with someone like this again felt good. It had been so long, and it distracted her from some of the sadness. It helped her escape her heartbreak a little.

As things wore on, she reasoned that it was just a dream. She wasn't betraying Tyler if she hooked up with Victor in a dream. As long as it never crossed into reality, it was reasonable. After thinking for a moment more, Kate gave in to desire and let herself indulge in her dream fantasy.

CHAPTER TWENTY-ONE

UILT WOKE KATE UP THE NEXT MORNING AS SHE thought about her dream of hooking up with Victor. She was thankful to realize, though, that she was still wearing her clothes. She was still in the guest room, a decent walk away from Victor's room, and there was no sign that a hookup had actually happened. It had all been dream.

She took a moment to enjoy being here now that she didn't have to feel guilty about it. The guest room was pleasant to be in, awash in white and gold. The cloudlike comforter felt like a puffy marshmallow that embraced her body, while the pillows had turned out to be even better than the ones she had at her house. Silk sheets were soft against her skin. She admired the environment Victor had created for his guests. It was certainly more than she was used to receiving at anyone's house, and she appreciated it.

As she forced herself out of the warm bed, she noticed the scent of bacon and coffee in the air, making her stomach growl a little. She promised herself she'd get breakfast as soon as she got home and went into the guest bathroom to freshen up a little bit.

After composing herself and washing her face, she noticed an unopened toothbrush and toothpaste with a note on it.

Just to make you more comfortable. Good morning!

It felt wonderful to brush the grime off of her teeth, though as she stayed in the bathroom longer, she noticed she felt a little sick and hung over. Her head pounded, chiding her for the night she had spent filling herself with poison.

"So worth it though," she whispered, thinking of the special connection she'd shared with Victor.

It was still the most fun she'd had in a while, so she was still grateful she did it. She appreciated the relief and fun it had offered her.

After deciding she wasn't going to feel guilty or bad about any of this, including the dream she had, Kate left the room feeling more confident and ready to tackle the day ahead of her. She went toward the kitchen where that delicious smell was radiating from, and the growl of her stomach was so loud she was sure Victor could hear it as he hummed away at the stove.

"Morning!" he said with a welcoming smile and cheerful voice. "How did you sleep?"

As Kate looked at him, she found she had to look away again quickly. What if he saw the evidence of her dream on her face? How would he react to knowing he was on her mind like that? She tried not to think of it as she grounded herself in the current moment. She tried to ignore how handsome he looked even first thing in the morning.

"I slept very well," Kate replied. "That bed is the most comfortable one I've slept in for some time. You certainly make sure your guests are cozy here."

"I try my best. I always want people to look forward to spending time with me. So, I do my best to make that a reality."

"I had a lot of fun spending time with you," Kate smiled. "Thank you for a great night. I really needed that after everything. I feel refreshed in a way that I haven't in some time.

Though I think I drank more than I should've. Sorry if I made a fool out of myself."

"No such thing," he insisted. "You have nothing to apologize for, I assure you of that. We both were a little drunk last night, so I'm sure in some ways we both acted a little foolish, but that's the fun of it. We're supposed to act a little foolish when we're drinking. We're supposed to let go a little and have a fun time every once in a while—which is exactly what we did. I had a fantastic time. I can't thank you enough for joining me last night. Your company is more than I ever thought I'd find in another woman. I'm so grateful we're friends."

Kate blushed at this. It felt nice to know that he enjoyed spending time with her. It made her feel less ashamed of so completely enjoying the time she spent with him.

"I'm grateful for our friendship too," she agreed. "But I do have work to do today, so I should get going."

"Nonsense!" Victor replied. "You must at least stay for breakfast—if you want to, of course. I made enough for two, and I certainly couldn't eat it all myself. I'm sure by now you must be hungry."

Kate's stomach growled again, very much agreeing to the thought of staying for breakfast. Victor's cooking did smell delicious.

"Come on," he pressed. "Stay, eat, and then I'll walk you to your car. We can enjoy the morning even more with some food in our stomachs."

"That would be nice," Kate relented.

Victor smiled as he turned back to the stove and they idly chatted about the day that lay ahead of them. Kate was surprised by how normal it felt to be spending the morning with him like this. It was comfortable and enjoyable to talk to him while he cooked and join him at his dining room table for conversation once the meal was done.

It was the best morning she'd had in a long time, and she felt less alone. Though she still missed Tyler and thought of him frequently, it was nice to have the company of someone else as well.

She actually found herself disappointed as breakfast came to an end. She wanted to spend more time with him. She wasn't ready to go home yet. But she certainly didn't want to come off as too clingy either, so she tried to hide this disappointment as they walked back to her car. The morning was so beautiful that it was easy to ignore anything unpleasant. Birds tweeted their approval as they danced between the trees. The sun seemed even brighter than normal, its warm rays enough to put her at ease.

"I really have enjoyed this," Victor said as the car came into view. "I'd love to do it again sometime whenever you're free. If you'd like that, of course. I don't want to pressure you into anything you don't want to do."

"I'd like that," Kate said. "I had fun too. I'd love to spend more time with you."

She didn't dare express how true this was. She didn't want their time to end at all. She was more captivated by him than she wanted to admit.

"How about next weekend?" he offered. "We could find something new and fun to do. Maybe this time during the day, so we have more time to spend together. If that's okay with you."

"I'd love to!" Kate replied a little too eagerly. Then she remembered something that she couldn't believe she had forgotten. "But I can't. My best friend is coming to stay with me from Friday until Monday. I have to spend all my time with her. I've missed her so much. Maybe we could get together after that though?"

"Of course!" Victor replied. Kate appreciated how understanding he was. "I'll keep in touch, and once you're free we'll get together again."

At that, they reached her car, and Victor opened her door for her. She was surprised and delighted by this chivalrous gesture. She started to think that maybe once she had healed, maybe things could change between her and Victor. Maybe something more than platonic could take place.

The idea of that surprised her. Was she really able to think of a world in which she had healed enough to date someone? She realized she was at least considering it, which disturbed her. It meant she was moving forward, which still invoked a sense of guilt.

Then, Victor opened his arms to offer her a hug. She hesitated then stepped forward to hug him. She once again noticed how much he smelled like Tyler and wished with her whole heart that her husband was the one holding her instead.

"Have a good week," he said as they parted.

"You too," Kate replied, feeling a little breathless.

At that, she got into her car and once again tried to compartmentalize her feelings. She couldn't let Victor get too thoroughly ingrained in her mind. She couldn't let her mind get too carried away with this relationship.

But as she drove away, she worried it might be too late. Victor was already in her mind and was working his way into her heart. It seemed like he might be there to stay.

CHAPTER TWENTY-TWO

THAT WEEK, KATE AND VICTOR TALKED EVEN MORE than before. They felt thoroughly attached to each other by now, and Kate found that she looked forward to his texts. It was nice to keep in touch with him throughout the day. It made her feel less lonely and more connected to the world of the living, distracted from what she had lost.

It made her week go by quicker as she worked on her book and prepared for Allison's visit. Finally, the day came that she was so looking forward to. Allison's car pulled into the driveway, and Kate rushed out to greet her.

"Hey, girl!" Kate called out as she hugged her best friend. "It's so good to see you!"

"Hey, you too," Allison replied with a wide smile. She stepped back from her friend to fully take everything in. "You look so much better than before. You look stronger, healthier, and happier."

"I *feel* so much better. I've been eating more lately," Kate explained. "I've been eating healthier foods too. I've also started running again, even doing a bit of weightlifting. I decided I wanted to be faster and stronger just in case..."

Kate paused. None of the creepy events in her home had happened lately, but the idea of someone possibly watching her still scared her. She worried that there was still a stalker out there following her, waiting for the perfect time to return.

She hadn't told Allison about any of that, though, because she didn't want her friend to worry about her any more than she already did. Allison was already uneasy about her interviewing people for her book. What if she attributed the strange stalking stuff to that work? Then she wouldn't be able to continue interviewing people without her friend nagging her, and she didn't want to deal with that.

"In case of what?" Allison asked, looking concerned.

"In case I ever need to fight someone," Kate teased, laughing it off like it was a joke. "In case I want to ever impress someone with my new, stronger body. You never know what's in store."

Allison smiled. "I like the sound of that. You were always so strong, but now it's becoming literal."

They laughed at that as Allison brought her bags into the house, but then Allison hit her with a complete surprise: "And is there anyone in particular you're trying to impress?"

Kate already knew that she couldn't hide the look that surely crossed her face as she thought of Victor. Was he someone she had in mind for a potential romantic future? Sometimes that seemed to be the case. He was on her mind more than she'd like to admit. She seemed to be unable to ignore it.

"I knew it!" Allison crowed, pointing at Kate's wistful expression with a taunting finger.

"I do have a friend," Kate admitted. "But I wouldn't say it's a romantic connection or anything."

"Is this the guy you went out to dinner with last week?" Allison asked. "Tell me everything!"

Kate nodded with a guilty expression. She still wasn't sure how she felt about Victor, but in that moment, she considered the possibility that talking to Allison might help her figure that out. So once Allison's bags were put up, Kate made them some tea, brought out snacks she had bought specifically for Allison's visit, and told her all about Victor.

As she talked about him, it became clear to the both of them that Kate saw him as more than a friend. She still felt self-conscious about it, but she could no longer deny that there were some strange feelings there that weren't exactly platonic. She didn't know how to deal with them.

"My advice is don't push yourself into anything until you're ready," Allison encouraged her. "If he's the right one for you, he'll understand your feelings and give you the time and space needed to process things before moving forward. You don't want to do anything you're uncomfortable with. I'll also say, though, that you shouldn't shut those feelings down out of guilt or a certain loyalty to Tyler. As difficult as I'm sure it is to face, Tyler is gone. He would want you to move on. He would want you to be happy. It doesn't make sense for you to be single forever. You're still so young. You deserve love."

"It's just daunting to think about," Kate said. "It's unfathomable to consider being with someone else right now. It hurts too much."

"Then don't worry about it too much right now," Allision advised her. "Enjoy spending time with Victor. See where it goes. If it works out it does, if not, it doesn't. Just try not to feel guilty no matter which direction your heart leads you in."

"Easier said than done," Kate muttered.

"Just don't let yourself lose out on the future because of the past," Allison said. "You were a great wife, Kate. In the future, you'll be a great girlfriend too. But now it's time to focus on you and do what makes you happy. That's most important. You can forget the rest."

Kate closed her eyes and took a deep, calming breath. "I'll try to," she said, even though she knew it wouldn't be easy. She reasoned that she could at least try to move forward without having too many expectations for herself.

She tried to cast all that aside as she and Allison enjoyed their weekend together. That day they spent a lot of time at Kate's house, catching up on everything and enjoying each other's company. The next day, they were determined to do something fun, so they took a road trip out to the outlet mall. Kate hadn't bought herself new clothes since before Tyler died, so she decided it was time to update her wardrobe a bit. It was time to physically change just as she had internally.

"You know, you seem far calmer now that you left the city," Allison noted as they ate ice cream in the busy food court. The sound of noisy shoppers intruded on their conversation as they avoided the semisticky table in front of them. It all made for a chaotic afternoon, which Kate didn't mind at all. She just loved being with Allison again. It felt like she was truly living lately.

"This move has been good for you," Allison continued. "It's so clear to see, and I'm happy for you. But I don't know…" Allison paused as a sort of uneasy look crossed her face. "I have kind of gotten the feeling today that we are being watched. Do you ever feel that way, or is it just all in my head?"

Kate froze with her ice cream halfway to her mouth. She had gotten so used to the feeling that she barely noticed it now, but it had been particularly strong that day. Kate *had* gotten the feeling that someone had been watching them. She simply attributed it to being surrounded by people.

"Maybe it's just because the mall is busy," Kate suggested, not wanting to scare her friend away.

"Maybe," Allison replied. She shrugged. "You're probably right. It's probably nothing."

They didn't discuss it any further as they finished eating, but the strange feeling still lingered over them. Kate noticed Allison looking over her shoulder more and being a little antsier as they continued shopping.

Then, as they were looking through dresses, Allison froze. She looked at the clothes rack pushed up against the wall, hidden by shadows. There were no other customers nearby, and no sales clerks anywhere near them. In fact, the store had been nearly empty since they'd entered.

"Something just moved in that clothes rack," Allison murmured softly.

They glanced over at it, but the dresses were so long they could easily be concealing a person. It made Kate nervous. Would someone really get that close to them?

"I'm checking," Allison stated. "I'm sure it moved. I'm not going crazy. Or at least, I want to see if I am."

"Wait," Kate stopped her with her hand on her arm. "What if you're right? What if it's someone dangerous?"

Allison looked her in the eyes with a scrutinizing gaze. "I knew it," she said. "You're scared of something."

"W-what do you mean?" Kate stammered.

"Something *dangerous*? In a public place like this?" Allison pointed out. "I can tell. This isn't the first time you've had this feeling, is it? Someone has watched you before."

Faced with a confrontation like this, Kate found it difficult to deny it. She didn't want to lie to Allison. So, she simply nodded.

"We're going to face this once and for all," Allison said. "If someone is following us, we're going to figure out who it is and put a stop to it." Despite Kate's protests, she walked right up to the clothing rack and pushed aside the dresses.

A little girl laughed as she delighted in being found in her hiding spot. "Don't tell anyone," she whispered.

Before Allison could respond, the girl's mother came over to get her. Some of the tension was released, but it couldn't be forgotten. Now that Allison knew something was going on, Kate suspected she wouldn't easily drop it. They left the store shortly after, and as Kate drove to the museum they'd decided to visit that day, Allison turned to her.

"Before we continue our day, I want to know what's going on," Allison demanded. "Something is clearly up. Don't lie or hide anything from me."

Allison had always been the stubborn one in their friendship. She was the firm oak tree while Kate was the willow, bending to the breeze. Kate sighed and told Allison everything. She couldn't look her friend in the eyes as she relayed the disturbing incidents that had occurred: the incidents with the keys, the flowers, and all the times she was sure things her house had been moved. She knew Allison wouldn't be thrilled that she hadn't confided in her sooner about it.

"I'm sorry," Kate said. "I know I should've mentioned it sooner, but I didn't want to worry you."

"Worry me?" Allison asked. "I have reason to be worried, but by not telling anyone, you're putting yourself at an even greater risk. None of this is good. It sounds like someone has been stalking you, and you haven't done anything about it."

"There's not much I can do. And I'm not even sure it's happening. It could be my imagination."

"And if it isn't?" Allison pressed.

"If it isn't, at the very least these things have been happening much less, so I'm not as worried about it. Besides, Brad's coming up next weekend. He's going to teach me some stuff to protect myself. And I'm taking a self-defense class. I do have pepper spray, too, like you said I should. I'm doing what I can to stay safe."

"I guess that's helpful," Allison admitted. "I just don't like the thought of you being in any sort of danger. It's terrifying. Who knows what could happen?"

"I'll be okay," Kate assured her. "I'm learning how to protect myself. I think my imagination has been a little overactive. But I swear, I'll make sure to protect myself. I will be okay."

She said it almost more to convince herself than to convince her friend. Allison looked skeptical, but they tried to continue their day in relative peace. The museum was a great way for both of them to get their minds off of things as they discussed the art and life in general. They followed it up with dinner, so they didn't get back until late.

When they got back to the house, they were happy and cheerful… that is until they reached the kitchen.

Kate had managed to keep the flowers from the field alive for a long time after that scary day when she had picked them. Once she had gotten over the fearful aspect of it, she found that she liked having flowers in the house. They brightened up her day and made her life a little brighter in a pleasant way.

Even though she hadn't gone back to that field ever since the incident, she did frequently go out to her own garden to pick bouquets for her home. The most recent were white lilies whose petals had been dying. She had been meaning to replace them but hadn't gotten around to it thanks to Allison's visit.

But now those lilies were purely white. Their petals were fresh. They were more alive than ever.

"Am I going crazy?" Allison asked. "Or did those flowers come to life during the time we were gone?"

"I see it too," Kate replied. And though it was scary to have Allison at risk with her, it did feel good to know she wasn't alone. This was the kind of thing she would've doubted before. She would've chalked it up to being all in her mind. She would've excused it as the petals not being as dead as she thought they were or that she'd replaced them and forgotten about it. There couldn't be any way this was truly happening.

But with Allison there to witness it, it all felt too real. Someone had come in and replaced her dying flowers with living, fresh ones. She knew she'd locked the door. She'd checked twice, the way she always did. They stared at the vase for a long time, wondering what to do.

"We should call the police," Allison noted. Though she didn't actually move to do so. "Someone has clearly been in your house while we were gone. We should call the police."

"And tell them what?" Kate asked. "That my flowers miraculously came to life? That's been my problem with this whole situation. I doubt the police would take the things that have been happening all that seriously. It's not like they've been particularly dangerous, and there's no evidence to show who it could be."

"Someone has been in your house!" Allison hissed. "Of course, that's dangerous!" Then she sighed. "Though I guess I do see what you mean. It would be a difficult crime to report. We wouldn't be taken seriously. We should be, but that doesn't mean we would be."

"Exactly," Kate agreed. They stood there for a moment longer. "Would you like some wine?"

The two women checked the house for any further signs of an intruder, carefully examining each room and crevice. After being unable to find anything, they gave up and went downstairs to grab glasses of wine, feeling defeated and at a loss for what to do.

They brought their glasses into the living room and made sure the curtains were drawn as they sat close to each other. Both were uneasy as they continued to look over their shoulders, just waiting for the attack.

"Did you ever follow up with Daniel Jenkins?" Allison asked. "I told you he's dangerous, and he was recently released. Maybe he's the one who's behind this. Do you know where he's been living?"

Kate shook her head. "I haven't really thought about him as a possibility, but it has crossed my mind. He lived all the way in like the Midwest, so I doubt he's nearby. Besides, he just didn't seem like he had any interest in me. I don't see him as a true suspect."

"Who else could it be then?" Allison asked.

"Maybe a stranger," Kate offered.

"That sure narrows it down," Allison griped. "Maybe we can ask the neighbors or something. But I don't know. Daniel's the most promising suspect to start with. I think you need to figure out what's going on with him."

"I will," Kate promised.

At that, Kate and Allison tried to resume their night as normal despite the dark cloud hanging over them.

The rest of the weekend was a great, fun, bonding time for Allison and Kate. Even though that fear still hung over them, they tried to ignore it and still have fun. By the time Monday came, they were reluctant to let go of each other.

They went out for breakfast that morning at Barb's before Allison took the long drive back home. Their conversation naturally turned to the fear Allison had of leaving her friend.

"I don't want you being in that house alone," Allison said, looking at her friend in worry. "I hope that once you find the opportunity to get the police involved, you do. You have to reach out to them if anything else happens. In the meantime, you need to continue to be vigilant. Do what you need to protect and take care of yourself. Take any precautions and steps needed to stay safe."

"I will," Kate promised. "And I'll check into Daniel, see if it's even possible that he had something to do with this."

"I appreciate that," Allison replied. "Just promise me you'll be careful. If he is behind this, that makes him even more dangerous. I really don't want anything bad to happen to you."

"It won't," Kate promised.

Still, a level of fear clung to Kate as she returned home for the day. She found that she didn't want to be there alone. She didn't want to have to guess what might happen next. It felt like it was a risk.

That feeling was only made worse as she walked up her front steps and saw that the door was open. She questioned herself, wondering if it was possible that they'd been in such a hurry to leave that she and Allison left without closing the door properly, the wind pushing it open in their absence.

It didn't seem likely with how paranoid they'd been that they would be so careless. They had been extra careful to make sure things were locked up and no one was following them. They were hypervigilant of their surroundings.

Considering the route this kind of thing had taken before, Kate didn't feel comfortable calling the police. She worried that no one would be there and they'd just think she was losing her mind. So, she got her pepper spray out and remembered what she had learned in her self-defense classes. Then, she stepped inside the house.

She vigilantly searched through all the rooms. She looked in every corner, behind each piece of furniture, under any spaces that had even the slightest possibility of hiding a human in them.

Kate found nothing—not even a clue or a trace of anyone having been in her house while she was gone. So, she finally gave up and made herself some tea. She started journaling her feelings as she tried to figure out what to do about this creepy position she found herself in.

CHAPTER TWENTY-THREE

K ATE REMAINED VIGILANT THROUGHOUT THE WEEK. She checked in with Allison every day to let her know she was okay. And though she still got the feeling that someone was watching her sometimes, she didn't find any more signs of that being the case. She still wasn't sure what to believe. She wasn't sure if she was going crazy or if there was someone to fear.

She kept in touch with Victor throughout the next few days as well. They talked continuously about increasingly deeper topics. She almost told him a few times about her worries about a stalker, but Brad was going to be there to visit soon, and she hoped that his presence might change things for the better.

As she waited for Brad to show up on the Thursday following Allison's visit, she realized she wasn't exactly standing on her own through this. She wasn't exhibiting the self-confidence that she'd been trying to cultivate. She kept waiting on people to show up to make her feel protected. In that way, she was embracing a sort of helplessness.

Kate hoped that Brad might be able to empower her a bit. She hadn't wanted to get Allison too involved as she worried about her safety as well. She worried about Brad, too, but she thought maybe the stalker wouldn't be as interested in him and they could figure out a real solution.

Seeing her friend step out of his truck did put her at ease. He looked so strong and muscular with his keen, green eyes piercing beneath his blond hair. He looked like the kind of person who could take on another guy if they got into a fight. She hoped she could rely on him.

"Welcome back," Kate said as she hugged him. "It's so nice to see you again."

"Nice to see you too," Brad replied, hugging her back even tighter. He stepped back and looked at her. "You look like you're doing much better compared to the last time I saw you."

"Thank you." Kate smiled. As she looked at Brad, she noticed the dark circles under his eyes and how tired and worn out he looked.

"I know, you don't have to tell me," Brad laughed. "I don't look like I'm doing as great as you are. Things haven't been easy."

"Well, come inside and we can talk about it," Kate offered. "You know I'm always willing to listen."

Brad followed her into the house where she made them each a cup of coffee. They took the coffee outside and settled onto the comfortable patio furniture.

"Garden's looking great," Brad noted, sipping from his cup as they admired the flourishing plants. "Honestly, you've done a fantastic job with it. Looks like you'll have a ton of tomatoes and peppers to harvest this fall."

"I have worked hard on it," Kate smiled, proud of the variety of colors and shapes that now surrounded her house. "It's been a good distraction from things. Very healing… and I'm always taking steps to do better. But we've spent so much time already talking about my struggles after the funeral. You were there for me through all of it. Tyler's death still bothers me, of course. It always will. That's something that sticks with a person. But you're dealing with something a little more current. So, I want to talk about that. How have you been holding up? Has the marriage recovered at all? Any hopes of a reconciliation?"

Brad looked away at that. Kate worried, wondering if she shouldn't have brought up the topic. Perhaps it was a sensitive one, and he didn't want to talk about it.

"It's been rough," he admitted. "I'm honestly so thankful to get a break from it to come out here and spend some time with you instead. Jade and I have been having trouble for a while. It's been something we've been trying to work on, but it seems like no matter how much work we do, it's not something that's easily mended."

"I'm sorry," Kate said. "I can't imagine it's easy."

"Like I told you before, I've spent some time out here by myself even before this—just to give her space and so I could be by the coast. I needed time alone. She needed time alone. We hoped it might bring us closer together as we grew to miss each other, but that just didn't happen. Instead of missing each other, we realized that our lives were more peaceful when we were apart. When we came back together again, the fighting picked up right where we left off. By then things were only getting worse. So, we decided to go through with the divorce."

"I'm so sorry," Kate replied. She knew what it was like to lose a spouse, but not a spouse who was still alive. Her heart hurt for him and the death of his marriage. "That must be so incredibly tough to deal with. Though I'm sure you tried your best to save the relationship."

"I did," Brad insisted. "I tried to be the best husband and best father. But it just wasn't working. Now we have to deal with custody and everything."

Kate was shocked at that. "You haven't been able to at least compromise on that?"

"Honestly, I didn't want it to be one more thing to fight about," Brad said. "For now, she has custody of him full time so he can stay at his same school. But once we get it formalized, custody will be a little more even. I want to find a new normal outside of this mess, and I hope this isn't what the new normal will be. I don't want to keep him away from his mother. I would never demand full custody, but I need to see my son. I hate being away from him like this."

"That's so awful," Kate empathized. "I'm really sorry you're going through this. It seems like none of the parties are happy with it."

"We aren't. But we can't seem to find a solution either, even though I'm really trying. I just want to get to a place where we can coexist and raise Tommy, even if we're not together. I just don't know how to get there," he said. And she could hear the effort in his voice. There was something about the way he said it that hinted at all the struggles he had been through and how hard it had been on him.

"Sometimes I feel like I'm not doing good enough," he continued. "Like, I'm trying to go about my life in the way that I should. I'm trying to process this divorce in the best way possible, keep up at my job, make sure I'm in a better place so I can be present once I can see my son again. It's not easy though. Sometimes I feel like I'm failing, slipping up no matter what I do. It's like life is rushing around me, and I can't keep up—like there's this darkness holding me back— and no matter what I do, I can't seem to fight against it. It's always there, reminding me of how my life has changed completely and what a challenge that has turned out to be."

"Without trying to put too much on myself, I think I understand where you're coming from to some extent," Kate ventured to say. "I don't know exactly what you're going through, but I do know what it's like to have my life twisted into that sort of upheaval—to feel the darkness closing in—and it's far from easy. Adjusting to a new way of life is a struggle."

"You seem to be adjusting well," Brad pointed out. "How did you do it?"

"Lots of patience," Kate said, surprised that now she was in the position to give advice on this when she was so used to being the one who needed that support. It felt good to be on the other end of things for a change. "I've had to have love and patience for myself. I've had to be motivated to want to get better because it's tough. Sometimes you get so comfortable in the darkness that the drive to get better all but disappears. I had to make that effort every single day—to make a choice that was going to send me in the right direction. I still struggle all the time. I'm still not even close to being fully healed. But I am feeling better. It just takes a lot of effort."

At that, Kate shared more tips on how to heal as Brad vented everything he was going through with the divorce and custody battle. Kate was grateful she could be there for her friend after everything he'd helped her through. He gave her a sense of purpose and helped her find meaning in the struggles she had worked through. She was proud that the knowledge she had learned in the struggle could be used to guide someone else.

Later that day as Brad went to the bathroom, Kate checked her phone and noticed a text from Victor checking in. She felt bad that it had been so long since she had seen him. She found that she did miss him.

Are you free at all today? I'd love to see you again. How about we grab dinner and catch up? I've missed spending time with you.

Kate's heart warmed at his text. It was nice to know he was thinking of her, too, and that she wasn't crazy in missing him. Maybe he felt the same draw to her as she felt toward him.

I have a friend in town, so I'm not exactly sure when I'll be free again. He's going through some stuff, so I definitely want to spend time with him. I'll let you know tomorrow when we can get together again. I'd love to see you soon!

Just as Brad was getting back, she heard her phone ping again.

That sounds great! I'm looking forward to seeing you again!

Kate was grateful Victor wasn't upset about their not being able to get together. She appreciated how understanding he was. It made her feel even more connected to him.

Knowing things were good between her and Victor allowed her to focus on her time with Brad. They had plans to go into Juniper Bay the next day, but for his first day, they stayed at the house, went for walks, talked, and just caught up in general. That night they made dinner together, and by then they were both feeling a bit better about things.

"I don't want to be too negative," Brad said. "So, I'm sorry if I've come off that way. There are good things going on in my life as well. It's not all doom and gloom."

"You don't have to worry about being too negative," Kate assured him. "You're going through a tough time right now, so it makes sense that you'd feel down. You were there for me, and I want to be there for you too. It's what friends do. But of course, I'd love to hear about the good things too."

"Well, I'm thinking of buying a new house in the neighborhood so I can be there for Tommy. You know how my father was. I don't want to be like him at all, distant and uncaring. So, I'm going to make sure I don't become that, no matter what it takes."

"That's really great," Kate enthused. "I know you'll continue to be a great father no matter what happens."

"I'm determined to," Brad agreed. "Though I have thought about moving closer to this area instead and just visiting my son as often as I can. I really do love it here. It's been a great place to escape to. I might need the fresh start after everything."

"Whatever you do, make sure you take the necessary time to choose," she told him. "You're going through a level of grief right now. You don't want to rush things because of that. That's how mistakes are made. I'd say listen to your heart and take your time. Give yourself time. You'll make the right decision for you and your son. I believe in you."

"That means the world to me," Brad said,

He gave Kate a smile filled with warmth and kindness. Though Kate was fond of Victor, she was delighted to be joined by this more familiar friend. It brought her a sort of comfort that someone who hadn't been in her life for as long simply couldn't give her.

Finally, as they wound down for the night, Brad had to bid her farewell and go back to his hotel room as he had a scheduled video call with his son.

"Really enjoyed hanging out with you, but obviously, he comes first," he said sheepishly.

"Wouldn't expect anything less," Kate assured him with a smile. "I admire a man who follows through on his word to his son. He needs you right now. I'm sure this hasn't been easy on him either. Tell him I said hi."

Brad smiled. "Will do."

The two hugged goodnight, and Kate had time to text Victor again. Even though they couldn't see each other, it was nice talking to him, and their bond was growing through these exchanges. She typed out a message to him and smiled as she hit send.

You're quickly becoming one of the people I'm closest to.

Confessing that to Victor made her feel vulnerable, but it was true. He was becoming one of her closest confidants, and she was grateful for his presence in her life. Her friends and family had helped her through the initial aftermath of Tyler's death, but Victor was helping her move forward. And she was quickly finding out that part was just as important.

The reply she received just about melted her heart.

You're one of the people I'm closest to as well. I couldn't be more grateful to have you in my life.

That night when Kate found herself dreaming of Victor, she didn't mind quite as much as she had before. It almost felt like the kind of comfort she had been looking for.

CHAPTER TWENTY-FOUR

"**Y**OU SEEM HAPPY," BRAD NOTED AS HE AND KATE went to breakfast at Barb's that morning.

Kate recalled how she had talked to Victor late into the night, sharing everything from the TV shows they were enjoying to the conflicting feelings they were dealing with regarding their deceased spouses. Whenever anything happened, she found that she wanted to tell him about it. She wanted him to know everything. It felt like she almost had a partner again, but she tried not to think about it like that.

"I'm just happy you're here," Kate said. "And I'm looking forward to hanging out together today. You said you had something different planned—something that will help me be safer."

"I do," Brad nodded. "But don't get too excited about it. I think it'll be fun, but I'm not sure you'll feel the same way. I do think it would be good for you, and I don't want to hear any protests about it. I'm only looking out for your best interest."

That got Kate curious. What could Brad be referring to? It sounded suspicious. But she trusted him, so after introducing him to the usual patrons at the café and enjoying a delicious brunch, she gave him her car keys and didn't protest as Brad started driving.

"We definitely have to take a trip to the beach after this," Brad insisted. "Our little activity might be something we need to decompress from. And there's something about the beach that draws me to it. Which is why I've come out here as often as I have. It's compelling. It's relaxing. It gives you space to think when you need it."

"I agree. I find it to be my safe space too. Though I guess sometimes it's too compelling to me. Sometimes I…" Kate paused as she debated how much she should tell Brad. She was used to opening up to him about a lot of things, so she decided to get vulnerable for a moment. "I guess sometimes I still have dark thoughts following Tyler's death."

"What kind of dark thoughts?" Brad asked, looking quite concerned.

"I don't know. It's tough. Mostly I've moved forward, at least as much as I could've by now, but every once in a while, I think about what it would be like to join him. To walk into the ocean and just keep walking. I'm learning how to enjoy my life without him, but maybe I don't appreciate it enough. Because sometimes I'm not sure that I'm totally committed to living. Sometimes I'm not sure that I really want to be alive."

The silence that followed made Kate second-guess herself. Had she shared too much? She hadn't even opened up about this to Victor. She was really making herself vulnerable in that moment, allowing Brad the room to think she was crazy and assess her in a hurtful way.

"That's understandable considering all you've been through," he said, totally surprising her. "I mean, I won't pretend that I'm not concerned about you… but I get it."

"I'm seeing someone about it," Kate rushed in. "I know it's not… well, it's not the most pleasant thought. I know that it's dark. But my therapist is helping me sort through the feelings. I *want* to feel better. I just sometimes have trouble with it."

Brad smiled, and the look of sympathy on his face could have split her in two. "I'm glad you've stuck with us. I appreciate you being here. You're so strong, Kate. You have so much to live for. Tyler would want that for you. He would want you to live. I hope you'll internalize the truth of that and keep fighting. I know you have it in you. I know you'll make it through this. You have so much support while you do."

"I feel it," Kate admitted. "I feel surrounded by lots of support, and I appreciate it. I appreciate you."

Brad smiled as they pulled into a parking lot. "Well, after this I hope you still appreciate me. Because I'm going to do my best to keep you safe and keep you grounded in the world of the living. Even if that means facing something you're unfamiliar with."

With that, Kate realized they were at a gun range. She automatically wanted to drive away. She knew she had promised Allison that Brad would help protect her, but she didn't want to actually go through with this.

"Guns are so powerful though," Kate protested as they sat in the car. "They can do so much damage. They can take a life. I don't want that power. I couldn't ever shoot anyone. I couldn't bring myself to, no matter how much danger I might be in."

"I think you'd surprise yourself if you ever found yourself in a life-or-death situation," Brad countered. "I've been in one myself, so I know that something totally different takes over in that moment when everything is on the line. Suddenly you become willing to fight in a way you couldn't before. Suddenly, you become sure you want to live."

"What do you mean?" Kate asked. "When were you in a life-or-death situation? Did you have to fight someone for your life? Or was it against nature or something? Did you ever have to use a gun?"

"That's a story for another time," he told her, getting a far away, uncomfortable look on his face. "Right now, it's time to make sure *you're* protected."

At that, he got out of the car, and after some hesitation, Kate followed his lead. She knew she wasn't getting out of this easily, and she reasoned it could be a good skill to have just in case the stalker turned dangerous.

"Cheer up," Brad urged her as they walked inside. "I know it's not exactly your hobby, but after everything you told me about the person who's likely stalking you, you should be at least a little interested in it. Don't you want to protect yourself?"

"Of course, I do," she replied. "But I have pepper spray, and I've taken self-defense classes."

"Pepper spray isn't going to do anything against a real criminal. And self-defense classes won't work against someone with a gun pointed at you. You need more protection than that."

Kate was still convinced that if it ever came down to it and she did need to protect herself in that way, she would just give up. She wouldn't be able to shoot anyone. This was a waste of time. But Brad was right. She should at least try to learn something new. It was something Brad wanted to do, and she wasn't so selfish as to insist they only did things she was interested in.

She stuck by him as they went into the shop, and she came face to face with dozens of guns of all shapes and sizes laid out in massive racks before them. She didn't even know where to begin, so she was thankful Brad was with her. Just seeing them was intimidating. She couldn't imagine what it'd be like if she actually had to use one. She just had to hope it'd never come down to that.

"We've got a first-timer here," Brad said as they walked up to the counter. "I want something for her that's easy to handle but puts a point across. I want her to be well-equipped so no one can touch her if she doesn't want them to."

The man at the counter looked at them skeptically. His eyebrows raised as he seemed to think this through. Then, he picked out a handgun for her and explained how to use it. After that, they went into the shooting range.

The room where the actual shooting would take place appeared cold, unyielding, and rather foreign to Kate. The stalls reminded her of a prison cell of some sort. The targets seemed to already be taunting her, judging her for being unable to hit them.

"I know I can't do this," she told Brad as she followed him to their designated area.

"I know you can," Brad assured her. "I have one hundred percent faith in you. You just need to have that faith in yourself."

Of course, having that faith in herself wasn't quite so easy, especially considering she had never done anything like this before. She wished it wasn't necessary. She wished Brad had chosen any other activity. But she listened to him and the instructor as they went over all the procedures one last time. And then with a deep breath, she leveled the gun at the target, got into the proper position, put her finger on the trigger, and pulled.

The bullet zoomed straight past the target, nowhere close to the paper, and Kate found herself off balance. She hadn't been expecting the recoil to be that bad. Her entire body was blown back so far that she had to step back to stabilize herself. Kate put the gun down and rolled her eyes as she looked at Brad, hiding her embarrassment.

"See?" she said, motioning to the undisturbed target. "I obviously can't do it. This isn't for me. There's no way I should be in charge of a gun. If I were aiming for something in real life, it would've gone super off track and maybe even hurt someone. I can't take a risk like that. It's not fair to whomever else could possibly be hurt by me."

"That's why we're not in a real-life situation," Brad explained patiently. "Because of course, if you were to be out in real life right now, you wouldn't know how to shoot properly. It would be disastrous. You wouldn't hit your aim, and someone could get seriously hurt. Right now, though, you don't have to worry about that. We're here to practice so you can get better at shooting."

"So everyone can laugh at me as I fail to hit the broadside of a barn?" Kate sniped.

"Kate, don't be so hard on yourself. It's your first time. No one does well at anything the first time they try it. We'll keep trying, keep practicing until you do better. You don't have to be perfect, but I want you to be competent in using this before we leave. You just need to have patience and give yourself more time to learn."

"I don't want to keep doing this though," Kate insisted. "I give up. It's not for me."

Brad looked at her, keeping his gaze locked on her eyes. He stepped closer in a compassionate way. Kate could tell by the look in his eyes that this was incredibly important to him.

"Please, Kate. I'm worried about you. It doesn't sound like you're in a safe situation lately, and that terrifies me. I can't imagine what any of us would do if anything bad happened to you. You mean so much to so many people. So, let's just try this. Try to take it seriously. Try your best. This just might save your life someday. It's a skill you need to have. Let's try again."

Kate sighed. She saw the genuine desperation in his eyes. He couldn't make her do anything she didn't want to do. Yet she could tell how much this meant to him. He really believed she was in danger.

Was she in danger? It often felt that way. Whoever was doing these strange things hadn't even tried to hurt her so far. But that was only so far. She couldn't know what would happen in the future, and it wasn't fun to try to guess.

She didn't like to think that she would ever need the protection of a gun. Then, she thought of Amanda. Amanda likely never thought she'd need a gun either. Kate certainly didn't think she'd ever end up like Amanda, but Kate didn't want to leave room for that chance either.

So, she listened to what Brad and the instructor tried to teach her. She took the responsibility of wielding a gun incredibly seriously and took the time needed to ensure she was doing it properly if she ever did need to use it.

Over the course of her training, she got better. Her aim got more on target to where she could at least hit the target now, even if it wasn't the exact spot she aimed for. She had more confidence that if someone was coming after her, she could hit them. But she still didn't think she could actually shoot someone.

The thought of actually killing someone, even if that person was attacking her, was unfathomable. She admired people who could defend themselves like that, she saw the value in it, but she would never be one of them.

Still, Brad insisted on buying her a gun against her protests. He usually would listen to whatever she said. He respected her in that way. But this time, he wasn't backing down. He picked out the proper gun regardless.

"Please," he said as he turned to hand the gun to her, "take it just in case. You never know what could happen. It's good to have as a precaution. You might never have to use it. I *hope* you never have to use it. You probably *won't* ever have to use it. But I want you to have it just in case you do. It would be reassuring to me to know you have it."

"Fine," Kate grumbled. "But if it comes down to it, I still don't think I could use this gun. I wouldn't want to hurt anyone."

"Let's hope you never have to find out," he said.

After their tense time at the shooting range, Kate wanted to do something that would get her mind off things, so they decided to take a trip to the beach. It was good for both of them to dispel a bit of that nervous energy as the waves calmed them and made them feel like Juniper Bay was probably safe.

"It really is nice to be here with you," Brad said, as the waves skipped alongside them, reminding Kate of their younger days. She was invigorated by the ocean's energy. "Life has been so stressful with the divorce, custody battle, and just everything in general. But out here with you, it feels like I have the time and space to be at peace. It's a much needed break from everything. I couldn't be more grateful for it. I couldn't be more grateful for you."

"I'm grateful for you too," Kate assured him. "With you here, I feel safer. I feel closer to the root of who I am. Like I remember the life I led before this. It brings me back to reality when things feel a little disoriented. I'm so glad you came to visit."

At that, they started reminiscing about the old days again and all they had gone through, the good and the bad. They laughed and bonded as the ocean watched them below. As they grabbed dinner, they kept up their nostalgic conversation. As they returned home that night and Brad left to go back to his hotel room to call his son, Kate thought about how lucky she was to have her friends. With them, she could get through anything. She could even convince herself that she wasn't in danger while she had a stalker.

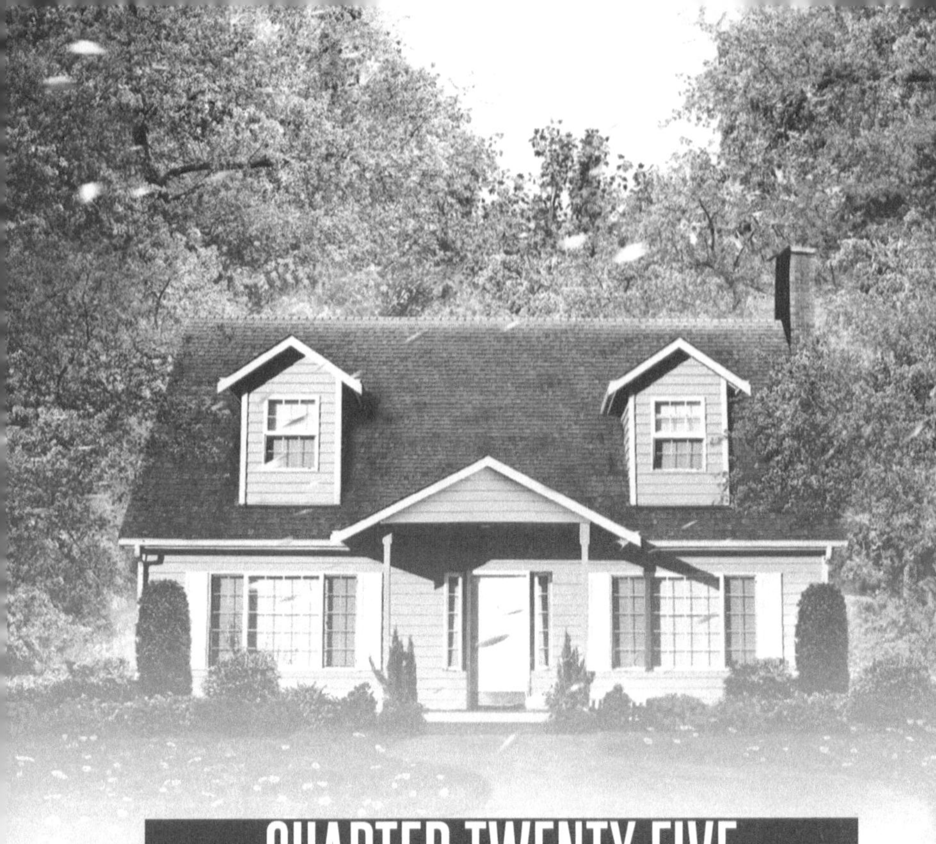

CHAPTER TWENTY-FIVE

VANESSA HAD BEEN A LITTLE DISAPPOINTED IN NOT seeing Kate at the meeting that night. She knew Kate's friend was in town, so she hadn't necessarily expected to see her there anyway, but her heart still sunk a little as the meeting began without Kate in attendance. She had hoped she would still make it.

She could use a friend lately. Kate was the closest friend she had these days, and she wanted to reach out to her more than anything as she tried to battle fears she couldn't tell anyone about.

They still texted regularly. They talked about their grief and the moving forward process. Vanessa was able to open up to Kate in a way that she couldn't with anyone else. She felt understood in a way that no one else was able to understand since no one she knew had gone through anything even a little bit similar.

Still, she held back a little. She didn't want to add more problems to Kate's shoulders. She had already been through so much. But she decided once she saw her again, she would finally open up. She would reveal the truth.

The truth was, the man following her was getting bolder. He had stopped going after her for a while. She thought she was safe because of it. She thought he would leave her alone. She was starting to feel comfortable.

Then, recently it had started up again. The feeling like someone was following her had gotten worse. Certain things in her house had gone missing. She saw shadows at times and heard strange noises.

For a while, she tried to convince herself that she was losing her mind. Her husband's death had caused such a fracture in her life that she was mentally unwell. She was paranoid without him here to keep her safe. It made sense in that way.

That morning, though, she had come home to flowers in a vase in her kitchen. There was a bouquet of white lilies freshly picked and expertly arranged. It terrified her. Whoever was stalking her could get into her house. He could attack her at any time.

She was lost and alone in this, and she wasn't sure what to do about it. So, she was going to turn to Kate. Then, at least someone would know in case something happened to her. And if someone dangerous was in Juniper Bay, every woman should know about it.

These thoughts were fresh in Vanessa's mind throughout the meeting. Being here didn't give her the same sense of safety and peace that it usually did. She couldn't process thoughts of her husband's death when worries about her own life haunted her.

She realized as she sat there and obsessed over the man stalking her that she didn't want to die. She thought she wanted to after her husband died, but not anymore. She had learned that she could live even in the wake of his death. She could attempt to move on. There was still good to be found in this life, and she wanted to enjoy it. When it was her time to speak, she decided to talk about this without sharing her stalking story, worried it might make others think she was crazy.

"I think I've improved," Vanessa started as the group listened intently. "I'm not crying all the time anymore. There will be hours when I don't think of him, which is a huge improvement over when I used to think of him every second of every day.

"It's in the small things. When something comes to my mind, I don't automatically think to tell him about it. I don't bear a consistent, heavy weight on my chest. I feel like I can breathe again. I can live again. I *want* to live again."

"That's the most important thing," Liam assured her. "That's the first big step to building yourself back up. You'll keep ruining your life if you're trying to live but don't actually want to. Your subconscious will continue to get in the way, preventing you from moving forward because it thinks you don't want to move forward. It will find a way to keep you stuck.

"Once you want to live, though, everything changes. Your natural instinct will come alive again. You'll do anything possible to live. Things will start naturally going better for you as your determination to do better makes even life's toughest challenges a little easier.

"I know it may be harder to believe in the beginning stages, but this is incredible progress you're making. You will find that in time, all the messes you've made will naturally begin to untangle themselves. Life will be even better. You will find your happiness. I know you will."

"I hope so," Vanessa said with a smile that felt genuine. "I feel the true sincerity of it. I feel like I'll be okay someday. I just … sometimes I worry that chance will be taken from me."

"What do you mean?" Liam asked.

"I don't know." Vanessa shrugged. "I guess sometimes I feel unsettled. Like maybe something bad will happen to me. I spent so much time wanting to die, but now I don't. I worry that the chance to live my life to the fullest will be taken away from me. Like maybe I didn't appreciate it enough before, and now I'll never get the chance to fully live my life."

The group was quiet for a moment. Vanessa worried she had shared too much. Would they now guess at her secret stalker? Would they think she was being dramatic?

"That makes sense," replied Jenna, one of the older women in the group. "When my husband died, suddenly the world became a scarier place. Even though he died from a heart attack, it felt like death could come at me suddenly out of nowhere at any moment. I think it was partially because he was my protector when he was alive. He made me feel safe in the world. Like someone reliable was looking out for me. With him gone, I was left to fend for myself, and I wasn't sure that I'd be able to do that. I got the feeling of danger no matter where I went, like someone was coming after me. Like someone was lurking in the shadows behind me."

Vanessa became more invested in everything she was saying after that. Could it be that she and Jenna shared a stalker? Maybe the same person was after them both.

"But as time went on, that feeling faded," Jenna continued. "As I became more confident and surer of my abilities, I felt safer in the world. There was no longer a murderer waiting in the shadows. Death wasn't stalking me anymore. I was free.

"I do think you'll reach that point, Vanessa. It takes time, of course. And it's going to hit you now more that you feel alive, but you will get there. And you'll find more certainty in yourself. You'll realize that this life is yours to live and it won't randomly be stolen from you. You will have time to enjoy it to its fullest. You're young. You have so much time to find happiness."

Her words were joined by affirmations and nods of approval, which made Vanessa feel better. She reasoned that Jenna was probably right. There wasn't any real danger. It was all in her mind. She had created a monster that was stalking her, and she could banish him. She just needed to rebuild her strength and confidence.

There was no stalker. There was no danger. Vanessa was safe, and she almost convinced herself of that.

The rest of the meeting went well for everyone. They shared their struggles, which made it easier because they didn't have to face them alone. The support they gave each other was invaluable, making Vanessa feel better about everything.

She didn't even get scared that night as she walked to her car and drove herself home. She didn't look over her shoulder as she went into her house. But as she faced her little terrier looking at her with expectant eyes, the familiar tendrils of dread found their way down her spine once again.

Vanessa glanced out her window. Summer was giving way to fall, so the sun had already fully set. If she didn't walk Leo now, it would be pitch black soon. With everything going on, walking him in the dark was the last thing she wanted to do.

Her eyes fell back to the dog, who was getting antsier, his round eyes furrowed in worry. She realized she didn't have much of a choice. She had to take him out or he would potty on the floor from holding it too long.

"You better know that I love you," Vanessa said as she went to get Leo's leash. The dog pranced around her feet, happy to have gotten his way.

Vanessa grabbed her pepper spray as she left the house and started down the street. She decided to stick to better-lit areas to avoid the chance of her stalker coming after her. She made sure to stay vigilant, look around her at all times, and be aware of her surroundings.

Though she used to walk while listening to music, she never did that anymore. She made sure to keep her attention focused on the walk at hand and nothing else. She wanted to hear every single sound.

But as she walked, she started to get the sense that someone was watching her. She felt those creepy eyes on her, crawling over her body, analyzing her every move.

"I know you're out there," she said aloud, just loud enough so anyone close could hear her, but quiet enough to not attract the attention of some random passerby. "You can't sneak up on me. I know you're there, and I'm calling the police."

At that, Vanessa took her phone out. She started to dial for help but then realized she didn't have any proof that she was being followed. There wasn't much she could tell the officers. She thought back to her conversation with Jenna and reasoned that she might be paranoid.

So, she dialed Kate's number instead. As the phone rang, she picked up the pace back to her apartment. Her steps quickened as she willed Kate to pick up the phone.

"Please," she mumbled. "Kate, I need you. Please pick up the phone. Please. Please. Please."

The call went to voicemail, and Vanessa cursed under her breath. She glanced around her, and while she still couldn't see anyone, she *felt* someone there. Even Leo seemed to be getting anxious as he walked faster toward the apartment.

Thankfully, they were close. Vanessa breathed a sigh of relief as the apartment building came into sight. She just had to go a little farther to get there. Then, she'd be home safe. She could convince herself this was all an overreaction. There was nothing to worry about. Everything would be okay.

"Vanessa!" a voice called out.

The male's voice sounded semi-familiar to her, but not familiar enough to where she could put a face to the name. She hesitated, wondering if she should turn around. What if it was a trap? What if it was the person who had been stalking her?

She realized that if it was, she was already in his grasp. Even if she kept walking, he could easily catch up to her. She could try running. She was a good runner, but what if he was faster?

After a quick rapid-fire succession of thoughts, Vanessa decided she had to at least see who she was up against. She had to know the threat.

She turned and was filled with relief as she faced a man she knew, thankful to be safe from the stranger haunting her.

"Nice night, huh?" he called over.

"Pretty nice," she smiled.

It was okay. Everything was going to be okay.

So, she let her guard down.

CHAPTER TWENTY-SIX

B Y THE END OF THE FIFTH DAY OF BRAD'S VISIT, KATE was feeling more at home in Juniper Bay and even more comfortable with Brad. They'd rekindled the easy, companionable friendship they'd had back in college, so they were closer than ever. And it was nice for her to have this break. She still got a little work done when he was talking to his son and spending time relaxing in his hotel room, but she spent more time bonding with him than anything else, which was what she needed at that moment.

As the time came for his visit to end, Kate grew sadder at the thought of him leaving. She had grown so used to having him here that she didn't want to say goodbye. She felt safer with him, more confident. She worried that once he left, she'd go back to being scared all the time, unsure of even herself.

So, that morning she was feeling a little clingier to him. She wanted to soak in as much time with Brad as possible before he left. They'd planned a hike that day, so as she got ready, her mind raced with every possible thing she could ask about staying safe.

As they drove up to the hiking trail, she peppered him with all sorts of questions about any tips he might have.

"You know, you make a compelling case for why I should be out here with you," Brad laughed as he pulled into the parking area of the trail. "Now you're actually starting to worry me. I feel like I want to be here just to make sure you're safe in whatever way I can."

"It's not like that—" Kate protested, but Brad stopped her.

"I mean, it makes sense. I do love the area, so I could be around anyway."

"What about your son?" she asked.

He shrugged. "I could just bring him up here on the weekends. Really doubt I'll ever get full custody of him. I would still make sure to spend plenty of time with him."

Kate found the idea of Brad moving closer comforting as they started walking beneath the leaves. The vivid oranges, reds, and yellows all around them rejuvenated her as she imagined a life where Brad lived nearby and she could see her friend all the time. She pictured them taking more walks just like this one.

"That would be nice," Kate admitted as they continued up the trail. "You have to make your own decision, of course, based on whatever's best for you. I'd never want to convince you of anything. It would be nice to be able to see you more though."

"It'd be wonderful to see you more too," Brad agreed. "I really have enjoyed spending all this time with you. I've always enjoyed spending time with you. You've always been such an amazing friend to me."

"And you've always been an amazing friend to me too," she replied. "It's rare to find one of those lifelong friends, but I really do feel like that will be us. We're the kind of friends who can go through things together and still get out on the other side in one piece because we have each other."

Brad and Kate fell into a friendly silence as they continued through the forest. They were alone out there that day, without anyone around to distract them from the conversation and view, so it felt safer to say things out loud that they wouldn't normally voice. They were protected in this space.

"I feel safe when I'm with you," Kate noted out of the blue. "I appreciate that. With the stalker and everything, I've been so afraid… but with you, I feel safer."

"I'm glad I can provide that feeling of safety for you," Brad replied with a warm smile. "You mean so much to me… I'm happy when I can give you any sense of happiness. I…"

As Brad paused, Kate glanced over at him and saw something strange in his eyes. It seemed that he wanted to say something to her that he was scared to say out loud. She hadn't seen him like that before. Usually, they would tell each other everything.

They had a certain familiarity between them that had grown comfortable over the years. For it to have seemingly faded now made her uncertain. She wanted to ask what was wrong, but all of a sudden, she felt like maybe that wasn't a good idea. Maybe they were inching into territory she didn't exactly know how to navigate.

"You?" she pressed with a raised eyebrow.

"I… have to admit that I think my feelings have grown for you," Brad finally confessed.

Kate was too shocked to respond at first. Sure, they were close. She enjoyed the closeness between them. But she thought they were close as friends, nothing more than that.

She replayed the last few days and saw the signs in their growing bond that could point to more. She'd missed them all at the time, which made her feel foolish now. She just thought Brad's feelings mirrored her own. He had to be mistaken.

"Well, I… your feelings might be difficult to navigate right now," Kate attempted, not exactly eager to hear where this was heading. "You are going through a divorce. You're stressed, under a lot of emotional turmoil, and dealing with a lot right now. It'd make sense for your emotions and feelings to be a little scattered. It must be difficult for you to know exactly how you feel about anything or anyone right now."

"That is true to some extent," Brad admitted slowly. "There is a lot going on. Everything is kind of everywhere as I try to make sense of my new life. And my thoughts and feelings toward people have shifted. But I don't want you to think that my feelings about you have changed just because of the emotional turmoil of my divorce."

That made her stop fully in her tracks and turn to face him. "What are you saying, Brad?"

"I'm saying… the truth is… I've had complex feelings for you since our college years, pretty much since the day I met you," he said. "Even back then I appreciated you being there for me so much; we had such a great bond, and you are a fantastic woman, Kate. You really are. I've always admired, respected, and appreciated you. It's what has helped us build a strong friendship. But even back then I wanted more."

"You never said that," Kate whispered, shocked that Brad could have been feeling this way for all this time.

"I was scared," Brad admitted. "I liked you so much that I was scared to ruin things between us. I still worry about that. I was trying to work myself up to it, but then you started dating Tyler, and you know Tyler and I were friends too. I liked you both. I respected you both. I respected you too much to get in between that, and you seemed so happy with him. I wanted you to be happy."

"You seemed happy with Jade too," Kate countered.

"I was. Jade and I got together after you and Tyler did, after I was sure there was no chance for you and me. And I loved her—I really did. My feelings for you faded as my feelings for her grew. At first, I had to bury my feelings for you. Then, they were buried so long they turned into something genuinely platonic."

"And that changed when Tyler died," Kate snapped. "Because now I was a widow and you could take advantage of that."

A flash of irritation passed through Brad's features, but he kept himself under control. "God, no. It's not like that at all. I'm not trying to take advantage of anything or anyone. It wasn't like right when Tyler died, I saw my chance with you. I'm not trying to get something out of his death. I'm not trying to replace him. Jade and I were already having issues before Tyler died."

"And you didn't tell me? You didn't tell anyone?"

He groaned. "What was I supposed to say? Things started going downhill a few years ago. We were bickering, clashing, not spending enough time together, all sorts of different things that contributed to where we are now. We just aren't a great match. And we tried to hold it together—we really did. I never thought of pursuing anything with you directly after Tyler died. My sole intention was to be there for you, help you through a tough time, and be the kind of friend you were to me."

"So, when did things change?" Kate asked.

"I think those thoughts returned when you told me the danger you were in," Brad explained. "It brought out a protective side of me, a side that wanted to be near you and keep you from all harm. And I thought about what it would be like to live closer to you, to keep you safe, to be by your side every day. I liked that thought. It led to me thinking about what it might be like if we were more than friends.

"Again, I did try to bury those feelings, though, because I've been scared. Not just of rejection. It would hurt to be rejected by you, but that's not the worst fear. I can understand if you don't feel the same way about me. I'm a grown man. I can handle that. I just worried about ruining the friendship. I'm still worried about that.

"I can accept you not wanting to be anything more than platonic friends with me. But I don't want to lose your friendship because I admitted to how I really feel. I value having you in my life so much. I would hate to lose you, especially when we're both still going through so much. It would be the worst time for us to part ways. So, I've waited.

"But the more time I've spent with you, the more these feelings have grown. I feel closer to you, more attached, and I've fallen for you. I really have, Kate. Things between us seem to come so naturally, spending time together feels so right. I want to keep you as a friend no matter what. None of this changes that. If you don't want anything more than friendship, then I respect that.

"Since I'm heading home soon, I don't think I could leave without at least trying. I had to admit to how I really feel. I had to give us chance… because what's between us feels too special to not say out loud and see how you feel."

Silence followed this. Kate wasn't sure how to react, so she was quiet as they continued hiking up the mountain. Despite the vulnerable conversation, things didn't feel awkward between them. There was a sense of contentment that made Kate wonder if Brad was right. Maybe there was something special between them worth exploring. Maybe things could be more than platonic after all.

"I don't know," Kate finally said as they neared the top of the mountain. "I'm sorry, but this is a lot, and I don't really know how to respond. I don't know what to say. I don't know how I feel about all this."

Even speaking the words made her feel more overwhelmed. It was so tough to even think of being with another man after Tyler died, let alone with a friend she had known all this time. There were just so many changes for her to try to comprehend, and it was difficult wrapping her mind around them all.

"I'm sorry," Brad said. "I shouldn't have even said anything about it. I know you're going through so much right now. It's selfish of me to add more pressure on you."

"No, you don't need to be sorry," she assured him. "I want you to feel comfortable telling me the truth about everything, including this. We're friends. This won't break us. We need to feel free to express ourselves. I appreciate the openness and honesty. It's just a lot for me to process right now... I need some time."

"I understand. I know it is a lot. I just figured it would be best to tell you. Like you said, it's best to be honest so it won't be even more complicated in the future. I really can accept if you don't feel the same way. Maybe we can just take a break from the subject, finish our hike, and go about our day. Take all the time you need to think about things, and if you don't feel the same way, we can forget I said anything."

"I'm not sure I want to forget about it completely without addressing it," Kate answered. "You did say it, and you deserve some sort of answer as to how I feel about it. I have every intention of responding. But I do think a break for now would be nice."

"Perfect timing too," Brad said, smiling. "Because look at that view!"

They reached the top of the summit to see the soft ways the early caresses of autumn were coloring the leaves, creating shocks of red, gold, and orange among the resilient green. A hint of the ocean could be spotted in the distance, while the plant life below remained wild and restless.

Kate looked at Brad as he glanced away into the safety of nature, and she wondered how exactly they should define their relationship.

Kate settled down with her cup of tea after a very long day. The awkwardness between her and Brad had been mostly smoothed over as they wanted to enjoy their remaining time together. But something had changed.

There was still something between them that had to be dealt with. Kate knew she needed to respond to his confession in some way, either by rejecting him or admitting to shared feelings… but she wasn't sure what she'd say. So, it lingered.

They parted earlier that night than usual just so they could have some space. And as she sat in front of the fireplace with her tea, she considered their relationship further. She had always cared deeply for Brad, but did she see him as more than a friend? Was she even ready for this after Tyler had died? Or was dating still out of the cards for her?

She certainly cared about Brad. There was something special between them. But how far should that go?

As she sipped her tea, her eyelids grew heavier. She leaned back in her chair, cuddled up with a cozy blanket, and dozed off to sleep.

Kate awoke to a knock on the door. Or at least, she thought she was awake. The whole world seemed gray, hazy, and a bit disoriented. It seemed like she was half awake and half dreaming. But she didn't feel frightened. Rather she felt comforted and safe—like somehow she knew everything would be okay.

As she went to the door, she was surprised and delighted to see Victor at her doorstep. She welcomed him in, eager to see him after being away from him for so long. She found she felt especially attached to him in a weird way after Brad's admission. Something about it made her want to pull him in even closer.

"I missed you," she said, unable to fully hide her true feelings in this haze, unable to question why he was there at all.

"I missed you too," he replied, hugging her tight. "That's why I had to stop by tonight. I had to see you. I had to talk to you. I've been staying away to give you space and time with your friend, but..."

"But I'm glad you're here," she assured him. "Spending time with Brad has been fun, but I have genuinely missed you. It's just different with you. You're different."

"I hope you mean that in a good way," he said with a smile that looked a little nervous.

"A very good way," she assured him. "I feel like I can relate to you in a way that I can't with other people. You understand what I'm going through not just as a widow but also as a person in general. We have a lot in common. Since I met you, there's just been something different about you and me..."

Kate paused as she realized how enthusiastic she was being. She worried she was coming on too strong, being overly friendly with Victor. It was difficult to keep control of her tongue in this state of mind. It felt like all the words she didn't want to say just kept coming out.

"I feel the same way," Victor assured her. "You're special, Kate. You really are. We're so similar in a lot of ways, which makes it easy to relate to each other. Yet we're also different enough to keep things interesting. I find you to be an incredibly compelling person. And ever since I met you, I've only wanted to get to know you better. I've wanted to explore this special bond between us."

Something changed in his eyes as they looked at each other that night. Kate thought she recognized the look. It seemed similar to the look Brad had before he confessed his feelings for her, but this time she was less nervous about what Victor would say. She was more nervous about how she'd respond because she knew her feelings weren't exactly platonic either.

"I like you, Kate. I like you a lot. Maybe even… maybe I'm overstepping boundaries here. I'm sorry if I am. I'm sorry if this makes you uncomfortable, but I think I might have feelings for you beyond just friendship."

Kate looked at him and still wasn't sure what to say, though her reaction was notably different from her reaction to Brad. She hadn't known Victor for very long at all, so he wasn't as neatly placed in the friendship box. But maybe that meant the category was a little more fluid. She wasn't sure how to feel or what to think. There was something undeniable between them, but she wasn't sure that she was ready for that yet.

"I love Tyler," Kate said.

Victor's demeanor fell a little at this, though he still didn't look away. He wasn't defeated.

"I know you do. That's okay. To be honest, I still love Evelyn. But I think… I think they would want us to still love them and move on with someone new. The right guy can do that. He can make new memories with you while respecting the old ones. And I want to be that guy for you. I want to be your chapter two."

Kate smiled at the phrase they used in their support group circle when talking about new romantic partners. Their chapter twos. There had been a point in time when Kate was certain she would never have a chapter two. Her whole book would just be Tyler.

Now, she wasn't quite so certain. Did she really want to live her whole life alone? What about this man in front of her? This man who reminded her so much of Tyler and yet was wonderful on his own as well. Was there room for him in her life outside of just a friendship? Was that something she could truly do now?

Victor stepped toward her, and in the haze, she felt like she couldn't resist. The thoughts that would usually keep her away from this sort of thing slid out of her brain as her mind narrowed to this one moment. She couldn't think of Tyler, or Brad, or if this was right or wrong.

She simply felt how she felt without any other complications. She simply felt that she wanted to be closer to Victor. She had grown used to sleeping with him in her dreams and even hooking up with him in her dreams at his house. And now he was here. It was like her dreams had come true, and something surged inside her at how happy that made her feel.

His touch seemed familiar to her by now as he gently caressed her cheek. She leaned into him. They grew closer as he brought her in for a kiss, and his lips on hers felt right. They felt natural.

"Be with me," he whispered, their bodies so close, and yet Kate felt like she wanted to be even closer. "Please, Kate. Let me be your chapter two. Be with me."

She couldn't say anything out loud. Though her filter was broken, something within her still wouldn't allow her to voice her agreement yet. She couldn't bring herself to say it out loud.

But when he kissed her, she couldn't resist. His lips were so warm against hers, so inviting, intoxicating. She remembered the magical dream of a night they had together at his house and wondered if she was still dreaming.

"If this is a dream, I might as well enjoy it," she whispered as their lips parted.

She held his gaze for a moment, and his eyes were so bright, so alive, so full of passion that she was certain she had to be awake. No dream could feel this real, this thrilling.

Unable to fully figure out what was true and what was merely her imagination, Kate gave herself to the passion of the moment. She allowed herself to enjoy it as she fell into Victor's arms and allowed him into her bed.

CHAPTER TWENTY-SEVEN

T HE NEXT MORNING, KATE KEPT HER EYES CLOSED AS she began to wake up. She thought about the moment she'd shared with Victor and the hookup that followed. It was all so thrilling, so scary, so many things all at once.

She wasn't sure anymore if she hoped it was a dream or reality. Though she found herself grateful when she turned and realized she was alone in the chair she had fallen asleep in. She was dressed. There was no sign that anyone had been here with her. It had all been a dream.

Knowing none of it was real took away some of the pressure Kate felt at having to process this, though it wasn't gone completely. As she got up and got ready for the day, she considered what her reaction would be to Victor if he did confess he had feelings for her.

In the dream, she hadn't responded, though she had slept with him. It was just a dream, so it wasn't the best indicator as to what she would do if faced with this in real life. Though Kate felt like it was still relevant. The fact that she kept having these kinds of dreams seemed to suggest that on a subconscious level at least, she was attracted to Victor in a more than platonic sort of way.

Kate allowed herself to really be open to the possibility. She still didn't think she was ready to date yet, but would that last forever? She was starting to suspect that she wouldn't be happy being single for the rest of her life. Eventually, she'd have to date someone again.

Could she possibly ever date Victor if he felt something more than platonic toward her? That was a tough question to answer. He was attractive, kind, supportive, fun, and a great listener. He was all the things she would want in a partner. If she did ever find herself ready to date again, he definitely fit the bill.

"What about Brad though?" she asked out loud as she sipped her coffee. "Could I ever view Brad as more than a friend?"

The difference in her reaction toward Brad compared to her reaction toward Victor was some sort of indication that maybe she didn't feel the same way about Brad. She cared about Brad a lot, but she wasn't filled with the same intense desire to be near him. She didn't have those strange dreams about him. So, that had to mean she didn't have the same feelings about him as she did about Victor, right?

"He's always been there for me," she mused. "Brad has been the best friend I could've asked for. He's protective, kind, fun, familiar. Things feel so right with him. They feel so comfortable. I don't know what to do!"

They had planned to have lunch together later that day, giving each other the morning to have a bit of space so they could process the intense conversation they'd had the day before. Kate hoped to come up with an answer for him by the time they met again. But with all of these conflicting thoughts, emotions, and dreams about Victor, Kate wasn't too sure how she felt. She wasn't sure what her answer would be, but she knew she had to figure it out.

First, she decided to try to call Vanessa back as a distraction. But the phone rang and rang with no answer. Kate shrugged, assuming she was busy, then turned her attention back to the impossible dilemma she was faced with.

That day, Kate had chosen a different place for lunch than she was used to. She regretted it the moment she walked up to the chic-looking brick building; she longed for the familiarity of the usual café as she faced such uncertainty between her and Brad. Being somewhere new was too much until she walked inside and felt a little more at ease.

The brick walls were decorated with tasteful yet simple artwork, while the ornate chairs and glossy, wood tables provided a sort of elegance. Inside The Coffee Haus, the smell of grinding coffee greeted her along with the low and soothing chatter of fellow patrons. Fresh wild flowers graced the tables. Brad was already waiting at a table in one corner, looking anxious as he stood to greet her.

They shared the usual greetings, but this time even those simple words felt strange between them. They gave each other a hug, which was much quicker than normal before sitting down at the table and glancing over the menu that was much fancier than their usual brunch spot.

"I think I'm going to go out of the box," Brad stated. "Try something new. I've never actually eaten arugula before. Or goat cheese. Usually, I like to stick to what I know, but taking a chance seems like it could lead to something delicious. May be worth the risk."

Kate nodded, wondering if the comparison to this strange place in their friendship was deliberate or not. "I think I'll do the same," she decided. "Lamb is a little extravagant for lunch, but I've never had it. I think I'll try a dish with it."

"That's the spirit," he smiled. "Trying to branch out a bit too?"

"I was talking to my therapist about this," Kate told him. "It's been so helpful to create new grooves and patterns that help me step away from my old life a bit and build something new."

"Very important," Brad agreed. "After everything that happened, I imagine you can't stay where you were before with things. You have to create something else or risk being dragged down into the past and stuck there forever."

"Absolutely," Kate nodded. "But also, you know, some things are nice when they stay the same. Because everything else changes so fast, it's also nice to have something familiar. It's good to know I have things that are stable and steady to return to. Things that are so great on their own that they don't need changing."

Brad nodded. "Yeah, that makes sense. It's a really important balance to strike between comfort and change. That's what I'm trying to do as I go through the divorce. Knowing when to hold steady—when to let go—and when to build something new as I walk down this strange path."

They were quiet as Kate took his words into consideration. It seemed like a good approach. She questioned herself. Was she doing well at fitting those patterns?

They ordered their food, both of them deciding to take a chance and try something new. The waitress smiled and bustled back to the kitchen, and they turned back to each other. Kate looked Brad in the eyes and tried to gauge her feelings for him. Even as she did it, she realized she had already made her decision.

"I don't want to just skirt around the conversation we had yesterday," Kate said boldly. "I know you said I could pretend like you didn't say anything, but I don't think that's possible at this point. I don't think it's something that can be ignored, and I honestly think that doing so would be a disservice to you. You deserve an answer, no matter how awkward the conversation might be. It's important we're on the same page with this."

Brad nodded his agreement, but he looked hesitant. He sipped his coffee and fiddled with his watch, his eyes wide with apprehension.

"I want to first start by saying, you don't have anything to worry about in regards to losing the friendship," Kate said, causing some of the tension to leave Brad noticeably. "I'm not upset by your being open and honest with me. Sometimes feelings creep up between people like that, and you communicated your feelings respectfully. That's all I can ask for. You expressed them well.

"I also want to say that I appreciate your presence in my life. You've been there for me every time I've needed you, and I hope you know that doesn't go unnoticed. We have fun together. You're so important to me. And I am drawn to you in a special, unique way. But I just don't think we'd work as a couple."

Brad nodded as he closed his eyes for a brief moment. He looked crushed in that moment, and Kate wished she could take his pain away. She wished she felt the same way as he did. She worried it might really devastate him.

When he opened his eyes again, though, he looked determined to get through this conversation peacefully. He looked strong and resilient. It made Kate feel safer in communicating her true feelings. Like things wouldn't break just because she couldn't date him.

"I'm just used to seeing you as my close friend," she continued. "And I like the familiarity of that. I find comfort in knowing that we'll always have each other. I wouldn't want a relationship to ever threaten that. I just really appreciate where we are in each other's lives.

"Plus, you were Tyler's friend as well. We were all close to each other. So, I don't think it'd be right for us to be together. I'm also friends with Jade, and I don't want to jeopardize that. Things just don't seem conducive to a good relationship. There's so much at risk. I just can't do it."

Things were quiet for a moment between them, and Kate worried what his reaction would be. She worried it would forever ruin the friendship. She desperately didn't want to lose him.

"I respect that," he finally replied. "It's not the ideal answer, but I can't force you to feel the same way as I do. I wouldn't want to. I'd only want you to be with me if that's something you chose willingly. And I accept that it's just not the same for you. I still value you as a person, and I'd want to have a close friendship with you regardless."

"Thank you for understanding," she said.

"Thank you for not letting… that… get between us. I'm glad I opened up about it, and I'm grateful you allowed space for that. The friendship between us is really special, and I'm forever grateful for it."

"Me too."

At that, the conversation fell into a more natural rhythm between them as their food arrived. It was awkward at first, with some noticeable tension. But they quickly smoothed it over because the friendship meant so much to both of them.

Partway through the meal, though, Brad got a phone call. He glanced at his screen, and his eyes narrowed a bit.

"I'm so sorry," he said, "but I have to take this."

"No worries," Kate replied, knowing it had to be important.

Brad stepped out for a bit while Kate continued eating, processing the tough conversation they just had. When he got back, he looked flustered and stressed.

"I have to go," he told her. His jaw was tense, and his eyes were suddenly clouded. Whatever phone call he'd just gotten had suddenly shaken him up. He took out more than enough cash to cover the full bill and leave a hefty tip. "But it was really nice seeing you, and I'd like to see you again before I leave."

"Of course," Kate agreed. "What's wrong? Anything I can do to help?"

"I'll explain later," Brad told her. "For now, I just really have to go."

At that, he left the restaurant abruptly, leaving Kate feeling a little shocked and more than a little worried.

By the time Kate got back home, her mind was abuzz with worries about Brad. He seemed so distressed as he left that she wanted to race to his side to help him. Though she suspected it was best to give him space right now. She knew he would tell her what was going on when he was ready.

In the meantime, she decided to work on her own thing for a bit. The thought of Brad leaving soon reminded her of her stalker and how she really needed to figure that out so she could feel safe once she was alone. So, she sat down at her desk and tried to map out how she might become more comfortable in her life again even when no one else was around.

As she thought about who might have reason to harm her, she thought again of what Allison had said. Her mind went back to Daniel Jenkins, so she decided to look him up and see what she could find.

It took a bit of digging to find any information on him since he was pretty well-protected. But during her research for her book on the dark side of psychology, she had come across a couple of people in law enforcement who liked her and were willing to help.

What she found was chilling. Not even a week after his release, Daniel moved to Juniper Bay.

Kate contemplated this for a bit, wondering what she should do about it. Daniel hadn't given off any red flags during her interview with him. But she also knew people can be manipulative and charming when needed. Through her research, she learned how often people hide the true threat of who they are until it's too late.

Was Daniel one of those people? He was a criminal, a murderer. He wasn't exactly the kind of person she could trust. And these things started happening around the time he was released.

She thought about it further, knowing Allison would kill her for the idea she had in mind. But she wasn't so sure she had another choice. She had to do something. She couldn't just ignore this forever. She didn't want to continue to live her life in fear. She wanted to figure out a way out of this for good and finally move on.

"I think I'm finally going to do it," she said to herself as she ate dinner alone that night. "I'll make another visit to Daniel. I'm not sure when, but I will. And I'm going to find out once and for all if there's any chance he's behind this. If there's any chance he's dangerous. I'm taking control of this situation."

CHAPTER TWENTY-EIGHT

THE NEXT MORNING, KATE FOUND HERSELF IN A GOOD mood as she waited for Brad to arrive. They had planned to go to the store to buy a bunch of ingredients and then come back to make a fantastic, elaborate brunch. Kate loved cooking, especially with him, so she was definitely looking forward to it.

She still had her obligatory cup of coffee before he arrived, then flipped through some recipes, trying to find the perfect ones. In the spirit of trying new things, she chose an asparagus, radish, and bacon frittata along with scallion pancakes topped with chopped fresh fruit. That day would be Brad's last day in Juniper Bay, and she wanted to make the most of it, cheering him up from whatever was bothering him and smoothing over any lingering tension over the unreciprocated feelings.

She looked down at her phone and realized that she still hadn't reached Vanessa since the day before. She fired off a text to her and waited for a response, but none came after several minutes. She made a note to better check in on her friend once Brad left and see what was going on with her. Then her mind went back to the fun morning that was planned.

The time that Brad had told her he'd arrive passed, and he didn't show. It really wasn't like Brad to be late to anything, but she figured he was just packing up his things or checking out of the hotel. She knew that he was stressed lately, which would explain the small change.

But when half an hour had passed, and she hadn't so much as heard a peep from him, Kate started to grow a little worried. She sent him a text to make sure things were okay and see when he'd be arriving. Still, there was no response.

By the time almost an hour had passed, Kate was increasingly concerned. She had tried texting Brad a couple of times and even tried calling him, but she still didn't get a response. So, she sent him a final text.

I'm heading to the store to get the ingredients. Then, if I haven't heard from you by the time I'm done shopping, I'm swinging by your hotel room. Not to be paranoid or anything. Just want to make sure everything's good.

With that decision firmly in place, Kate headed out to the store with Brad still on her mind. She walked into the grocery store and soon became distracted by all the chatter. It seemed like people were overly talkative that day, approaching each other more freely. Kate was curious as to why, but she didn't know anyone well enough to ask until she spotted Barbara in the produce section.

Barbara automatically waved her over as she approached, and they gave each other the usual, quick hug. She looked more tired than normal, a little drained. But Kate didn't read too much into that. She was older, so it made sense.

"How are you doing, dear?" Barbara asked. "Have you been making sure to stay safe?"

"Of course," Kate answered, though that had been growing difficult. She still tried her best. "After what happened to

Amanda, I've been extra vigilant. We don't need another trag-edy in Juniper Bay."

"I'd hoped for the same. Such a shame…" Barbara said.

That made Kate frown. "What do you mean?"

"Haven't you heard?"

"Hm?"

"It was just this morning. Or at least, it was discovered this morning," Barbara clarified. "Who knows when it happened."

"I haven't heard anything about what happened this morn-ing," Kate replied, her concern growing. "What's going on?"

"It's shocking. Terrible and gruesome. I'm not sure I want to share it. It's so upsetting."

Kate didn't want to deal with any more upsetting things, but she did want to be aware of any trouble she might come across. Plus, despite what she said, it did seem like Barbara was a little more eager to share this story than she was willing to let on.

"I'm strong and used to upsetting things," Kate assured her. "And it's safer for me to know what's going on, especially if something terrible has happened. Please do share."

"Okay," Barbara sighed. "You're right. It is better for you to know. Hopefully, you don't know her."

"Know who?"

"Vanessa Harrison."

Kate's heart skipped a beat at her friend's name. She real-ized then that she hadn't heard from her at all since that missed phone call, which was strange since they usually texted most days. She pulled out her phone and realized that the text she'd sent earlier had not even been opened, and a tendril of icy fear slid down her spine.

She'd been so distracted by what was going on with Brad that for the most part, it slipped her mind. She hadn't made much of an effort to check in. She felt deeply guilty for it, but she simply had been focused on other things. She hadn't thought much of Vanessa over the past couple days. She just kept telling herself she'd reach out once Brad was gone.

"You do know her," Barbara said, her face softening in empathy. "I can see it in your eyes."

"I do. I still want to know what happened to her though. I need to know. Please, tell me."

Barbara closed her eyes for a moment, then reopened them. "She was found dead in a hotel room," Barbara explained. "Naked and chained. The suspect is on the run."

The world blurred around Kate as she became dizzy. It couldn't be. There had to be some sort of mistake. Vanessa was one of the kindest people she knew. She couldn't imagine anyone wanting to hurt her. It made no sense.

"That can't be," Kate insisted. "Who would do such a thing?"

"I think they said his name is Brad Jackson," Barbara replied. "I didn't get a glimpse of the face when it came up on the news. But he must be from out of town. No one we know would do such a thing, and…"

Barbara paused as she looked thoughtful before more empathy flooded in. Her eyes widened as Kate's world crashed.

She felt like everything she knew was being ripped away from her out of her control. She had to be in a nightmare. None of this could be true. There had to be some sort of mistake.

Her mind flashed back to the day she found out her husband had died. It was a similar, sinking feeling. Back then she also couldn't come to terms with it. That had felt too awful to be true. And yet it had turned out to be the truth. Tyler was really dead.

So, what if this was the truth now as well? What if Brad really was a murderer? How could she exist in a world in which Brad killed Vanessa?

"You introduced us to a Brad," Barbara said quietly. "Please tell me it's not…"

Before Kate could answer, she was running away from Barbara and out of the store, leaving the groceries in the cart behind her. She didn't want to know, and yet she had to know. She had to reassure herself that it wasn't true.

As much as she liked Barbara, she knew Barbara could also be a gossip sometimes. The information she gathered had to be false. There was no other explanation.

Kate sped on her way to Brad's hotel as she desperately tried calling him multiple times in a row without any answer.

She became more worried as time ticked by. It became more difficult to convince herself that this wasn't true.

Then, her worst fears were confirmed as she pulled up to the hotel and saw police cars and an ambulance sitting in front of it. The entrance was taped off with caution tape with people surrounding it.

"It might not be him," Kate assured herself. "It can't be him. It's got to be another person at the hotel. It must be. They must be mistaken."

She pushed through the crowd to the caution tape where a police officer was standing. He had a stern look on his face as he warned the crowd to stay away.

"I just need confirmation," she told him as she approached him. "Is Brad really the one who did this? Brad Jackson. It's not him, right? Please tell me it's not him."

The officer crossed his arms over his chest as he analyzed her. "Do you know him?" he asked.

"Yes," Kate said quietly, no longer quite as eager to know the answer. If she didn't know if Brad was involved in this, she could convince herself it wasn't true. If she didn't know, she didn't have to deal with this. Though deep down she knew she couldn't avoid it forever. "I'm the one he's been in town to visit."

"We're going to want to talk to you," the officer replied. "Wait here a minute, and I'll get someone to meet you at the station."

Just then, Kate's phone pinged. She checked and saw a text from an unknown number.

You're next.

You don't know who you're dealing with.

Kate put away her phone as she walked into her house, feeling more scared than ever. She hadn't told the officers about the threatening texts though she knew she should have. She knew they'd attribute them to being from Brad, and it would only make him look worse. She wasn't sure why she cared about

making him look worse, but she did. She still wanted to protect him.

Once she locked the door behind her, she checked her
whole house, making sure every window was locked and every
room was clear. She couldn't afford to be snuck up on right
now. She was still waiting for that monster to come get her at
any moment.

Finally, after she was sure she was home alone, she sank to
the floor in her bedroom and started sobbing. She brought her
knees up to her chest as if she could hold the pieces of her heart
in if she just hugged herself tight enough. She curled up and she
cried over the threats, the questions with the officers, and the
slow realization that Brad was mixed up in this.

Still, she couldn't believe he was a killer. Sure, Vanessa was
found in his hotel room. He had gone missing as well, which
made him look even guiltier. And now Kate was getting threatening texts after she had rejected him. There was plenty of evidence against him.

Kate knew him though. She knew him better than she knew
most people, and she just couldn't convince herself that he
would do this. She knew people could be sneaky and manipulative, but to this extent? There were no signs. It didn't make sense.

It just didn't fit. And though Kate knew she had to at least
be open to the possibility that he had done this to avoid being
blindsided, she also wanted to explore other options. She
wanted to believe that maybe he had been set up. Maybe someone else had killed Vanessa and…

That's where her thoughts stopped. Because if someone
else had killed Vanessa and set Brad up, it didn't look good for
Brad now. He was nowhere to be found. She couldn't help but
worry he might be dead or trapped now too.

There was still hope though. He was missing, not dead. She
just had to figure out what had truly happened. She had to clear
his name. She had to get to the bottom of this.

Kate decided that she absolutely had to talk to Daniel
Jenkins. He was the best suspect so far. He was the only murderer she knew who was living in town. They already knew he
could be dangerous. So, maybe he had grown a strange fixation

on her and was in turn jealous of Brad. Maybe he was responsible for all of it.

But didn't that mean she was giving in to the stigma against him? Didn't that mean she was hoping to blame this man for something he may not have ever been involved in? She wrestled with that in her mind, but she knew it couldn't be Brad. That wasn't right. She had to hope it was someone else.

She clung desperately to that hope as she called Victor that night and told him about what happened. He listened to her empathetically and supported her just as he always did.

"I'll come over right now," he offered. "We can have dinner together, watch a movie, do anything to get your mind off of things. You deserve some time to unwind and try to feel better."

"That would be nice," Kate said. "But I think I need some time by myself tonight for a little while if that's okay. We can get together once I've had time to process this more. I really would love to see you."

"I'd love to see you too," Victor replied. "But I respect your need for space right now, so of course, we can get together when you're ready. Just… promise me you'll stay safe in all of this. Whoever is behind this seems to have a connection to you, and I don't want to see anything bad happen to you. You're so important to me, Kate. I want you to be protected always."

"I will stay safe," she promised. "I'll do my best. I've learned a lot about self-defense, so someone wouldn't have it easy if they attacked me. I have pepper spray."

"You do seem like a fighter," Victor chuckled. "I wouldn't want to go up against you."

Though Kate still was nervous. Vanessa and Amanda had been strong as well. They still hadn't been able to protect themselves. So, could she really say for certain that she would be able to keep herself safe?

She wasn't super convinced of it. She liked to think she'd be able to protect herself, but she didn't feel totally confident that she'd be okay. She was still worried about talking to Daniel.

Yet she knew she had to work to clear Brad's name if he was innocent. He would do the same for her. So, she got off the phone with Victor to call it an early night in preparation for throwing herself right into danger.

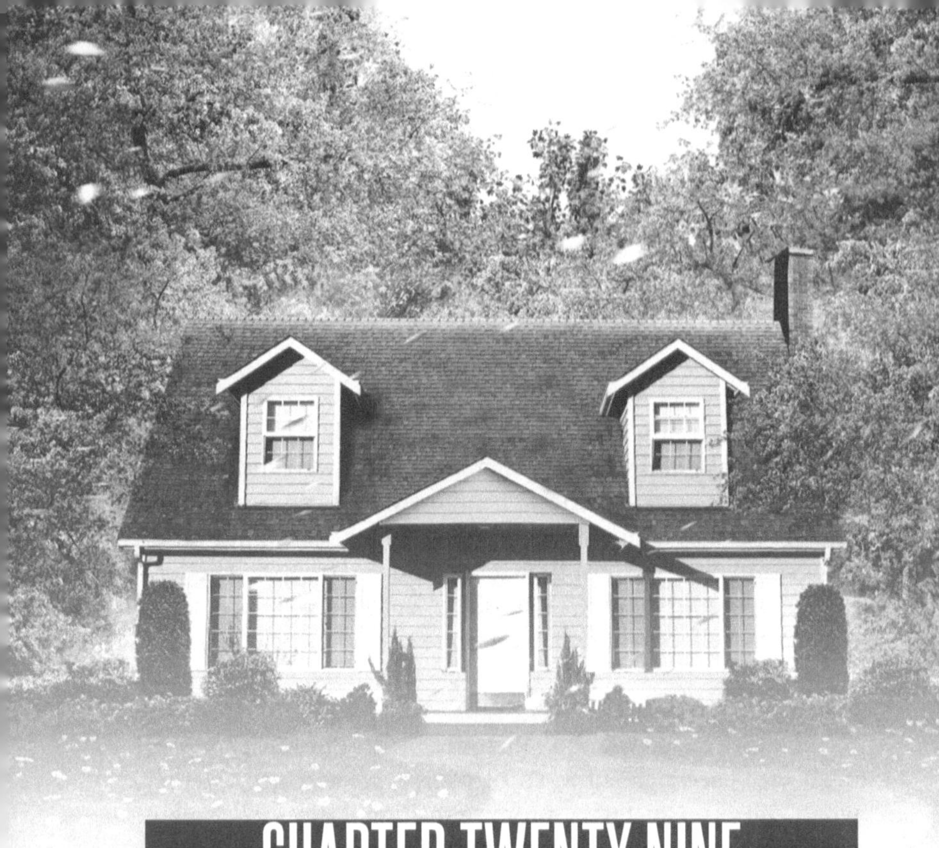

CHAPTER TWENTY-NINE

THOUGH SHE KNEW SHE HAD TO DO IT, KATE second-guessed her decision multiple times the next day. She was more scared of Daniel than ever, and she questioned her ability to even get answers. If he was the killer, it wasn't like he was going to flat-out admit it to her. Visiting him might even make him angrier. It might make the target on her back even bigger.

Still, she wasn't sure what else to do. So, she forced herself to get in the car and drove over to his apartment, hoping that she wasn't putting herself in danger for no reason.

The building was modest but still nicer than Kate expected. She wasn't sure how a murderer who certainly wouldn't be able to get a job to afford a place on his own could end up in an apartment like that. Was he finding other ways to make money?

She couldn't recall if the women who had been killed were robbed too.

It made her even more nervous as she walked up to the building and realized she had a problem. To even be able to see Daniel, he had to buzz her in when he had no real reason to want to talk to her again. It might even be more suspicious if he allowed her in. It could be a trap.

She kept her hands on the pepper spray she brought with her. Her gun was in her purse as well—just in case—but she still didn't think she could use it. She still wasn't sure that she had enough protection.

In a surge of strength, she buzzed the buzzer for his door and waited for a reply. He didn't unlock the door, so she tried again, this time deciding to speak into the speaker.

"Hi, Daniel," she started. "It's me, Kate. I was hoping you'd have time to talk to me again."

The lock clicked open, but there was still no response from Daniel. She hesitated. Though this was what she wanted, she was still terrified. And she realized something very important in that moment: as much as she missed Tyler, she no longer wanted to die. Not doing anything seemed like just as big of a risk, though, so she took the chance and walked inside.

Walking down the hallway was a struggle. She second-guessed herself with each step she took toward his door. But her determination drove her forward, and suddenly she was at his door. She knocked on it, and moments later, there he was. Daniel greeted her with a smile that was so friendly it was off-putting.

"Kate Larose," he said simply. "I've been thinking about you. How's your book coming along?"

The way he said it made her shiver, but she nodded. "It's in progress," she said.

"That's great. You know, I'm surprised to see you again," he said. "But our last conversation was so pleasant, so it's a nice surprise. Please, do come in."

Daniel stepped back and allowed Kate into an apartment that was nicer than she was expecting. It was tastefully decorated with colorful décor in shades of green, blue, and gray with pops of yellow mixed in and bits of gold and silver. Everything was clean and tidy and looked surprisingly mature. She'd been expecting a bachelor pad, but this was much nicer.

"Welcome to my home," he said. As he turned, he smiled again. "You look surprised."

Kate shrugged, deciding to opt with honesty that she hoped he would be responsive to. "I just assumed it might be difficult to gain employment after everything. It seems like it would be difficult to afford this apartment."

"Impossible," Daniel agreed. "No one is going to hire me. My grandparents were kind enough to pay for this place. My grandmother decorated it. I think they feel guilty for what happened. Or embarrassed. Or both. It's enough for their grandson to be a murderer, let alone homeless. And no one wanted me to live with them so, it's easier to just stow me away somewhere and not have to think about it. I'm not complaining though. Would you like something to drink or eat?"

"No, thank you," Kate replied. The last thing she wanted to do was to be drugged or something while she was in his apartment. "I just wanted to have a quick conversation with you. Catch up with how you're doing since you were released. I'm sure it hasn't been easy to get adjusted."

"That's for sure," he admitted. "There's a huge difference being in the real world compared to being in a mental institution. And what's normal shifts so easily that being in the institution became my normal for a long time. It's real life that's difficult for me to face now, but it's worth it. How about we have a seat? My brand-new couch is the most comfortable thing my grandmother picked out."

Kate was a little unsure about going even farther into Daniel's apartment. The farther away she was from the door, the less safe she felt. But she had committed to having a conversation with him, and that came with some risks that she couldn't escape.

So, she agreed and followed him into the living room. The couch really was comfortable, and she admired his grandmother's taste in picking furniture out. However, she wasn't sure what she thought about a murderer living in such luxury. It was sure to be a controversial topic she planned on putting in her book … if she got out alive, of course.

"It certainly is cozy," Kate agreed as she sat across from Daniel. She'd brought her notebook and pen, so she made a show of taking notes for their conversation, even though her real purpose was very different. "It must be nice to have these comforts you didn't have at the institution. The adjustment must be easier than it was compared to getting used to the hospital."

"To some extent, yes. Of course, I'd never choose to go back. I plan on staying well away from that. Now that I'm properly treated, I'll never commit a crime again. But it's weird because I still feel like I can't leave my apartment. I'm worried I'll be recognized as a murderer and be attacked. I'm much less safe out here than I was in there. And I guess I deserve it, but it's not easy. There's more fear that comes with being released."

"I can imagine. Speaking of leaving, though, I'm curious as to why you chose to live in this area. It might be easier for you if you were surrounded by family. But instead, you chose a town that's closer to the facility than your family. That seems like an odd choice to me. Is there anything in particular that influenced your choice?"

Daniel smiled in an unsettling way that made Kate worry that he saw right through her. How would he react if he knew she was there because she suspected him of murder? It certainly would make things more complicated and dangerous.

"It does seem to be an odd choice," Daniel admitted. "I can see why someone on the outside would be caught off-guard with that decision. But when you look at it, it makes perfect sense.

"The main reason is I'd be easily recognized back in my hometown. People know me—they know what I've done. If I dared do something as simple as go to the store, I'd be attacked immediately. Her family and friends are there. They want revenge. I'd end up dead before the year's end. I could never start over there.

"Here, it's less of a worry. The people here don't know as much about my crime, and they are less likely to recognize me since the case wasn't super publicized in this area. I'm planning on dying my hair, getting glasses, doing small things to obscure my true identity. Here, that should be enough.

"Plus, it's a lovely area. I love the ocean, and it's soothing being so close to it while also being surrounded by trees that make me feel protected. Juniper Bay is a little closer to the facility, which is how I found out about it. But it's also far enough away to give me some distance from those old memories. It's the perfect place really."

He had her there. The explanation made sense. Him living there didn't necessarily mean it had anything to do with her. But he still wasn't in the clear. Kate just wasn't sure how to go about getting the other answers. How could she find out the truth without flat-out accusing him of murder?

"Have you been able to enjoy nature a lot since you've been here?" she asked. "I know I have. There's this particular running trail I'm fond of. Maybe you've heard of it. It's by a small park and follows a creek."

"The one that branches off from the park where the young woman got murdered," Daniel replied with a grin. "I suppose you think you're being clever, don't you? Asking these simple, friendly questions in order to get to the answers you're truly seeking. So discreet."

Kate started fidgeting as she realized she wasn't being as discreet as she needed to be. He was on to her, that much was obvious. It was dangerous. Suddenly, she was in the worst position, and her mind raced trying to figure a way out of it.

"You think just because I murdered someone before, I might do it again. And since I moved to the area where these women were killed, I'm the natural suspect. Even though you seemed to really listen to me when we talked, empathize with me, you still see me as a monster. You still think I'm dangerous."

"That's not true," Kate insisted. "I don't see you as a monster. I know you made a mistake due to your mental illness. But that's been treated. You've clearly improved. You're no longer dangerous."

"Oh really?" he asked. "That's what you think?"

Kate nodded, but she could already tell her expression was giving everything away. He slowly leaned down to Kate's purse. Her heart thudded in anticipation. She wanted to stop him, to fight him. But she worried fighting would only make things worse. He was closer to her purse than she was. He would be able to grab the gun before she could. And suddenly, with her whole heart, she regretted bringing it. What was supposed to keep her safe was now putting her in danger.

"If you really thought that, then why would you bring a gun to my house?" he asked, pulling the gun out of her purse.

Kate froze as she scrambled for an answer. "I always carry a gun with me. Especially after the murders. I don't want to be next. It's nothing personal against you."

"I'm not sure I believe that," he mused as he held the gun in his hands. He examined it as if it were something fascinating to him, inspecting it idly. He could shoot her at any moment.

Then, he looked straight at her. He pointed the gun at her. "I believe that even in this moment, you're scared I'll shoot you. Be honest. You've already lied to me so much, and I don't appreciate it. You're terrified of me."

Kate's eyes stayed glued to the gun. "You do have a gun pointed at me," she answered. "I'd be scared of anyone pointing a gun at me."

"That's fair." He shrugged and moved the gun away from her. "Are you scared now?"

Their eyes stayed locked and Kate suspected that he could tell when she was lying. He was far too perceptive.

"Yes," she admitted. "You still have a gun in your hands. Who wouldn't be scared?"

"And if I put it down, are you going to come after me? Will you try to shoot me or leave? Will you tell anyone about this?"

"I couldn't shoot you," Kate admitted, though she hated how true that was. Even if Daniel was threatening her life, she knew she couldn't shoot him. She wasn't strong enough to bring herself to do it. "I don't know why I even brought the gun. I have no intentions of harming you. I'm not going to leave or tell anyone about our conversation. I really do just want to talk to you."

Daniel looked at her with a scrutinizing gaze, and Kate hoped with her whole heart that he could see the truth of her words in her eyes. She suspected that if she couldn't convince him, things were going to end very badly for her. And he was unstable enough that it was very possible that she couldn't convince him.

"Okay," he finally said. "I'll put the gun down. But don't underestimate me. I will stop you if you try to kill me. By any means possible. I'd rather be locked up in jail than dead. I want to live."

"So do I."

Daniel seemed to respect her for that. He finally returned the gun to her purse and pushed it away from himself. Finally, she was able to breathe again, but she was starting to realize maybe she had underestimated Daniel. Maybe she was in over her head. She hadn't quite realized all she had gotten into as Allison's warnings rang through her brain.

He was dangerous. This was dangerous. She should've never come here, but it wasn't like she could up and leave now. She had to stay through this. She had to show she trusted him. She had to see this through.

"So, what's the real reason you're here?" Daniel asked. "Remember that I only want the truth. I won't tolerate anything less than that."

"I'll be honest," Kate promised. "I'm here because of the recent murders. Though I will say that in talking to you before, I truly did believe you. You didn't seem dangerous. I wasn't worried upon leaving you that you'd do something awful. You seemed to have changed. I went into that with a fully open mind."

"So, what changed to make you think I would do this now?" Daniel asked, looking truly curious. "If you thought I had changed, why was I the first person you thought of when there were murders in town?"

"I guess because I can't think of anyone else who would've done it," Kate admitted. "You're the only murderer I know."

"Why do you think it's someone you would know? That's what's really got me curious. Why would you assume that this person is tied to you?"

Now Kate was getting increasingly uncomfortable and uncertain. She wasn't sure how much she should share with Daniel—how much was safe to share with him. If he was her stalker, though, he would already know the answer. If he wasn't, then it was safe to tell him.

"Because I think I'm being targeted by the same person who killed them," she finally said. "Someone has been stalking me lately. I knew both of the women who were murdered. I don't know for sure that these things are related or that the killer is tied to me, but… I think they also framed my friend."

Daniel smiled as he shook his head. "So, that's what this is about. It appears that your friend did this, and you can't face it, so you're trying to blame someone else for it. I can see why you'd feel that way. It is difficult to accept that someone we know would be capable of such things. Speaking from experience, though, it can happen. I'm sure this may be difficult for you to believe, but the people in my life never thought I'd be capable of murder either. They were shocked when it happened. People are surprising in the worst way sometimes."

Kate internalized this as she questioned herself. Was she simply in denial about Brad? Was this all about her refusal to accept this?

"Well, there's this," Daniel replied, lifting his pant leg up to reveal an ankle monitor. "Do you think you're really the only one who thought perhaps the local murderer was behind this? Of course not. The police already talked to me, and the ankle monitor proved I couldn't have done it. They were able to track exactly where I was when it happened, which was here, of course. I rarely leave."

Kate felt silly at that. Of course, Daniel was already a suspect. Of course, he would pop up on the detectives' radar, and they could investigate more thoroughly than she could.

"Plus, there's the proof on my laptop," Daniel noted. "And my sleeping app. My laptop shows that I was using it during the times that the women were murdered and asleep shortly after. I'm sure it'll prove I couldn't be stalking you if you'd like to take a look at it. I was probably here during the times you were being watched."

She didn't want to admit to Daniel that she was still suspicious of him, but she did want that information. The police didn't know about her stalker. They wouldn't have investigated that so thoroughly. She had to know for herself if it was true.

So, she allowed Daniel to show her the information. He was on his laptop a lot and on his home network, which ruled him out for many of the times she felt like she was being watched and when the stalking incidents happened.

"Not to mention, if I was seen at your house, you would be contacted," Daniel concluded after he had shown her all of the information. "Those keeping track of me would be suspicious if they spotted your location with the information taken from my ankle monitor, and they would check up on it. I can't do anything without them analyzing it. I'm sorry you're having to go through this, but I don't know who your stalker is, and it certainly isn't me."

Facing all of this information meant that Kate had to believe him. There was no way he could be the stalker or the murderer. He was right. With investigators keeping such a close eye on him, they would have noticed his activity, and he would have been in trouble for it.

"I'm sorry," she said, looking him straight in the eyes so she couldn't shirk away from this. "I shouldn't have assumed it was you just because of your past. I don't want you to think that I'm oblivious to the mental health component in all of this. I know you've worked through your struggles. I do believe you. I believe in your ability to change."

"It's okay," Daniel replied. "Truly. It hurts to know that I'm not widely trusted and that I will be the first suspect when something like this comes up, but I also know that it's for good reason. I killed someone. I have to accept that. It's the biggest regret of my life. I killed someone. I can never take that back. I have to deal with the consequences for the rest of my life, including being suspected in horrible things like this. And I deserve it.

"But I hope you do fully accept now that I didn't have anything to do with it. I am sorry you're going through this, but it's not me. I would suggest at least being careful, though, because it's not me. Which makes it more dangerous because it sounds like you have no idea who else it could be."

Daniel was right about that. Kate was rather disappointed that Daniel wasn't her stalker. Sure, that meant she was safe while she was in his house. But that also meant she didn't know who might be doing this. She didn't know where else to look.

As she left Daniel's house, her mind went back to Brad. Could he really be the one behind all of this? He had mentioned coming to the area recently, and Vanessa's body was found in his hotel room. Plus, he admitted he had feelings for Kate. Did that lead him to stalking her? Was he now furious because she rejected him?

Kate wasn't sure what to believe as she drove away, but she felt more afraid and vulnerable than ever.

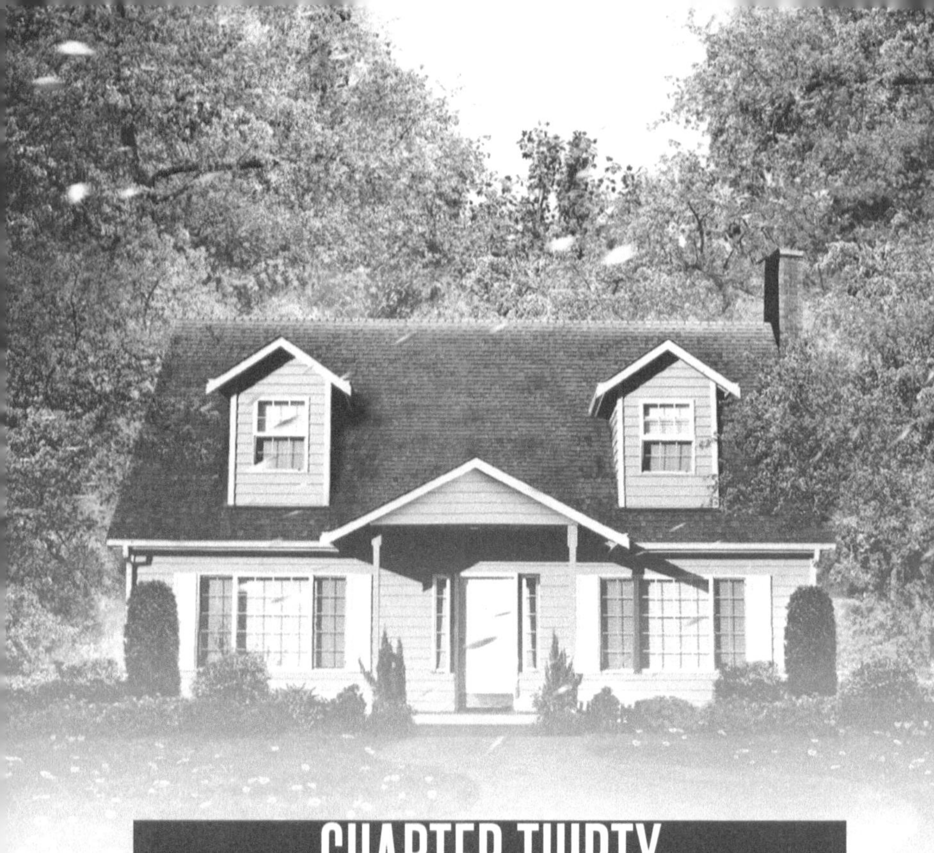

CHAPTER THIRTY

As Kate drove home, thoughts of Brad flooded her mind. She still couldn't completely believe it. She didn't want to. Yet she couldn't turn away from the proof that was staring straight at her.

This only got worse as she drove up to her house and saw red paint all over her front door. She stayed in her car, staring at the door that was wide open, terrified of what might be waiting inside. Finally, she called the police, knowing it was well past time to do so.

Kate waited in her car with the doors locked as her heart beat loudly in her chest. It had to be Brad. She couldn't ignore it any longer. She had rejected Brad, and now he was turning against her and doing these horrible things to scare her. He was responsible for this. He killed Vanessa and Amanda. She had been blinded this whole time to his true intentions.

As she waited for the police, she called Victor. She found that she couldn't stand being alone in this. It was all too much. She needed the help of a friend to process it. She quickly told him what happened, her hands shaking as she did so.

"I'll be right over," he promised.

"You don't need to do that," she assured him. "The police are coming. I'll be okay."

"But they can't give you the kind of moral support a friend can," Victor reminded her. "It's no problem at all. I'm coming over."

The police showed up before Victor did, which was a little disappointing to Kate despite her protests that he didn't need to come at all. She longed for his presence as she went through this without him. She got out of her car and approached them, still grateful to be with people she could feel safe around.

"We're going to need you to stay outside the house," Officer Maddison warned her in a gentle tone. She had introduced herself in a kind way that made Kate trust her, assured this was a safe place. Her gray eyes were like cozy, rainy days, and she had blonde hair that stayed perfectly in place. "I'll stay out here with you while Officer Bradley and Officer McKinney check out your house."

"Thank you," Kate replied, glad that this was finally out of her hands. She hoped things might actually change with the help of professionals.

"It's no problem at all. While you're waiting, would you mind telling me what's been going on lately? Is this the first time you've had trouble like this?"

Kate decided that now was the time to open up about everything. This showed it clearly wasn't all in her mind. She *did* have a stalker, and she wanted the officers to know all about it so they could catch him.

When the house was cleared and they knew for sure no one was inside, they moved inside the house where Kate continued to talk as Victor quietly joined them and offered his support by sitting by her side.

"And you locked the door?" the officer asked.

"Every time. I double-check it. Sometimes triple-check it. There are no other keys than what I keep on my person at all times either."

She explained all the events that had happened: the flowers on her table, the random times it seemed things were out of place, and all the other times she'd been sure someone had been watching her.

"That all sounds terrifying," Officer Maddison admitted once Kate was done speaking. "You must've been worried for quite some time now. I really wish you would've come to us sooner. That's what we're here for. We're here to help."

"I wish I would've as well," Kate replied. "It's just tough to know what's real and what's not in such a crazy situation."

"I understand that," Maddison said. "And right now, all that really matters is you did come to us. We're going to help you feel safe again. We're going to catch whomever did this. All of Juniper Bay has been turned upside down since that first young woman was found murdered, but we're going to get to the bottom of this. We will make sense of all of this. We will make sure Brad is caught and punished."

Kate thanked the officers many times for their reassurance. She believed they would do the best they could, though she couldn't help but worry if their best was good enough. This stalker seemed determined to get to her. So, would she be the next woman who was murdered?

This fear grew even stronger as the officers left the house and it was just Victor and her in her house. She worried about what might happen once he left too. She was terrified that the stalker would come back and the red paint might be blood this time.

"I'm so sorry for all you've been through," Victor said, giving her a long hug that made her feel a little better. "That's so awful. You've been tormented, and you don't deserve it. How about you come to my place and spend the night in the guest room? It'll give you a safe place and hopefully make you feel better about all of this. You can come back home in the morning."

Kate hesitated. She didn't want to be a burden and intrude on his life or anything. Yet she also couldn't imagine staying here after everything that had happened. The last thing she wanted was to be alone in her house that night.

"That would be wonderful," she agreed. "Thank you so much for the offer. Thank you so much for being here for me."

"Anytime," he promised her. "I'll always be here when you need me no matter what. You never have to be alone because you always have a friend in me."

Kate felt even more assured knowing she didn't have to face this on her own—knowing she always had backup. She still missed Tyler more than ever during this time, but she was grateful for Victor's presence in her life and his unwavering support.

"You know, this all means so much to me," Kate said as she followed Victor into his house. "Your friendship means so much to me."

"And your friendship means so much to me too," Victor assured her. "You're special to me, Kate. So, it makes me feel good, useful, and just all around happy whenever I get to help you. It really isn't a problem or any type of inconvenience at all. How about I make you some tea to help calm your nerves, and then we can unwind from all of this?"

"That would be lovely," she replied.

She joined him in the kitchen and started talking about her feelings more as he made her tea. Once it was finished, he handed her the warm cup, and she sipped it. Something about that simple act made her guard slip a little as the reality of it all hit her hard.

"I just don't know what to do," she said, as she looked up at Victor, who was standing abnormally close to her. "I'm just so scared all the time, and I don't want to be. I want to feel better. I want to feel freer. I want to feel safe again."

"I know," he said. "I want that for you, too, and I'm so sorry you're going through all of this. But this will get figured out. Life will get easier."

She nodded, but before she could stop them, the tears started falling. She was surprised that they came during this time when she felt safest, but the safety allowed her to experience those emotions. So, in that moment, they refused to be held back.

Kate started shaking as she cried with Victor there to gather her in his arms. He held her close, and she felt safe, comforted, and not so alone. As her tears subsided, he kissed her forehead in a gesture so sweet it warmed Kate's heart.

She looked up at him and his beautiful eyes, his kind smile, and that handsome face that had grown to be so familiar to her. "Thank you," she whispered. "For everything. I…"

In that moment, she was gripped by a strange feeling. She thought back to all the dreams she'd had of Victor, of the huge role he was now playing in her life. She thought about how long it had been since she had been able to bring someone close to her… how much she missed having someone physically with her.

Then, before she could think about it any longer, she reached up and kissed him. His lips were warm and soft against hers, just like they were in her dreams. And for a moment, he froze. She worried she was crossing boundaries. Maybe he didn't want her in the way she wanted him. Maybe she had misread the whole situation.

Then, he kissed her back. His lips moved against hers, and it was even better than in her dreams because this time she wasn't in some foggy haze. Her mind was clear and willing. She knew she wasn't sleeping. This was real, and though the guilt was still there, Kate wanted him.

Kate's hands slipped around Victor's neck as his arms wrapped around her waist. The kiss grew more passionate, and Kate could feel the direction these touches were going in. She worried for a moment that it was too soon. The guilt remained, reminding her of Tyler, of her vows, of the fact that she still loved her husband.

By now, though, Kate was learning to move on. She realized she could still love Tyler while being with someone else. Moving on didn't mean she didn't care about him. It simply meant that he was gone and she had to find a way to live a fulfilling life without him. She hoped that's what he would want for her as it was what she would want for him.

So, she gave in to her urges as she allowed herself to explore Victor's body and allowed his touch to wander over hers. She succumbed to her desires, knowing very well this wasn't a dream. This was real life, and she wanted him. She wanted to move on.

Passion swirled around them and consumed them, and before they knew it, they were lost in a tumbling mess of arms and legs and heads and kisses and emotion.

When it was done, they lay in his bed with her head on his chest as the reality of the situation set in. She couldn't believe what she had done. There were no regrets.

"I want more than just this," Victor whispered into the darkness. "Though that was an incredible experience, I want more than just a hookup. I have feelings for you, Kate. Real, strong, feelings. I'll understand if you don't feel the same way, but…"

"I do," Kate interrupted him. "I have feelings for you, too, and I also want this to be more than a hookup. I want to explore where this might go. I want to be with you."

Those words were even more difficult to say than hooking up with him had been. It was crossing the line from animalistic, base desires—something that didn't have to mean as much—to admitting she wanted a partner. She wanted to move on. She wanted to be with Victor.

They were scary, vulnerable, confusing words. Yet she realized as she said them just how much she meant them. This was what she wanted. She wasn't sure if that made her a bad person or not, but it was how she felt, and she couldn't easily shy away from that.

"I want to be with you too," he assured her, easing over some of the fear and tension. "I really do, Kate. I want to be with you."

They snuggled together and fell asleep peacefully in each other's arms. Despite all of the crazy things going on, Kate felt happy. She felt safe, and for the first time in a long time, she felt like things might really be okay.

CHAPTER THIRTY-ONE

KATE WOKE UP THE NEXT MORNING WONDERING IF HER conversation with Victor had all been a dream like it was before. But when she turned over, he was still there. They were still naked in his bed. This wasn't a dream. This was her reality now.

She still was uncertain about this reality though. Despite what he told her, she wondered if this was just a hookup for him and if he had been saying just what she wanted to hear. She was worried this might affect the close bond they had. She questioned herself and if she should've gone through with it.

But when Victor woke up, all those fears were dashed. He kissed her, held her, and made her feel much better. They cuddled the morning away before he got up to make them breakfast. As he cooked, Kate helped him and caught herself staring at him. She just wanted to convince herself he was here to stay.

She wanted to appreciate the man she had connected with during this crazy, turbulent time she still had difficulty making sense of.

Luckily, she had plenty of time to come to terms with what was growing between them, because Victor didn't turn away after the hookup. Instead, it brought them closer. Once they had admitted to their feelings, Kate and Victor found it hard to hold back. So, they dove right into a relationship that was loving, passionate, and fulfilling for both of them.

They started texting more often, seeing each other frequently, and spending time together almost every day. They often spent the night at each other's houses. And though they both knew they were taking things faster than usual and becoming super close, they wanted it. They had waited a while to move their friendship to the next level, and now they were ready to fully allow themselves to feel and experience every bit of it.

However, things weren't perfect in Kate's life yet either. She still received random, threatening text messages. Strange things still happened. It seemed her stalker hadn't gone away, and Kate was increasingly worried about it. Each time she received a threatening text, she forwarded it directly to the police and let them know each time she felt something was amiss.

Police officers started patrolling around her house more, convinced that Brad was the killer and stalker. They thought maybe by sticking to her, they might be able to find him. But as soon as they started doing this, the stalking incidents ceased. It drove him away from the house and out of her life. Still, she worried.

"I do wonder if he'll ever come back," Kate said, as she and Victor worked in her garden, gathering the last of the harvest before winter set in.

It was a familiar conversation between them. Kate tried not to let Brad's disappearance take up too much of her life. But she couldn't help that it still remained on her mind sometimes. She couldn't seem to quite shake it.

"He has left you alone for quite some time now," Victor reminded her. "I think he knows that coming after you will only lead the police to him. I can't imagine that he'll want to get any closer."

"Maybe you're right," Kate replied. "I guess I just... I do wonder if Brad is truly the person behind all of this. It still doesn't seem like him. I still can't wrap my mind around it. There's got to be some sort of explanation... which would mean I'm being stalked by someone I don't know. That being-lost-in-the-dark feeling is unsettling."

"I mean, you thought you knew him for so long. Sometimes people are really good at hiding their true intentions. Monsters lurk all around us. It's possible you just didn't see the kind of person Brad was until it was too late. He could've been fooling you this whole time."

"I guess. I don't like to think about it, but I suppose that is a possibility."

"Either way, I'll do my best to keep you safe. As long as you're surrounded by people, he'll be less likely to strike than if you're alone."

Kate was well aware of that fact. For a moment she wondered if that was part of the reason she spent so much time with Victor. She did feel safer with him around. She wondered if they would've gotten just as close if it weren't for all of this.

Before she could think of the implications of that for much longer, she was interrupted by a phone call. She answered it quickly, her stomach twisting at the voice on the other end of the line.

"We wanted to call to give you the heads up before you could hear about it through the town gossip or on the news," Officer Maddison said after exchanging the normal greetings. "Brad has been found."

"He has?" Kate asked, hardly able to voice the words as her whole body flushed in chills and panic. It was a relief, sort of. Still, she worried. "Where is he? Is he okay?"

Kate surprised herself by asking that. After all he had done, she knew she shouldn't care if he was okay. But unfortunately, she still did. Part of her still thought he could be innocent.

"He's not okay, but you will be safe from him," Officer Maddison replied. "We found his body in the creek by the running trail near your house. He had a gun shot to his head. We think he committed suicide out of the guilt over what he did to Amanda, Vanessa, and you."

Kate's whole world crashed down at this. She still didn't want to believe that Brad was behind it, so knowing he was dead shook everything within her. She wanted him to be alive so he could give some sort of explanation. She wanted him to be proven not guilty. She wanted this to be some sort of sick nightmare.

"Thank you for telling me," she whispered.

At that, she hung up the phone without another word. She looked at Victor, who was looking at her with concern.

"He's dead," she said. "Brad is dead."

Then, she fell to her knees on the soft ground. She curled up into herself as she cried for Amanda, Vanessa, and Brad. She sobbed as she thought of the friend she lost, the friend who wasn't who he said he was.

After all the years they'd spent together, she still couldn't believe he betrayed her like this and killed those innocent women. She had never seen it in him. And now it felt like their whole friendship was a lie. It felt like her life was ruined.

"I'm so sorry," Victor said as he wrapped her in a hug. "I can't imagine how tough this is. I'm sorry."

He let her cry into his chest for a little while, and she was grateful for it.

"Hey, think of it this way," he offered gently. "You're safe now. No one is going to come after you. You never have to be afraid again. You're safe now. I'm here. And you're safe. And I love you. I love you so much. I'll do anything to make you happy again."

At that, Kate's crying subsided for a moment. They had never told each other they loved each other before. But in this pain, where everything else was unbearable, she looked at Victor and realized the truth.

"Thank you," she said between tears. "I love you too."

They held each other even tighter as they tried to make sense of the grief and horror Brad had left behind.

The next day, Kate ran along the running trail before going to see Victor. For some strange reason, she wanted to be near the spot where Brad had been found. She wanted to feel connected to him one last time. She needed to say her goodbyes.

Her chest tightened as she kept running along the creek, wondering where exactly he had been found. Then, she came across the yellow caution tape marking off the area. Though the officers weren't there anymore, the space was still blocked off. It was still a horrible reminder of the awful things that had taken place there.

Kate slowed as she approached it, then stopped completely. She thought she was going to be sick as she looked at the blood-soaked ground, knowing this was a piece of Brad that was still there. Grief gripped her as all the pieces of their memories dug into her fragile heart.

"Why did you do this?" she asked as she stood in front of the crime scene. The tears were streaming down her face, but she angrily wiped them away. "Why did you kill them? Why did you stalk me? Why did you kill yourself? It didn't have to be like this. What about your son? Didn't you ever think of how devasting this would be for him?"

The wind whispered his confession, but Kate didn't want to hear it. She blocked her ears off to any idea of why he might do this. She didn't want to think of any signs she might have missed. She didn't want to entertain any thought that this could be real.

Even as she was denying it, though, the truth hit her hard. This *was* real. Brad had done this. There was proof he had. He was a monster. She hadn't seen it before all of this, but her friend was a terrible person.

As she stood there, it started to rain. It felt like the sky was crying along with her, so she waited a moment longer before running back to her car so she could find refuge in Victor's arms.

As she stepped into Victor's house, he welcomed her with open arms despite the fact that she was soaked. He held her close, and it made her feel a little better. Though nothing could fully heal her, his embrace eased her heart a little.

"I'm so sorry this has been so tough on you," he said as they parted. "I had an idea."

"What kind of idea?" she smiled, still not able to let it reach her eyes.

"A good one," he chuckled. "Why don't I go to the store and get us some ice cream while you get changed into one of my shirts. We'll put your clothes in the dryer and snuggle up with a movie. Your choice, of course."

"You're so good to me," Kate said, giving him a kiss. "Too good to me. I don't deserve it."

"You deserve everything," he assured her. "Everything the world has to offer. I'll always try the best I can to make you happy."

With that, he kissed her and left to get their ice cream. Kate watched him leave, then went to his room to grab a shirt. She stepped into his closet and breathed in his familiar scent which calmed her. She went through his shirts and found the comfiest, soft blue T-shirt.

Then, she realized her feet were freezing. She decided she needed a pair of socks to go along with it, so she started going through his drawers, unsure of where his socks were. Finally, she found them and searched to find the smallest pair. Suddenly, she paused.

Her hands caught something unexpected that she picked up. It was a photo—of *her*. She immediately recognized it and froze. It was of her trip to France with Tyler, a trip that happened four years ago.

Her mind whirred with the possibilities. Why would he have this? How did he get it? She hadn't known him for long enough for him to have it, and even if she had, it would be strange.

Panic set in at the thought that maybe something was wrong, though she wasn't exactly sure what that something was. Then, she tried to calm herself. She realized her emotions were heightened thanks to everything else that was going on lately. She had been stalked, had a friend who was a murderer, Brad had died, Tyler died. Perhaps there was a simple explanation for this silly photo. She couldn't project the worst possible motives onto Victor when so far, he hadn't shown any signs of doing anything wrong.

She didn't want her panic and suspicions to ruin something possibly good, so she grabbed the pair of socks and the shirt and changed, taking the photo with her. As she sat in the living room, she tried to think of how she might broach the topic. She didn't want to come off as accusatory or angry. Yet she did also want answers. She needed answers to ease her mind.

Before she could fully formulate a plan, the door opened. Victor came in with ice cream and pizza, smiling brightly as he brought the food over to the coffee table.

"I hope you're hungry," he announced. "I thought we might want something solid to eat along with the ice cream. We'll eat our emotions and hopefully feel a little better by the end of the night."

"That sounds perfect," Kate said with a smile. He went to the kitchen to put the ice cream in the freezer, and her demeanor instantly faltered the second he looked away. "First I have something to ask you about though."

"Oh?" Victor asked, coming to sit on the couch with her. "You know you can ask me anything. What's on your mind?"

Kate took a deep breath. She didn't like the thought of causing conflict between her and Victor, but she had to get answers. So, she took out the photo. She saw his face fall, showing that he clearly recognized it.

"I found this when I was looking for some socks to wear," she said. "Why would you have this? It was taken years ago."

Victor looked immensely uncomfortable as they sat in silence for a moment. Kate desperately hoped for any sort of explanation that would clarify this in a reasonable way. She wanted to be sure that Victor wasn't hiding anything. She needed him to be the hero he had always been.

"Well, I'll admit that it's mine," Victor said finally. "But it's not anything creepy. Or I mean, maybe it's a little creepy but it's nothing nefarious or anything. I just… I found it on social media."

"And you had it printed?" she pressed skeptically.

"I mean, I have a printer here. I was just curious about you after we first met. It was my way of getting to know you better. I honestly liked you a lot from the start. I was fascinated by you before I could even admit that to you. So, I did my research. I did a little internet stalking."

Kate's throat closed up at the word "stalking," but he held his palm out to try to calm her down.

"I know that sounds not… great, but I don't think that's that weird, is it? Lots of people research the person they're interested in. Social media stalking is a cliché, but it's a cliché because it happens all the time. It's embarrassing, but I was curious about you. I thought we had a connection even in that first encounter."

Kate softened a little at this because she'd felt the connection too. Even during their first encounter she'd felt drawn to him. She'd had those dreams about him, those intense fantasies—and those were things she'd never told him about either. How could she judge him for that when she didn't even want to tell him that she'd been aching for him for so long?

Knowing he felt something there sooner was a bit of a relief. It made her feel less crazy for feeling something that was shared between them rather than something she made up in her mind. Still, it didn't feel like it explained everything. Stalking someone on social media might be normal. Keeping a photo of them was a little strange.

"You printed out a picture to keep in your dresser though," she pointed out. "That's not exactly something everyone does."

"I guess not—not technically," he admitted. "But in a way we do. We have access to pictures so easily online. We can go and look at and relook at old photos whenever we want. I just really liked this one of you, and I didn't want to continue to stalk your social media. So, I printed it out as a reminder of you and kept it close as I got to know you.

"I had forgotten all about it by now, honestly. I stopped looking at it after a while since I knew it was a little strange and I could just see you in person. But I promise there are no ill intentions behind it. I just liked you. I was attracted to you. This was just how I dealt with it."

Kate considered his explanation. It was a little strange, but it made sense, and a picture was harmless. It was actually kind of cute that he was so interested in her so early, especially considering how early she had been fantasizing about him.

"It's okay," she assured him. "It caught me off-guard, but there's nothing that bad about it. I can't punish you for something so small and harmless. I was just curious. Now, let's dig into that pizza while it's still hot."

Victor smiled. "I hope you like pineapples."

"Love 'em," she replied.

"Somehow, I just knew it," he said. "I got the vibe from you and took a risk and, well... seems like it paid off."

"Oh, it's a vibe, is it?"

"Something like that."

At that, they curled up on the couch together, and Kate soon forgot about the photo as she leaned into Victor for comfort.

By the next day, Kate was feeling a lot better and had completely overlooked the incident with the photo. She knew she needed Victor now more than ever, so she didn't want to even begin to question him. She needed his security and safety for things to feel right.

With her mental health improving a bit, Kate used this time to go back home after breakfast that morning and spent the whole day working on her book. It had been difficult for her to focus; her head had been especially cloudy after Brad's body had been discovered. Writing was always so difficult to do when everything else in her life was erratic and crazy. But thanks to the comfort of Victor and her own inner strength, Kate was finally able to get back down to it and make progress with her writing.

About halfway through the day, she paused. She was writing a book about the dark side of mental illness. It reminded her that she had experienced her own brush with this recently regarding Brad.

Brad had suffered from mental illness for as long as she had known him, and she suspected this had been an extension of whatever suffering he'd experienced before meeting her as well. It made her wonder if his mental illness contributed to his actions. Did he have a story to tell as well? Was it her responsibility to put his story in the book alongside the others?

She was uncertain about that. Just thinking about Brad was painful. She couldn't imagine how tough writing about him would be. And despite how close they had been, she wasn't even sure that she knew the whole story. Surely a lot was missing if he was capable of murder. She wouldn't have guessed that he was capable of that, so maybe she couldn't portray an unbiased opinion of him.

Still, she decided to at least try writing some of it out, and she found it almost therapeutic to do so. It helped her process some of her thoughts and feelings and see where things might have gone wrong... though it was still difficult to believe he could do such things.

By that night, she was exhausted from the emotional toll of it all. Her energy had been completely zapped by having to invest so much of herself into her writing. All she wanted to do was make her tea and go to bed.

So, of course, as she reached into her cabinet and pulled out her usual tea, she found that she had drunk it all. Her tea was completely gone.

Kate checked the time. It was far too late to go to the store, so she decided to just make a warm drink of lemon and honey instead. She went around as she did every night and checked her doors and windows, double-checking that each of them was locked. Ever since Brad's death, she hadn't experienced anything weird, but now it was just a habit. And that was fine with her. She took sips of the lemon and honey water as she did so. It made her feel far less tired than normal, but she still forced herself in bed at the normal time. Since she had forgotten her sleeping pills, she fell into a much lighter than normal sleep.

This sleep wouldn't last long, though, because a couple of hours later, a noise awoke her. A noise coming from the closet.

CHAPTER THIRTY-TWO

I T TOOK KATE A MOMENT TO FULLY AWAKEN AS HER EYES fluttered open. She was certain she had to be dreaming, just like she had those strange dreams shortly after Tyler died. But she felt more awake than normal, clearer, less dreamlike.

Whatever was going on felt all too real and tangible. So, Kate kept still and quiet. She was certain she had heard something. But all that greeted her was silence.

She thought about getting up to check, but if it were just a dream, she'd feel silly. And if someone was in there, checking would be dangerous. So, she froze, unsure of what to do.

As she waited, something in the closet moved, she was sure of it. Then, slowly, the closet door opened. She panicked. Was she about to die?

She decided it very well could be her stalker who hadn't tried to harm her so far. She reasoned that he could simply be wandering through her house, so it would be best to pretend to be asleep and then call the police as soon as it was safe to do so.

Kate was betting her life on this, but she didn't think she had any other options, so she waited for the perfect moment. Then, she caught a glimpse of the intruder's face as he peered out of the closet.

She jumped to her feet in an instant. It was too strange to believe. But there he was.

"Victor?" she said.

He looked over at her like he was startled to see her. Then, his face smoothed over.

"Kate," he said in a soothing, calming voice as he approached her. "What are you doing up? Let's get you back to bed."

He tried to hug her, but she was in no mood for hugs. This was beyond strange. Why would he be in her house at this time of night? Why would he be in her closet?

"What are you doing here?" she asked in a demanding tone.

"You're just dreaming," he assured her. "Let's get you back in bed all cozy, and we can cuddle."

Kate thought about the haze she was normally in when she went to sleep lately, ever since she had moved into this house. And it worried her. In that haze, she suspected she would believe him. It would make sense to her that she was dreaming. She also had difficulty telling the difference between her dreams and reality. All the things she had shared with Victor in her dreams had felt so real.

Was that what was going on now? She questioned herself. Was she dreaming?

She looked at Victor and saw his features clearly. She saw how he was acting his normal, soothing self. But she knew something was wrong. She knew she wasn't dreaming.

"I'm awake," she said sternly. "I'm more clearly awake than I have been in a long time. And I want to know why you're trying to make me think I'm asleep. I want to know what you're doing in my house."

At that, Victor's demeanor changed yet again. Now, he looked startled and perplexed. It was as if he fully expected her to buy his story that she was sleeping. He didn't know how to deal with it now that he was being challenged about it.

Each moment was making Kate feel more uncertain about this whole thing. It was beyond strange and had moved into truly concerning territory. She couldn't imagine that he had good reason to be in her house. Even though she cared about him deeply, it was unsettling having him here. And his reaction to having been found out was even more disturbing. Why would he lie to her?

"I'm sorry," Victor said sheepishly. "I should've been honest with you when you first saw me. I just didn't want to come off as a creeper or anything. Which I know that's what this looks like. It looks like I'm one of those creepy guys being stalkerish in the middle of the night."

"It sure does," she snapped.

He nodded but seemed determined to apologize. "The truth is, you seemed so upset after what happened with Brad that I was worried about you. I couldn't sleep because I kept thinking about you being in this house alone, scared, sad, and vulnerable. I remember how dark you were directly after Tyler died, and I worried that darkness would come back in the wake of Brad's death.

"So, I decided to come over and just check on you. I just wanted to make sure you were okay and that nothing bad would happen to you. I didn't want to leave you alone during such a vulnerable time. Your door was unlocked, so I decided to come in and make sure you were sleeping peacefully."

It made sense to some extent, but it was still alarming to Kate. A deep part of her wanted to believe him. He meant so much to her. She didn't want to lose him now. Not over this. Not if he was genuinely worried about her and simply showed it a strange way.

It was still off-putting though. "But why were you in my closet?" she asked.

"Well, your door was unlocked," he reminded her. "And I thought that was strange and a bit dangerous. Who knows who might've come in. I know you're safer now that Brad is gone, but there could be other dangers. There's still that risk.

"So, I checked the rooms, including the closet, to make sure no one else had gotten inside. I can't imagine what I'd do if anything bad happened to you. I would never forgive myself for not doing more to keep you safe. That's all I'm trying to do. I'm trying to keep you safe."

Kate looked at Victor and saw a genuineness in his eyes. She felt that he did truly care about her. She truly cared about him. And she didn't want to break that connection that she had yet to find with anyone else.

"You should get some sleep," he said. "I know you've been on high alert lately. There's so much going on. You need your rest. I'll go sleep on the couch so it doesn't make you uncomfortable. We can discuss this more in the morning when we've both gotten some sleep and have clearer heads."

Kate hesitated. She wasn't sure that she was ready to let this go quite yet. But she did think it might be valuable to have some time away from Victor so she could process how she felt about this. She certainly wasn't comfortable enough to have him in her bed currently.

So, she didn't protest as he gave her one last look before leaving the room. Once he left, Kate felt more confused than ever and a little empty as she looked around the room and tried to process the fact that Victor had been in here and had given her strange excuses.

Because she hadn't left her door unlocked. She knew she hadn't.

As she came to terms with this, she thought about the random photo she had found in his dresser. Sure, she had moved past it by then, but it was still something that lingered in her mind. As she put the pieces together, she found herself getting a little paranoid.

"What if *he's* my stalker?" she whispered quiet enough so only she could hear it.

She tried to push the suspicion to the side. There was no way Victor was her stalker. He had always been so kind to her, so supportive, so there. She couldn't imagine him doing anything to harm or scare her.

Still, once it was in her brain, it was difficult to get out. His explanation still didn't sit right with her.

She glanced over at the closet as she debated this in her mind. She decided she'd check inside the closet to make sure nothing was disturbed and that he didn't leave anything in there. She was strict with herself and promised herself that if there were any signs that Victor's story wasn't true, she'd call the police on him even if she didn't want to. She'd do whatever it took to get to the bottom of this and keep herself safe, no matter what that meant for him... or for them.

Kate took a deep breath as she walked to the closet. She wasn't sure what she'd find, but she wasn't looking forward to it either. She didn't like being this suspicious. It felt all wrong. This whole thing felt wrong.

As she stepped into the closet, her body tensed. She imagined Victor in there watching her. It sent chills through her body. She started looking through things, glancing around and trying to find something that would suggest he had been lying.

But after a thorough search, she didn't find anything. It didn't look like Victor had been hanging out there at least, so she reasoned maybe he was telling the truth. Maybe he had just gone in there to check like he'd said. As strange as his story was, maybe he was just trying to protect her.

She moved to step out of the closet, feeling the relief that came with knowing she wasn't dating a bad person... until she stepped forward and saw Victor glaring at her.

CHAPTER THIRTY-THREE

Years ago…

“I KNOW YOU'RE CHEATING ON ME,” VICTOR SAID, HIS voice deep and low with frustration. “I've adored you all this time. I've quite literally been *obsessed* with you. I've done everything you've ever wanted, given you the world, and you cheated on me.”

“I don't know what you're talking about,” Evelyn replied, impatient with the same conversation they had over and over. “I would never cheat on you, Victor. You know that. I know you haven't had the best luck with women before, but we're married, and I take that very seriously. I would never hurt you like that.”

“Wouldn't you?”

"Please, let's talk about this calmly. Usually when you're suspicious of me cheating on you it's because some other insecurity has popped up. We've gone through this before. Usually it's because you're stressed, anxious, or not feeling like we've spent enough time together. Is that what this is about? Do you think we haven't spent enough time together lately?"

"That's not at all what this is about," Victor snapped. His anger was rising at her words. He didn't like her saying that this could be influenced by something else. He didn't like being accused of overreacting about something.

No. He knew she was cheating, and nothing she said could convince him otherwise. He knew her words were part of a clever ruse she had created and had been maintaining ever since they got together. That's all it was though. It was a mask to hide her true, awful nature.

"I know you're cheating on me with Cole," Victor said. "I've seen you together, acting close and whatnot. I know you went out to lunch with him yesterday afternoon."

At that, Victor got a reaction he wasn't expecting at all. Evelyn smiled. It was the most sickening smile Victor had ever seen, and he had to clench his fists to keep himself from lashing out.

How dare she smile when he was confronting her with something so awful? Was she really so heartless? Did she not care about him at all?

"Cole is my coworker," Evelyn reminded him. "Of course, I spend time with him. We have become friends as well. So, sometimes we take our lunch breaks together and go out to grab food. It's nothing you need to be worried about. I would tell you about this stuff more often if you didn't overreact like this."

"Overreact?" Now Victor was fuming. "I'm not overreacting! You're cheating on me! I know you are. I've been loyal to you, faithful to you, devoted to you. And you've betrayed me!"

"Victor, Cole is gay," Evelyn said patiently. "He would never be interested in me or any woman. Which doesn't matter anyway, because I wouldn't do that to you whether or not he was gay. I'm not that kind of person."

Victor blinked, stunned, and Evelyn sighed heavily. "I really need you to trust me more. I don't want to keep having these same fights with you. They're not healthy for us; they're just going to erode our relationship, which isn't healthy. I want to be with you and only you. No one else matters to me. I would never betray you … I promise."

Victor was soothed by this for a moment. If Cole was gay, that meant he didn't pose a threat to their relationship.

Then he thought about it a little more. Just because Evelyn said he was gay, doesn't mean he was. She could just be saying that to get him off her back. It could be another lie she was indulging in.

"I want to see proof," Victor decided with his arms crossed over his chest. "If he's gay, there must be a picture of him with a partner. Bring up his social media. I want to see the pictures."

Evelyn faltered at that, and Victor automatically knew she was lying. "I can't," she admitted. "Cole hasn't come out to his family yet, so there are no pictures of him with his boyfriend on social media. I've seen him plenty of times around the office, as he can be his true self around all of us, but …"

"So, it's a lie!" Victor insisted, raising his voice. "I know you're lying! Just tell me the truth. I can't stand this anymore, Evelyn, I really can't. I know you're having an affair!"

Then, Evelyn did the worst thing she could do. She had already lied to him, treated him with contempt, and accused him of overreacting. But then she rolled her eyes in such a petulant way that Victor saw red and couldn't regain control of his sight again.

"I can't do this anymore with you," Evelyn sighed. "I really can't keep doing this. It's draining, it's toxic, it's exhausting, and …"

Before Evelyn could say any more of those traitorous words, Victor's hands were around her throat. Evelyn's eyes widened in surprise. Victor had never gotten violent before. She never thought she was in danger when she was with him.

She tried to scream, but he just squeezed tighter.

"I hate you! I loved you so much, and you betrayed me!"

"Please," she croaked. "I can't breathe. I—I—"

Victor's grip tightened as the memories flooded over him. All the times Evelyn had lied to him, all the times she cheated on him. He knew she was unfaithful, unreliable, and never actually loved him. Not in the same way he loved her. This couldn't be forgiven.

He couldn't break his iron grip as she struggled in his hands. Her fingers clawed at him, but he didn't stop. He couldn't stop.

Until finally, Evelyn stopped moving. Victor removed his hands, and she fell the floor. He fell with her and sobbed, shocked and unable to fathom what he had just done.

It had been over a year since Evelyn died, and Victor still thought of her every day. Though she was gone, she remained in his mind. She remained part of his everyday life, and he wasn't sure he'd ever be able to escape her. His guilt haunted him, and he still had difficulty coming to terms with what he had done.

So, he threw himself into his work. He took on as many construction projects as possible. And the latest one was one he enjoyed, which made it more tolerable. It was a nice home that this guy Tyler was building for his wife. He thought the gesture was sweet enough to make all the hard work worth it. He knew that if he ever fell in love again, he would do something like this to give the woman of his dreams the house of her dreams.

He worked harder on this particular project than he normally would, knowing it was being built for a good cause. He stayed later, he put his heart and soul into it. And then, one day everything changed.

"This is my inspiration," Tyler said as he and Victor talked one day before going about their work. "She's beautiful, isn't she? And smart, kind, talented, passionate, loving. She's everything you could want in a woman. I'm lucky I get to call her my wife."

Victor nodded, unable to speak as he looked at Kate's picture. She was gorgeous, an angel having fallen to earth. And the way she smiled made it even better. The brightness of it, her friendliness. Everything about her was perfect. She had black hair and blue eyes… just like Evelyn.

She was perfect.

That day, he cursed Tyler for having this gorgeous work of art as his wife. He liked to imagine that if she had met him first, she would've chosen him instead. She would love him in the way she loved Tyler.

The feelings only grew stronger as he started to notice her showing up at the construction site to bring Tyler lunch, just say hi, and check out the house with him. Victor watched from a distance, too nervous to introduce himself. But she saw how friendly she was to the others, how kind and bright. She always brought this certain light with her when she visited, and the whole crew worked harder and happier in her presence. It was a feeling that remained even after she left.

Once Victor learned she was a writer, he went out and bought her book immediately. He read through it throughout the night, unable to stop to even sleep. And he fell in love with her work. She had a magical way of writing words that drew him into everything she was saying. He couldn't turn away from it. He couldn't turn away from her.

After he finished the book, he knew he had to get to her. He had to know her. He had to see her. He had to have her.

"You're creepy, you know that right?" he told himself as he walked onto the work site the next morning. "You're turning into a stalker. You're the kind of person others warn each other about."

Yet as he looked at the house, he was already imagining the work he could do if he could get his hands on it. As they were building, he reasoned he could find ways to incorporate secret hideaways and passages to get into the house. He could find a way where he could watch her, where he could see her from afar.

That had to be enough to soothe his obsession. He knew he could never be with her, not considering how devoted she was to her husband. He doubted she would ever leave him. But if he could watch her, that would be enough. If he could be near her, she could be safe and keep her life, keep her husband, while his strong desire to have her to himself would be soothed.

Or so he hoped.

After long days spent working on the house, Victor came back later at night to do his own work, designing creative ways to be able to get into the house. He spent much of his time figuring out how to be closer to her, how to ease this ache in his soul.

His exhaustion only made things worse though. It blurred his mind and fueled his obsession. Whenever he saw her with Tyler, it felt like he was being stabbed. Watching their hands intertwined together was torture. When they kissed, it was a heartbreaking death.

Finally, one day he couldn't take it any longer. He couldn't keep seeing them together—it felt like when Evelyn was cheating on him. He knew he had to do something. So, he went into Juniper Bay and walked. He kept walking as his mind ran rampant, wondering what he could do about this.

As he decided to dip into an ice cream parlor to eat away his emotions, he paused and saw something that destroyed him. There was Cole walking out with another man.

"It can't be," Victor whispered. "It can't be."

"Victor!" Cole said, as he spotted him. He looked at him with deep sympathy. "I didn't expect to see you here. How have you been? I know it's been tough ever since… well, how are you holding up?"

"It is tough," Victor admitted. "But I'm trying to move forward. I think Evelyn would want that. How have you been? What brings you all the way out here? Seems a bit far away from home."

"My boyfriend Dustin and I wanted to get away for the weekend," Cole explained. "I don't think the two of you have met, have you?"

"No," Victor croaked, his heart shattering as he held polite conversation with the proof that Evelyn had died for no reason.

When he went home that night, he stalked Kate on social media, convinced she was his salvation. If he could just be with her and treat her right, then he could make up for what he did to Evelyn. He could have the happily ever after he always imagined.

First, he had to get Tyler out of the way. He had to orchestrate a workplace accident. Sadly, a life might have to be lost for him to reach his dreams. He didn't want to hurt Kate, but there were no other options.

Once Tyler was out of the way, Victor was able to finish setting up the house so he could keep an eye on Kate. He installed cameras and secret entryways so he could always watch over her. Everything was just to protect her and keep her safe. He had caused her husband's death, but that was a necessary sacrifice. It was up to him now to take care of her, and this was the best way he could do that. He was being helpful.

Once she moved in, he was able to tamper with her tea so she would be sleepy and disoriented at night, making her pliable to his advances and giving him the opportunity to be with her in the way he wanted while making her believe it was all just a dream.

Having this contact with her helped him be patient and not come across too eager as he approached her. It allowed him to build a steady relationship with her and keep his obsession hidden.

Sure, it sounded creepy, but it was what she needed. It was what she deserved. Kate needed to be with a good guy like him, not some loser like Tyler who couldn't even provide for himself. He only did it to protect her. To make her dreams come true. Didn't she see that? Didn't she want this?

Now, as he looked down at her, his heart broke over the waste this had been. He thought they had something special. He thought they were soulmates, meant to be together forever. He thought he did everything right. He thought for sure this would work out perfectly.

But she didn't trust him. Even after all he had done for her. He saw it in her eyes. She was suspicious. She didn't trust him. She was going to leave him. He just couldn't let that happen.

CHAPTER THIRTY-FOUR

"**W**HATCHA UP TO?" VICTOR ASKED IN A SING-song tone that made Kate panic.

The person she saw in front of her wasn't the man she had grown to know. This guy looked intimidating, unpredictable, and dark. Even though she was in her own closet, she felt like she had just been caught doing something wrong.

"I had a nightmare," Kate replied, too scared to tell the truth. "It made my skin kind of sweaty and gross. So, I thought it might be good to get a change of pajamas is all."

"Weird, you don't look sweaty to me," Victor said. "Don't tell me you're lying to me, Kate. I would hate for you to lie to me. We're honest with each other, right?"

Kate searched his eyes for some hint of the man she had grown so fond of. Knowing Victor well enough, she suspected he'd be able to tell if she lied. Lying right now could be the worst thing.

"I just wanted to make sure everything is okay," Kate admitted. "I do believe you; it was just strange to find you in my closet. So, I was just checking. I didn't find anything, though, so it proved you were telling the truth. There's nothing nefarious going on."

"Of course, there isn't," Victor replied. He sighed. "I guess I do see where you're coming from though. It is strange, and I did lie. I'm sorry about that. Maybe we can just forget both of our lies and go to bed?"

Kate nodded, unable to speak. She wanted to know why he had come back into her room. She wanted to know the truth about him. She was smart enough to know that now wasn't the time to question him. She needed to get safely away from him first. She needed space to find a chance to leave.

Victor stepped aside so Kate could leave the closet, but she didn't want to leave the closet. She didn't want to walk past him because it made her feel nervous and uncertain.

With the way he looked at her, it made her think maybe this was some sort of test. If she left the closet, it would prove that she trusted him. Maybe he'd leave her alone. Maybe he'd let her go. She didn't have much choice, so she proceeded to walk past him… very slowly, and…

Before she could react, he lunged toward her, grabbing her roughly as Kate fought against him. She squirmed as she cried out, and he wrapped a rope around her wrists.

"What are you doing?" she demanded. "Let me go! This is insane!"

"You haven't seen insane yet," Victor snarled as he picked her up and threw her onto the bed. He used the ropes to tie her wrists up to the bed post, holding her securely in place despite how much she fought it.

As he was tying it, though, she remembered a trick she learned in her self-defense class to contort her body in different ways to make sure the rope was looser without him noticing it. It still wouldn't be easy to escape the binds, but she wanted to give herself a fighting chance. She knew she desperately needed some way to escape from this.

"You know, I really thought you were different," he said, as he stepped back and looked at her. "I thought you appreciated everything I did for you. I thought you saw the work I put in, and you loved me for it. I really thought I made the right decision when choosing to pursue you.

"I guess I was wrong again though. You're just like Evelyn. You pretended to care about me, pretended like you trusted me, pretended like you loved me. But it was all an illusion, wasn't it? You don't trust me at all. You don't care about me. And what's a relationship without trust and loyalty? You were just looking for proof that I did something wrong. You wanted to turn me in to the police."

Kate froze at his words as she realized the darker implications. She wondered if maybe Evelyn had once been in this same position. Maybe Victor becoming a widower hadn't been a tragic accident. Maybe it was a path he chose.

"I took such good care of you too," he continued. "That's the worst part. Didn't you notice you slept better once you moved here? You had a better life. That's all because of me and how I looked out for you."

Kate thought about how well she had slept since moving into the cottage. She thought about her hazy sleepiness, those strange dreams where she wasn't sure what was real and what wasn't.

"You drugged me," Kate whispered. She thought about how she was clear minded now. So, what had changed? Then, it hit her. "My tea."

"You say that in such a negative way," Victor hissed. "Like I did something bad to you. I helped you sleep, and I helped you get used to having me with you. I know you enjoyed our cuddling sessions. You curled up to me so willingly, so eagerly. We got closer that way. Yet you don't even seem thankful for it."

Kate's stomach twisted at Victor's admission. It sickened her to think of him crawling into her bed when she was drugged. She couldn't believe how might nights they had cuddled without her realizing it was truly happening.

And what about when they'd hooked up in her dreams? Was that all real too? Had they slept together without her true consent? The thought of it sickened her and traumatized her.

"I even took care of that little disturbance," he continued. "When Brad kept pushing the issue, clearly wanting you when you didn't want him, I helped rid you of him. That way you didn't have to keep dealing with him. He threatened what was between us, and I took care of him. You didn't even see it though. You didn't appreciate that either. Instead, you mourned his death so deeply… as if you didn't even care that he tried to replace me. After all I've done for you."

The room spun, and Kate's heart broke. She didn't want to believe it. She couldn't believe it. But this meant Victor was involved in Brad's death. Her friend was dead because of her— because of the monster she'd brought into her life. She could never forgive herself for that. But it was too late now to make amends. She could never bring him back.

Her thoughts reached even further as the horror unfolded. Vanessa and Amanda. Brad had been suspected of killing them. So, was it really Victor all along? He *was* her stalker. He had been all along. He killed Brad. He seemingly killed his wife. It only made sense that he was the monster behind those other deaths as well.

Kate wanted to scream, but she knew it wouldn't help. She wanted to fight against her binds. She wanted to rage, cry, put a pause on life so she could process this. But she didn't have time. She had to think of a smart reaction.

"I'm sorry," she said, looking up at him with pleading eyes. "You're right. You did all of this for me, and I haven't appreciated it well enough. I've been thankful for you from the start. I've loved you for quite some time now. But I didn't even know all you were doing for me. Now that I know, I can treat you the way you deserve to be treated. I can admire, respect, and love you the way you've earned."

Victor looked at her skeptically. "Doubtful," he huffed. "I know the kind of woman you are. Now that I've confessed my true intentions, you'll twist it. You'll go to the police. You'll get me arrested and sent to prison for the rest of my life."

"I would never do that," Kate insisted, trying to look shocked. "I love you, Victor. I've been falling for you from the start."

Kate reached into her heart and tried to toss aside his betrayal, tried to look past his murders. She needed to see him the way she had all this time. She had to convey that she adored him for it to sound genuine.

"I've been able to open up to you in a way that I wasn't able to with anyone else," she admitted. "After Tyler's death, you gave me so much love and support. You helped me want to live again, and I truly do appreciate it. You mean so much to me, Victor. I don't want to lose you. I can't lose you. No matter what you did, I forgive you. I know you were only trying to do what was best for me. I appreciate you looking out for me like that. No one has ever loved me like that."

Kate's heart twisted at these words. She knew it wasn't right. The last thing she wanted to do was be with him. But she had believed it at one point in time, so she hoped that was enough to make it sound genuine now.

"I'm not sure I believe you," he replied. Though Kate could see in his eyes that he wanted to believe her. He needed her to want to be with him just as much as he wanted to be with her.

"I'll prove myself to you," she insisted. "You can keep me tied up, and I'll still prove myself to you. Kiss me, and you'll see. You'll be able to feel my true feelings. You'll know that I do want to be with you."

Victor hesitated, looking like he was at war with himself. Of course, he knew the truth. He had to know she wouldn't want to be with him after what he had done. But he wanted to believe she wanted him. He wanted her to need him.

So, he allowed himself to at least entertain the idea that she could still love him. He walked over to her and kneeled on the bed beside her. He looked in her eyes, and she tried to cast aside all thoughts but love for him. She tried to view him in the way she had before the revelation.

He leaned down slowly, gently, as if he was terrified of her rejection. He paused with their lips inches apart.

"I know it doesn't seem like this right now," he whispered, "but I love you, Kate. I really do. That's why I had to kill Tyler."

Kate trembled; every muscle and every nerve in her body cried out in agony in as the emotion hit her like a sledgehammer. Everything threatened to spill out. She felt her heart breaking over and over and over again, like she was being dashed against the shore and held down to drown at the same time. Her mind spun and her throat closed up and her vision went blurry.

But she had to remain still. She had to find a way through this. It was what Tyler would have wanted for her.

"I love you too, Victor," she finally whispered.

With that, their lips met, bridging the gap between them. Kate pushed everything else out of her mind as she kissed him back as if nothing had ever happened between them. She leaned forward with passion, with love. She kissed him like her life depended on it.

It seemed like he bought it. He kissed her back with just as much intensity as he moved his body over hers. Beneath the façade, having his weight hovering over her was repulsive. She wanted him away from her. She wanted nothing to do with this.

But she swallowed the feeling. She played into the romance. She kissed him more passionately, feeding into his desires.

In a natural way, she moved her body, causing her wrists to strain against the binds in the way they might if she wanted to touch him. She used her body language to show how much she wanted to touch him without ever requesting the binds to be released.

She knew if she acted too eager, he would see right through her. He had been hesitant in approaching her because he wanted to slowly gain her trust. Now she had to use his own tricks against him to escape from him.

Finally, he noticed her straining. He noticed her body language, and she felt his body responding to hers. He wanted her. He still wanted her desperately.

"Stay with me," he begged, vulnerability coming out in his words. "That's all I've ever wanted … is for you to stay with me."

"I will," she promised. "I want to be with you. I want to hold you. I want to stay."

He looked her in the eyes, and she hoped her acting ability was up to par. She channeled that old side of her that loved him, and finally, he nodded.

"Just don't go," he promised. "I love you, but I love my freedom more. If you try to escape and call the police, I will kill you. It will prove that you're not the person I fell in love with anyway, so I truly wouldn't hesitate."

"I understand," she replied. She understood all too well that he meant every bit of it. So, she stayed still as he untied her right wrist.

She hoped he would untie both, but he only allowed her that one bit of freedom before he went back to kissing her. She touched him as gently and seductively as she could while secretly scanning the surrounding area.

When he wasn't looking, she tested the binds of her left hand. They gave way a little, showing the technique had worked. If she got just a moment to free them, she would be able to save herself. Or at least she could give herself a fighting chance.

Finally, she spotted a weapon. She angled her body so he wouldn't notice as her hand left his back in a quick motion and grabbed the bedside lamp.

Without thinking about it long enough to know if it would really work or not, Kate smashed the lamp over Victor's head, causing him to fall to his side and tumble on the floor. She quickly reached up for her left hand. The chase was on.

CHAPTER THIRTY-FIVE

T HE TECHNIQUE KATE USED TO KEEP HER WRIST LIGHTLY bound did wonders, allowing her to free herself quickly. Before Victor could gather himself together, she was flying off the bed and scrambling for the door.

She thought about grabbing her gun, but she still wasn't sure that she could shoot him even if she wanted to. So, she bolted for her keys which lay on the kitchen counter.

Before she could get to them, though, Victor came barreling out of the room with an animalistic roar. He was in obvious pain mentally, emotionally, and physically. Kate knew she wouldn't survive if he got ahold of her.

He lunged for the keys at the same time as she did, scaring her away from them. She knew she couldn't win in a physical fight, so she decided to flee out the door.

Just like she thought, the door was locked. It took her only a second to unlock it, but Victor was bearing down quickly behind her. Her only chance was to dart out into the night and hope he couldn't catch up. She had been running every day lately, so she hoped she could run faster and farther than he could.

He gained on her quickly, but the darkness engulfed her. Clouds shielded the moon and the stars, making everything even darker than normal. Kate used this to her advantage, running to the tree line to hide. She didn't dare look back to see how close Victor was to her.

She thought about where her closest neighbor was. They were quite a ways away, seeing as the property had been chosen for its seclusion. She felt hopeless, helpless, desperate.

Yet she realized with greater urgency in that moment that she didn't want to die. She wanted to live. She wanted to build a real life away from Victor.

So, she kept on running. She ran through the trees, falling multiple times as she tried to be quiet. She didn't look back. She didn't give up. She just kept on running.

Finally, a light broke through the darkness. Kate raced out from the trees and stumbled onto a lawn. She ran to the closest front door, hoping with her whole heart that someone was home.

She pounded on the glass desperately. "Please!" she cried out. "Someone help me! Please help me! Please!"

The house remained dark and silent. It was late enough in the night to be well past most people's bedtimes. So, Kate hit the door harder. She cried out louder as she kept glancing over her shoulder, waiting for Victor to pop out at any moment.

And then he came out of the trees, stalking her with dark purpose. The clouds shifted above and the moon shone through. Something glinted in his hands, and Kate's heart sank as she realized it was a knife. She cried out in terror again as he came out of the woods and started crossing the street, never once looking away.

Just as she was about to bolt away, a light turned on. She heard someone coming down the stairs, and the door swung open. A middle-aged man looked at her with concern on his face and a gun by his side.

"What's going on?" he asked. "We heard you calling for help and—"

"You have to help me!" she wailed, tears streaming down her face. "Someone's after me! Please! He's going to kill me!"

The man looked over her shoulder behind her and frowned. "Who?"

Kate's entire body shook violently as she slowly turned her head back around, expecting to be face to face with a killer.

But he was nowhere to be seen.

"Someone is after me," Kate finally said after a couple deep breaths. "Please, you have to let me inside. We have to call the police."

The man ushered her inside as his wife came down the stairs. They closed the door and locked it as the man called the police.

"Well, this is quite the introduction. I don't usually have random people showing up on my doorstep. I'm Stephanie," the woman said. "And I want you to know you're safe here. We're not going to let anything bad happen to you."

"I'm Kate, and I'm so sorry about this. I live just down the street. I don't mean to bring danger to your home. I just didn't know what else to do, where else to go. I don't have my phone, and I couldn't get to my car, and..."

"It's okay," Stephanie replied, pulling Kate into a much needed hug. "Like I said, you are safe. We'll make sure you're okay. I'll make you some tea, and we can sit in the living room while we wait for the police officers to come."

Kate was reluctant to have tea after knowing hers had been drugged for so long. But Stephanie seemed nice enough, so she followed her lead and curled up with a blanket on the couch.

It didn't take long for police officers to arrive, and Kate told them what happened. A few officers quickly went to her house while Officer Maddison stayed behind to comfort her. Finally, the other officers arrived back at the neighbors' house and talked to Officer Maddison before she turned to Kate.

"It looks like Victor has disappeared," she told her. "We've searched the area, and he's gone. We're not giving up though. We're going to keep looking for him. For now, is there anywhere you can stay that might be safer for you? I wouldn't suggest going back to your house yet."

"I can stay with my family," Kate decided. "But it's late, so for now, I'll stay at a hotel."

"I can bring you there," Maddison replied. "And we'll set up watch for the night just in case he returns."

Despite knowing there were officers watching over her, Kate felt alone and vulnerable in her hotel room. She sat on the bed, drenched in shock as she considered how the last few days had gone.

She couldn't believe Victor had been behind this all along. She couldn't believe she didn't see it before… that it was all a façade.

Worst of all was coming to terms that Victor was a murderer. It didn't escape Kate's notice that Amanda and Vanessa shared similar features to her. She knew Brad had been killed because of her, her husband had been killed because of her, and maybe Amanda and Vanessa had been killed because of her too.

Darkness engulfed her as she lay back on the bed.

"This is all my fault," she said to the empty room. She could feel the presence of their ghosts crowding around her, making it difficult to even breathe. "It's my fault, and I'm so sorry. It's my fault you're dead. I should be dead."

The thought reverberated through her mind. It struck a chord and hit home as the truth of it sunk in. She dipped back into the dark days that had followed Tyler's death—when she felt like life wasn't worth living—when she wanted to die as well.

Did she want to die now? She assumed she probably didn't, which is why she'd fought so hard for her life. But she wasn't sure she wanted to live either. The guilt was too heavy. This was all too much.

She curled up into a ball and sobbed under the pressure of everything, unsure of if she'd ever be able to emerge from the darkness she was drowning in this time. Or if her light had been stolen for good.

Kate was grateful to be embraced by the loving arms of her family the next day. Returning home felt like a huge relief as she found safety with them. She still worried a bit. She worried that she'd be bringing danger to them just by her presence. She had already brought so much danger to the other people in her life. She wouldn't be able to bear it if something happened to them. That would be a step too far. A step she couldn't recover from.

"It's okay," her mother assured her with a hug. "No one is going to come here. We won't let him hurt you. You've been through so much, and now is your time to unwind and feel safe. I promise you, Kate. It's going to be okay."

Kate nodded but didn't quite believe it. She went through her days in a numb haze, still unable to fully fathom the nightmare her life had become. As the week went by, though, she started to slightly emerge again. She started to feel like her old self again.

"Still no news," Officer Maddison said a week after the attack. Kate had checked in every single day, yet every answer was the same. "We've been searching for him and will continue to, but we haven't found him yet. It seems like he's extra practiced at evading law enforcement."

At that, Kate was disheartened as she set down the phone. She didn't want to stay with her parents forever, putting them at risk. She also wanted time to decompress and be on her own for a bit. She needed space to process this.

She spent a couple more days at her parents' house before deciding it was time to go back home. She had to face this. She couldn't stay away forever.

"Are you sure you want to do this?" her mother asked her as she packed up her things. "You're always welcome to stay here for as long as you'd like."

"I know," Kate replied, giving her mother a hug. "But I feel like I need to do this. I need to get back to my normal life. Victor has disrupted things so much. I can't let him continue to get away with it. I need to move forward. I need to finally be free of him."

"Are you sure?"

"I'm sure," she said. "I have a gun. I'll install cameras. I'll do whatever I have to do. But I will not let him hurt me ever again. I promise."

Kate's mother hugged her like she might never see her again, which was unsettling to Kate. She knew she was taking a risk, but she didn't want to think about it like that. She wanted to believe that everything would be okay.

"Nothing bad is going to happen," she told her mother. "Victor is gone. I am safe. I just need to move on with my life."

Despite exuding confidence as she talked to her mother, Kate felt something different as she drove back to her house. The thought of approaching the same place where she had been stalked and terrorized was intimidating and frightening.

What if he came back? What if he killed her this time? What if he tortured her? She had never been in that kind of pain before, so she couldn't even imagine what that would be like.

She tried not to imagine it any further as her house finally came into view. It looked normal from afar. Everything was in its rightful place. There were no signs of the traumatic things that had happened there.

Kate knew that looks could be deceiving though. Victor knew how to get into her house. He'd drugged her. He'd hurt her. He'd betrayed her. He'd could do it again.

"He won't dare come back again," Kate said as she got out of her car. "Especially not so soon after everything. I'm safe. I'm safe. I'm safe. I'm also starving."

Thanks to her putting off her return for so long, the sun was already setting. It was dinner time, and Kate had brought groceries with her so she could cook herself a full meal. She knew she deserved it, and she hoped it would be a nice way to settle in again.

She grabbed the grocery bags and braced herself as she walked into her house. It now seemed eerie with the lights off. Even once she turned them on, the home seemed a little shadowed.

"Is anyone here?" she called out, feeling stupid as she did. It wasn't like Victor had ever announced his presence before. It was never that easy.

She was careful as she brought the groceries into the kitchen and set them down. Then, just to ease her mind, she decided to look through the house. She started with examining the kitchen, then went into the living room.

There, her heart stopped and fear froze her. Victor was waiting in the living room for her, looking up at her with a nasty glare and the knife in his hands.

CHAPTER THIRTY-SIX

K ATE WASN'T SURE WHAT TO DO. VICTOR WASN'T extremely close to her… yet. But she had seen how fast he could run, and this time he had a weapon. He was surely even angrier than last time. He could kill her easily. She could die.

"Welcome home, Kate," Victor said with a sneer. "It's so nice to see you again. I'm honestly surprised you came back, but I suspect it's that bond we have. You couldn't stay away for good."

Kate's stomach twisted at the thought of them having any sort of bond. She didn't feel anything special with him. She didn't want to be near him. But as long as he thought that, she hoped she still had a chance of getting out of this alive.

"It's too bad you can't see it," he continued. "You can't feel the way we're connected. You can't believe in the true, pure love that should be between us. You're blinded, and it's sad. I never wanted to have to hurt you. I only wanted to love you, protect you, cherish you."

"I'm sorry," she said, though she already knew that wasn't going to work this time. "I shouldn't have betrayed you. You frightened me is all. But I'm glad you're back so we can make things right."

"How stupid do you think I am? You really think I'm going to fall for the same tricks again? I have more pride than that. I have more self-respect. There's no way I'm going to let you charm your way into betraying me again. You had your chance, and you blew it. I should've known then what kind of person you were, but I was blinded too. I was blinded by my love for you. I'm not anymore. I see everything clearly.

"You never loved me. Just like Evelyn. She didn't love me either; she didn't trust me; she cheated on me. She led me to you, and you were supposed to be my salvation. That was your destiny, but you've turned away from it. You ruined me. You ruined everything."

"It doesn't have to be ruined," Kate insisted. "We can still be together. I can forgive you and..."

"And the police are already after me. They're not going to let me go so easily. I'm sure you already told them what I've been involved in. You want me to go to prison. You want me to be locked away forever. This is the fate you've chosen for me, and you want me to just forgive that?"

Kate looked around helplessly. She knew she was stuck. She couldn't reach in her bag to call 911, and even if she could, there was no way the police would get there in time to stop him. There was no way she was going to convince him out of it this time, so she had to find a way to escape.

Her only chance was the gun. It was upstairs in her room by the bed where she had left it from before. She wasn't able to use it then. She wasn't ready. But with that knife pointed at her, she thought she might be able to. She might be able to fight him to protect herself.

Victor stood and stepped toward her. "You're going to die, Kate. Tonight. There's nothing you can do about it. My life is ruined regardless, so first, I must have my revenge."

At that, Kate threw the groceries hard at him and bolted toward the stairs without a second thought. Her drive to live was the only thing propelling her forward, and she hoped it would be enough to get her out of this mess.

She had to at least try. She reasoned she would be dead regardless, but she had to at least try to fight him. She didn't want to die.

The bag of groceries only delayed him for a few seconds before he pursued her, his footsteps heavy and loud behind her, threatening what would happen if he got ahold of her. It was a race to the stairs, and she clambered up them, not pausing to look back until she felt the stab at the back of her leg just as she was reaching the top.

She let out an agonized shriek. The pain was unreal, unlike anything else she had ever felt. She fell to the floor and knew she was done for. She knew the race was over, and she lost.

But her will to live didn't stop as he approached her. She thought back to what she had learned in her self-defense class, and as he lunged at her with the knife again, she maneuvered around him, using the techniques she'd learned to catch him off guard and push him, landing her fists where it would hurt the most, sending him tumbling down the stairs.

He cried out, but she knew he was still more than able to come after her, so she scrambled up despite the excruciating pain in her leg and her blurring vision. She ignored the warm trickle of blood flowing out of her calf. She ignored her body begging her to stop and rest.

With the blood loss, she was aware that she might die anyway. He might catch up to her. She wouldn't win a fight against him. He was stronger.

She clawed her way to the top of the stairs as he regained his footing and stormed up the stairway. She heard him closing in behind her, and he lunged again just as she was approaching her nightstand where the gun waited to protect her.

He sent her sprawling to the ground, desperately lashing out with his knife as she evaded him. She worried that in taking a moment to grab the gun, she might be giving him the opening he needed to fatally stab her.

So, she kneed him in his stomach and then reached for the gun, hoping she would have the strength to use it. She still wasn't sure that she could shoot someone, even for her own survival. She didn't want to kill him. She didn't want to be responsible for anyone's death.

But before she could think about it further, her finger was on the trigger. Victor gathered himself with the knife in his hand lunged for her, aiming straight for her heart.

Kate twisted around and pulled the trigger.

The weight of his body was blown backward under the pressure, taking them both by surprise. He fell against her legs, crushing them beneath his weight.

She cried out in pain, panicked that she hadn't stopped him, terrified he would rise again … and land the killing blow.

But a second passed, and then a minute, and then another, and he stayed on the floor, unmoving. Kate dug herself out from under him and finally staggered back downstairs to get her phone and call for help, hoping she wouldn't bleed out before this nightmare could end.

It was over. It was finally over.

Her vision wavered as the red and blue police lights came into view and the sirens echoed in the night. As Officer Maddison kneeled next to her, she could only vaguely hear her calling for a medic.

"I got him," she whispered. And then the world went black.

For the first time in a long time, she dreamed of Tyler.

EPILOGUE

Three weeks later…

"WELCOME HOME!" ALLISON SAID CHEERILY AS she brought her stuff into Kate's house. "Isn't it beautiful? I can't wait to start our lives over here."

"I'm just so glad you're going to be living here," Kate said as she hobbled in on her crutches. "It's going to make me feel so much safer than being alone."

Lucky for Kate, Allison's lease had ended shortly after the incident with Victor. Allison hated her apartment, and she didn't have anywhere else to go; at the same time, Kate was so traumatized by everything that she didn't want to be alone.

She debated selling the house she almost died in—the house she had killed someone in. But Tyler had built it for her. Selling it seemed like it would be disloyal to him. And she wanted to move on. She wanted to get away from Victor's grasp. He had destroyed her life for far too long. But he was gone now. He could no longer hurt anyone again because Kate had stopped him. She would never allow him, or any other man, to hurt her again.

"How are you feeling?" Allison asked.

"Well, the doctor says hopefully the wound should be healed up—"

"Not that," Allison pressed with a soft chuckle. "How are *you* feeling?"

"It's hard to say," she said honestly.

Allison gave her another hug. "Well, until it gets better, I'm here. I'll always be here."

"I can't tell you how much this means to me," Kate attempted. "I really…"

"Nope. Don't even mention it. This is the best arrangement for both of us," Allison said. "I'm looking forward to getting settled in and living with my best friend. I can't imagine a more perfect situation."

Kate couldn't respond to that because she could think of a more perfect situation. For a moment she thought about what her life would be like if Victor had never entered it. She considered how things would be better if Tyler was there with her, if they could have their happily ever after that they both worked so hard for.

But he was gone. All of it was over. And this was the best she could do now. She had made great progress in moving forward, but after everything was revealed with Victor, it was going to be hard to get back there again. But this time, she knew she could do it. And she didn't need a man to help her at all.

The two women sat on the couch to relax for a moment. Kate looked up at the photos of Tyler with a heavy heart.

"I feel so guilty," Kate admitted. "Tyler is dead because of me. Vanessa and Amanda are dead because of me. Brad is dead because of me, and now his son has to live without him forever. The worst part is, I didn't have faith in him. I was convinced for a long time that he didn't do the things they said he did. But eventually, I caved. I believed he was a criminal, a monster. I'm the worst friend … the worst wife."

"You're not," Allison promised. "None of this is your fault, Kate. Victor got obsessed with you—there's nothing you could have done to prevent that. You didn't ask for this to happen. You did what you could to stop him, and I'm so proud of you for it. You are amazing. You are safe. I love you, and things are going to get better. They're going to be okay."

Kate hugged her friend and hoped for a better future where she might finally be able to work through all of this. She closed her eyes and saw Tyler smiling at her. And when she spoke, it was like his voice joined hers, and the two of them spoke in unison: "Things are going to be okay."

AUTHOR'S NOTE

Thank you so much for reading *The Woman in the Cottage!* As a new self-publishing author drifting into the vast ocean of published books, your support is what buoys me and helps me get noticed among all the rest. This book marks my first published work. And I am both incredibly happy and extremely nervous by the prospect of you having read it. It is a culmination of a lot of time, effort, and encouragement from loved ones pushing me to publish it. I hope that my book entertained and thrilled you and that you will return to read the next one. With my first published book behind me, I am going to be working hard to bring you many more in the future.

If you can please leave me a review for this book, it would mean so much to me. Writing is my one true passion, and your review and word of mouth will continue to make writing more books a possibility for me. And I promise that I won't keep you waiting too long.

Best regards,
Cara Kent

P.S. I will be the first one to tell you that I am not perfect, no matter how hard I try to be. And there is plenty that I am still learning about self-publishing. If you come across any typos or have any other issues with this book please don't hesitate to reach out to me at cara@carakent.com, I monitor and read every email personally, and I will do my very best to rectify any issues that I am made aware of.